THREE CHILDREN IN DANGER

A GRIPPING HISTORICAL NOVEL ABOUT A DARING ESCAPE FROM NAZI GERMANY

ESCAPING THE REICH
BOOK ONE

MARION KUMMEROW

Three Children in Danger: A gripping historical novel about a daring escape from Nazi Germany

Escaping the Reich, Book 1

All Rights Reserved

Copyright © 2024 Marion Kummerow

Cover Design: Jane Dixon Smith

Images:

Background: Shutterstock

Children: Shutterstock

This book is copyrighted and protected by copyright laws.

No part of this publication may be reproduced or transmitted in any form or by any means, electronic, mechanical, photocopying, recording, or otherwise without prior written permission from the author.

This is a work of fiction. Names, places, characters and incidents are either the product of the author's imagination or are used fictitiously, and any resemblance to any actual persons, living or dead, organizations, events or locales is entirely coincidental.

CHAPTER 1

BERLIN, DECEMBER 1942

Holger listened as the two women debated his future—and that of his younger siblings. Much to his dismay, he only understood fragments of their conversation since his seven-year-old sister, Hertha, chattered incessantly.

With all the authority of his twelve years, he glared at her and hissed, "Shh. I'm trying to listen."

"Mutti always says eavesdropping is forbidden." Hertha made a face that was probably meant to intimidate him, revealing her two tooth gaps in the process.

"Just be quiet for once!" he snapped at her, putting a finger to his lips. His little sister simply didn't understand when to follow rules and when it was wiser to ignore them. Like now, for instance, as Frau Lemberg and Frau Goldmann were in the kitchen discussing what should happen with the three siblings.

"You have no right to order me around, you're not Mutti." Hertha wasn't giving up without a fight.

Deep in his heart Holger loved his sister dearly, but at this moment, he itched to clamp his hand over her mouth so she would finally shut up and he could eavesdrop on the adults in peace.

But as he'd learned from experience, doing that would never work. Although he was much bigger and stronger than Hertha, the little imp had learned to defend herself against her two older brothers and would create a screaming scene until one of the adults rushed to her aid.

Then Hertha would put on her "I'm-a-sweet-innocent-girl" face and the adults would inevitably scold him for causing trouble. Unfortunately, Hertha possessed the talent to wrap people around her little finger, so he and ten-year-old Hans usually got the short end of the stick.

"Please. I want to know what's going to happen to us. Surely that must interest you too, doesn't it?"

Finally, Hertha seemed to understand the severity of the situation and her endless chatter fell silent.

Holger crept closer to the kitchen door and waited, his heart racing as he listened intently. Frau Lemberg had been his school principal before the Nazis had closed the Jewish school she owned several months ago. Until yesterday, the five members of the Gerber family had shared an apartment in a Jewish house in central Berlin with the Goldmanns, the Falkensteins, and the former prima ballerina, Delia.

He still shuddered at the memory of the SS raiding the building and arresting everyone who'd had the misfortune to be at home. Thanks to a mysterious black-haired woman named Roxy, he and his siblings hadn't been abducted too.

None of the residents in the house had seemed to know that Roxy lived in its drafty attic, where she had hidden the children while the SS wreaked havoc on the apartments downstairs.

"The children can't stay here," said the strict, yet friendly, Frau Lemberg, who had been very popular with her students.

"Just for a few days, until we find another place for them. Please," begged Frau Goldmann.

A throbbing pain shot through Holger's chest, so strong he

had to lean forward to avoid toppling over. The evening after the raid, his parents hadn't returned home from work. When Frau Goldmann had visited the police station the next morning to ask about them, her sad expression upon returning had told Holger the awful truth: His parents had been deported to the East, probably never to be seen or heard from again.

Inside, Holger's heart felt like it was wrapped in ice, cold and heavy, each beat a reminder that his parents were gone. He clutched at the aching hollow in his chest, trying to make sense of how a single day could change everything.

Then the terrifying memory of the SS hit him again, the crashing of doors, and the eerie stillness that had filled the air when they were no longer there.

Mere hours later Frau Goldmann had ordered them to pack their satchels and brought them to Frau Lemberg's place, because it was no longer safe to stay in their old apartment. She feared the SS might return any moment to search for the missing children.

Holger bravely squeezed his eyes shut until the grief subsided, because neither Hans nor Hertha could see how severely he was suffering. As the oldest of the siblings he had naturally assumed the role of head of the family, after they had effectively become orphans. The self-imposed responsibility for his younger siblings weighed heavily on his shoulders.

Just as another wave of grief threatened to overwhelm him, he reminded himself of his new role and pulled himself together. Straightening his shoulders, he vowed to protect Hans and Hertha until that stupid Hitler was eventually defeated by the Allies.

Holger was so preoccupied with his pain that he forgot to keep listening and startled when the kitchen door handle was pushed down. The creak brought him back to the present, and he left his listening post with a quick jump. He certainly didn't want to be caught eavesdropping.

The door opened a crack and Frau Goldmann's voice rang

out, "In any case, thank you for trying. I wouldn't have brought the siblings to you if I thought they were safe in our apartment."

Holger wanted to slap himself. Lost in thought, he had missed the women's plan for them and now had to wait until someone told him. Which might mean waiting a long time, since in his experience adults seemed to believe kids were too young to understand their plans anyway.

But he was twelve and understood very well what was going on in the world. Besides, as the eldest, he bore the responsibility for the well-being of his younger siblings. Shouldn't he rightfully expect to be let in on the adults' plans?

Frau Lemberg's answer was so quiet he understood but fragments: "... keep overnight ... can't help ... pick up again ... SS ... premises ... dangerous."

Fear crept into his veins. Even though Frau Goldmann had praised him for his quick-witted response when the SS man had stopped them on their way here, he much preferred to avoid the police. One never knew what they might do. Instinctively, his hand reached for the yellow Star of David on his jacket until he remembered that Frau Goldmann had removed their stars before they'd set out for the Lembergs, so they were allowed to use the bus. Since she wasn't Jewish, she had impressed on them the importance of pretending she was their mother if a patrol asked.

Shortly after, the kitchen door opened fully and Frau Goldmann stepped out. "Will you listen to me, please?" She waited until Holger, Hans and Hertha fell completely silent, three pairs of eyes riveted to her mouth. "You will stay with Frau Lemberg for a few days until she finds a safe hiding place for you."

"What about you?" asked Hertha.

"I have to return to our apartment. I'd love to keep you with us, but you're not safe there anymore. If the Gestapo searches for you, they'll check first at the place where you are registered." Frau Goldmann stroked Hertha's hair. "If that happens I'll tell them that you moved to the countryside long before the raid. I'm keeping my fingers crossed for you."

"How will our parents find us?" Hans asked.

Holger stared at him open-mouthed. How could Hans believe that Mutti and Vati would return anytime soon? No one knew for certain what happened to those who were taken away, but one thing was sure: they disappeared forever. No one who had been picked up by the SS and put on a train heading east had ever be seen again.

"Frau Lemberg or I will tell your parents where you are if they come searching for you," Frau Goldmann replied. From her tone, Holger realized that she didn't believe that would ever happen and had only said it to reassure Hans.

Indeed, it worked, because Hans broke out into a huge smile and turned away.

Holger had never quite gotten used to the fact that his brother seemed to live in his own world and often didn't notice what was happening around him. In that respect, he was the complete opposite to the constantly chattering Hertha or to Holger himself, who firmly lived in the here and now.

"Be good and do what Frau Lemberg tells you to do. The war can't last much longer. After it has ended, things will become better." Frau Goldmann bade her goodbyes pressing Holger's hand slightly longer than necessary. "Take good care of your siblings, will you?"

"Of course, Frau Goldmann." He puffed out his chest. "Please thank Roxy for hiding us."

Frau Goldmann's eyebrows shot up.

Damn, now he had let the secret slip. Roxy had impressed upon them not to tell anyone about her existence. He bit his tongue, waiting for the inevitable interrogation.

Fortunately, Frau Lemberg intervened: "Frau Goldmann, you'd better leave, it won't do good if someone sees you here." Then she turned toward the children. "Come with me. I'll show you where you are going to sleep."

Holger swallowed a lump in his throat at the prospect of being taken to an unknown place. To hide his fear, he barked at Hans and Hertha, "Hurry up. Grab your satchels and follow me."

Their new lodging was a storage room, just big enough for a makeshift bed using rough blankets instead of a mattress, but at least they had a roof over their heads. Frau Lemberg would allow them to play in the living room or in the back of the garden during the day – as long as they disappeared into the chamber instantly whenever someone approached the little house.

After Frau Lemberg had left the three alone, Hertha whined, "I'm so glad I have the two of you."

Heart aching, Holger hugged his little sister tight. Hans joined them and wrapped his little arms around them both. They stood huddled together in an unbroken circle until Hans said, "I'm glad you two are with me."

"We'll never separate," Holger assured. "We'll always stay together."

"Promise?" whispered Hertha.

"Promise," Holger and Hans answered.

CHAPTER 2

Baumann sat in Pastor Perwe's office. The sparsely furnished room contained only the essentials: a wooden desk, a few chairs and a rack full of books. The pastor's shoulders sagged, the worry lines on his forehead deepening the longer he stared at the papers in front of him. The two men had known each other for a few months, ever since Perwe had succeeded Birger Forell as pastor of the Swedish Victoria church in Berlin.

Baumann came from the working class, having worked his way up from a simple toiler in the locomotive workshop to mechanic, then to foreman, and finally to workshop manager. As an old communist, he maintained a healthy aversion against authority and especially against the Nazis. He didn't trust representatives of this government one iota, even though after Hitler's rise to power, he had been forced to realize that open resistance was not a viable attitude.

So he and his comrades had decided to go underground to help those persecuted by the Nazi regime. Despite being a pronounced atheist, he had started to regularly attend church. Although certainly not to pray.

Before Perwe's arrival in Berlin, Baumann had worked with Birger Forell, who led a network of helpers for refugees, persecuted people and those in hiding. Forell had long been a thorn in the Gestapo's side until they'd finally expelled him from Germany a few months earlier.

Fortunately, Perwe shared his predecessor's mindset and seamlessly continued his work.

"You look worried," Baumann said, prompting a deep sigh from the pastor.

"Indeed I am." The time in Germany had visibly taken its toll on the pastor. His usually calm and composed gaze was filled with unrest. "Every day, more people come to us seeking help and protection. I honestly don't know how I can do right by all of them."

Baumann nodded. He empathized with the pastor's desperation. The situation was getting worse on a daily basis, with Jews in particular never safe from persecution anywhere. He himself had taken a half-Jew, David Goldmann, under his wing. On David's first day at work, Baumann had given him the nickname Kessel and made sure none of the other workers knew about his heritage.

Such measures wouldn't have been necessary with the seasoned employees, but new men were constantly assigned to the workshop, and he couldn't be sure of their loyalties.

At that moment, there came a knock at the door. Pastor Perwe's wife entered, her cheeks sporting heated red dots. "Two policemen from across the street are here and want to speak to you, Erik."

Pastor Perwe narrowed his eyes to slits. "We've never had problems with them before."

"I think you'd better hear them out," Baumann chimed in. Although he despised the government, he strove to maintain a good relationship with the police and other officials. This had often proved useful in resolving minor problems.

"Alright, please tell the policemen I'll see them right now," Perwe instructed his wife. "Let's hear what they have to say."

Shortly after, another knock came at the door and Frau Perwe entered with two men in Ordnungspolizei uniform. Baumann breathed a sigh of relief. Orpos, as the ordinary policemen were nicknamed, were generally less fanatic Nazis than SS men or the Gestapo. Both Orpos were beyond fifty years, their paunches and chubby cheeks making their appearance more sluggish than threatening.

"What can I do for you?" Pastor Perwe asked in a friendly tone.

The senior policeman glanced briefly at Baumann, who didn't bother to introduce himself, while nervously twirling his cap between his hands. "My name is Gruber, and this is my colleague Ahrens. You may know that we serve at the police station across the street."

The pastor nodded. "Of course, gentlemen. We're very grateful for the pleasant relationship."

This seemed to calm the policeman, because he finally stopped twirling his cap. "Well, Herr Pastor, it's just that... we have come to warn you."

"Warn me?" Perwe pursed his lips, giving the officers a brooding look.

"Yes, I mean... Please don't misunderstand. We mean you no harm." Gruber broke off.

"And yet you want to issue a warning. How am I supposed to interpret this visit?"

Baumann could practically smell the tension in the room. The priest had guts; not many people dared to challenge a representative of the Nazi regime. Although Perwe was a Swedish citizen on official business and thus protected by diplomatic immunity, it still took considerable courage to act so boldly.

"No. Well, yes." Herr Gruber took a few seconds, before he

continued. "We've been informed that the Gestapo is planning to pay your parish a visit. It seems you've been denounced for illegal activities."

Pastor Perwe leaned back and folded his hands over his stomach. "We're doing nothing wrong here."

In this moment Herr Ahrens chimed in. "We agree with what you're doing, but the Gestapo has different opinions. We came to warn you. So you can take precautions and make sure that in the next few days, no one knocks on your door who shouldn't be found if a search takes place."

"I greatly appreciate your concern. Our parish stands on Swedish territory. The Gestapo is not allowed to enter without my government's consent."

"We didn't know that," said Ahrens.

Pastor Perwe had the grace not to dwell on their lack of knowledge. "I thank you nonetheless for your visit; one can't expect this kind of goodwill these days."

An awkward silence fell over the room, giving Baumann goosebumps. Waiting was not his forte. The tingling in his thick, strong fingers almost drove him mad, but he held his ground.

This wasn't his show; he was just a silent observer. In fact, he shouldn't even be here. Why would an atheist be in a parsonage, let alone a Swedish one? Even the dullest policeman – and these two seemed smarter than most – could figure out that Baumann hadn't visited Pastor Perwe to confess his sins.

The tension stretched on, filling the room, settling on the men's shoulders until Baumann struggled not to sag under the weight. The policemen seemed to feel the same way: Herr Gruber intently studied his toecaps, twirling his damn cap between his hands once again.

Still, no one spoke a word. Baumann almost sent up a prayer to a God he didn't believe in, just so Pastor Perwe would cut their agony short. Then, finally, Herr Gruber cleared his throat. "My colleague and I have been observing for some time what you're doing here and who's coming and going." He broke off, sending a pleading look to his colleague.

Baumann took a deep breath, clenching his hands into fists. If necessary, he would defend the pastor with his bare hands. He appraised the two policemen: desk jockeys, as their paunches and chubby cheeks revealed. He, on the other hand, possessed the muscles of a prize fighter from hauling heavy spare parts around the locomotive workshop on a daily basis.

Involuntarily, his gaze wandered to Gruber's hip. At the sight of the empty holster, he suppressed a grin. Thanks to the strict rule that all weapons had to be handed over to the sexton at the entrance to the parish the two policemen would be hopelessly outmatched in close combat.

However, he hoped it wouldn't come to that. After a fistfight against the police, he'd have to disappear and would no longer be able to help the pastor with his work for the persecuted. So Baumann stayed still and waited, no matter how much he yearned to intervene. With a touch of nostalgia, he remembered the good old days of class struggle, when one was allowed to join in an honest brawl without ending up in a concentration camp afterward.

Herr Ahrens chimed in. "We've long disagreed with what our government is doing. Therefore we appreciate that people find shelter with your church. Especially our Jewish fellow citizens."

Herr Gruber took over. "Officially, of course, we have to agree with Hitler's actions. But that doesn't stop us from turning a blind eye every time a person we should arrest shows up at your door. However, we can't do that while the Gestapo is at our premises, or we would endanger ourselves. I'm sure you can understand."

Baumann's hands clenched tighter. What exactly did the pastor and his helpers, including Baumann himself, do every day? They endangered their lives to help those in need. The Orpos were too cowardly to take action. It was all well and good to disagree with Hitler's insane ideology, but if they did nothing about it, they were accomplices of the system, even though they might not be obstinate Nazis. The government only managed to stay in power because the majority of citizens looked the other way when things got uncomfortable.

"That's very generous of you and I greatly appreciate your willingness to help," replied the pastor, who always found the right words. "It would probably be advantageous if we agreed on a sign, something you might use to warn us of an upcoming Gestapo visit without endangering yourselves."

The policemen's faces immediately brightened. Inwardly, Baumann harbored a slight rancor against their cowardice, although he grudgingly accepted that Perwe's idea was brilliant. Just what might such a warning sign look like?

It had to be obvious yet inconspicuous, something everyone noticed, whether approaching the entrance to the Victoria Parish from the street or while inside keeping watch. Honestly, Baumann couldn't think of anything.

The pastor rubbed his chin. "My wife has long admired the pretty plants on your windowsill."

"Thank you. Gardening is my hobby." Herr Gruber beamed from ear to ear.

"My wife probably isn't the only one who enjoys looking at the flowers. Perhaps you could discreetly change something whenever you need to send us a warning?"

"An excellent idea that will surely help us find a solution." Herr Gruber put a finger to his nose. "I water the flowers almost every day, and I just have to open the window to do it. I've even bought a small watering can that sits right next to the window on a filing cabinet, so it's always within reach."

The pastor furrowed his brow in thought. "Hmm. Perhaps you might leave the watering can standing between the flower pots to signal imminent danger?"

"As I said, it usually sits on the filing cabinet next to the windowsill." Gruber ran his finger over his nose. "I don't think my colleagues pay attention to it and a stranger certainly won't be suspicious if it's not in its usual place. Alright, if we get word of the Gestapo approaching or any other danger, I'll put the watering can between the bush roses and the spider plant."

"In case one of our colleagues does notice, you can always pretend you simply forgot the watering can there," Herr Ahrens chimed in.

"They're so uninterested in my plants, I'm quite certain that won't happen. Remember last year after my vacation when all the flowers had withered, even though I had explicitly impressed on Schmidt to water them every second day?" Herr Gruber gave a dejected gaze, while Herr Ahrens nodded. Then they both eyed the pastor.

"That's how we'll do it." Pastor Perwe stood up and shook hands with the policemen. "Thank you very much for your willingness to help. I truly appreciate it."

After the policemen left, Baumann remained alone with Perwe. The pastor returned to his seat behind the desk with deliberate slowness. Once seated he folded his hands under his chin, thoughtfully gazing out the window.

Baumann knew this routine and used the time to go over the conversation in his mind. The pastor was a much better judge of character than he was. If Perwe trusted the policemen, Baumann would too.

"Baumann," Perwe finally spoke. "This warning sign is only valuable if those seeking help know about it."

"You instruct your helpers and I'll spread the news on the street," said Baumann. The few remaining Jews mostly frequented the same places and information traveled fast through the grapevine. If he relayed the news about the warning sign strategically, it would spread like wildfire among the people living in the underground.

"Be careful. If you get caught, an important pillar of our network will fall."

Baumann's chest swelled with pride. He never would have

thought that he, of all people—the boy who had received his fair share of beatings from his pastor during his school time—would be praised by a representative of the church.

"I always am." Baumann would do his best to ensure the information didn't fall into the wrong hands, for *Greifer* – Jews betraying other Jews to the Gestapo – and other traitors were lurking everywhere.

CHAPTER 3

Countess Sophie Borsoi entered the elegant dining room of her friend Baroness Annemarie zu Steinfeld. The room was adorned with heavy velvet curtains, which served both to comply with the blackout regulations and to keep out the icy December cold.

A massive chandelier illuminated the long, festively set table and the fireplace provided cozy warmth. Sophie rubbed her hands, which had grown cold despite her wearing thick leather gloves.

The aroma of roast and fresh herbs filled the air. Annemarie, about twenty years older than Sophie, moved in the same circles, so she knew most of the guests present. They included an illustrious company of old friends and people related to her extended family in one way or another, some of whom she hadn't seen in years.

Annemarie greeted her warmly, her blue eyes shining with joy. "Sophie, how wonderful that you found the time to attend!"

"You know I love your invitations," Sophie replied with a guilty shrug as she had sorely neglected her friend during the past months due to the double burden of her studies and work. "It seems not much has changed."

"Except for the times, my dear." Annemarie said it with a bitter smile. "But let's not spoil the mood. Come into the dining room, I'll introduce you to some people."

Sophie followed her to the table, where the other guests had taken their seats.

Annemarie stopped at the empty seat next to a young, delicate and handsome man. "This is Reinhard Busch, son of the industrialist Fritz Busch," she introduced the man and bent forward to whisper in Sophie's ear: "You two would make a good match."

Sophie rolled her eyes. She neither wanted nor needed a romantic relationship – she barely found the time to meet her existing friends.

Reinhard Busch stood up, and she extended her hand in a friendly greeting, whereupon he blew the perfect hand kiss onto it. Standing, he looked even taller and slimmer. "I'm pleased to finally meet you, Countess. Especially since my father considers you the black sheep of your family."

"I'll take that as a compliment. I don't share my family's political views, if that is what you're alluding to." Sophie had never made a secret of her critical stance toward the Nazi regime. Not only Germany's titled society, but practically the entire nation including the Gestapo, knew of her aversion to the Nazis.

"Me too, I don't approve of the prevailing opinion." Herr Busch slightly bowed his head and adjusted the chair for Sophie to sit down. "However, I don't trumpet it to the winds the way you do. It's easier to act when no one suspects you."

His response left Sophie speechless, which didn't happen often. While she was still pondering how to counter the implied criticism, she was rescued by her table neighbor to the left.

"Countess," said Herr Kleist, an older gentleman with gray hair and sharp features. "How are your esteemed parents?"

"As well as can be expected under the circumstances. My father complains that most of his farmhands have been drafted and that the prisoners of war assigned to his estate neither speak German nor have experience with farm work." Sophie's father owned a huge estate in East Prussia, which included a horse breeding farm.

"The war has caused problems for all of us," Herr Kleist replied.

"What about you? Are you still working with the education commission?" Sophie asked, trying to steer the conversation back to safer ground.

The man heaved a dramatic sigh. "I was politely pushed out because my views weren't progressive enough."

By progressive, Herr Kleist obviously meant National Socialist, as he too was a declared opponent of racial politics in particular.

"The Nazis are becoming more unpalatable every day," complained Frau von Riedel, a conservative older lady. "Their influence reaches everywhere. One can hardly breathe, let alone take a single step without being watched."

"Yes, and who knows how much longer we'll be able to speak so openly," Annemarie added. "The Gestapo has ears everywhere. Just recently they visited my house looking for banned books I supposedly own."

"And did you have any?" Sophie asked.

"Of course not." Annemarie put on an innocent face. "Still, I'm angry. I'm pretty sure I know who ratted me out. It's the cousin of our dear friend, Countess Knevel. Needless to say, I've never invited him again."

Reinhard Busch took Annemarie's outburst as an opportunity to join the conversation. "A stark warning not to trumpet one's critical views and to carefully consider in whom you confide views that might cause you trouble."

Sophie gazed at him, feeling singled out. She took her wine glass and sipped the delicious drink to dispel the oppressive heaviness pressing down on her chest. The Nazis' reign of terror hovered like a monstrous shadow over Germany. Where would this lead if she couldn't even trust her friends or family any longer?

Her gaze fell on the young man sitting at the other end of the table who had been introduced as Eugen Habicht. He was in his mid-thirties, with dark hair and serious eyes. So far, he had hardly participated in the conversation, despite listening attentively. The mysterious air about him deeply touched Sophie.

As soon as the meal ended, the guests stood up and wandered into the salon, where they gathered in small groups. Sophie seized the opportunity to strike up a conversation with Herr Habicht.

"How do you know Annemarie?" she asked him.

"We used to be neighbors." He offered no further explanation, instead giving a slight bow. "It's an honor to meet you, Countess Borsoi. I've heard a lot about you."

"Hopefully good things," Sophie replied coquettishly.

"Well, that might be debatable." His deep eyes seemed to devour her. It struck a chord within her, urging her to please him.

"You shouldn't believe everything you hear about me. There's a lot of gossip in our circles."

A smile appeared on his lips that lit up the room, setting Sophie's heart ablaze. "I hope most of it is true; I'd be inconsolable if it turned out you shared the same mindset of most Germans."

"In that case, everything you've heard is true."

"I'm glad to hear this."

"Me too." No sooner had the words tumbled out of her mouth than Sophie chided herself for being stupid. Herr Habicht must think her very silly, or arrogant, which wasn't any better. "I mean, I'm glad you feel the same way."

"As a Jew, that's almost a given."

"You're Jewish?" Another response that didn't do justice to

her intelligence. Sophie groaned inwardly, hoping Herr Habicht's high opinion of her wouldn't evaporate too quickly.

"I am." The smile vanished from his face to be replaced by a sad expression. "And I must say, it's not a pleasant experience."

"I'm sorry," she murmured. "What's happening in our country is abhorrent."

"Yet nobody stands up against it. The most anyone does is rail against the Nazis behind closed doors. Always careful that nothing reaches the public."

Under his scrutinizing gaze, discomfort spread through her limbs. It certainly wasn't her fault that Hitler had come to power; God knows she had recognized the dangers a decade ago and warned about them. "You need to be understanding with the people, you just heard how dangerous it is to express a critical opinion."

"More dangerous than being a Jew?" he challenged her.

Ashamed, Sophie cast her gaze at the floor. "Certainly not."

"Talk is all well and good, but it won't change a thing. Action is needed to end this madness. Take this gathering here: a group of intelligent, highly respected people who are too cowardly to act according to their convictions."

"It's far too late for action; the surveillance state is everywhere. Any proactive measures should have been taken years ago," Sophie protested feebly.

"That's easy for you to say, Countess. You're not suffering under the persecution. You can comfortably lean back and lament the terrible conditions. You come from an influential family. Your protest in the right places could make a huge difference if you go about it cleverly."

His words hit Sophie like a slap and she felt her cheeks grow hot. "I'm afraid you overestimate my capabilities."

"Do I? Or are you just as much of a coward as everyone else?"

Sophie considered herself anything but a coward, yet – or perhaps because of it – she felt called out. Deep in her heart, she recognized the truth in Herr Habicht's assessment. So far, she had talked a lot but hadn't acted accordingly.

Fortunately, at that moment, Annemarie came rushing over, sparing her from having to answer. "There you are, monopolizing the charming Eugen."

"Esteemed Baroness, I must take my leave. It's not advisable for someone like me to be out on the streets too late." Eugen offered his hand to Annemarie, blowing an air kiss to her right and left cheek.

"Dearest Eugen, it was lovely to see you. Please keep in touch," Annemarie replied.

"I will do my best." Despite the casual words, Sophie knew what he was alluding to. Day by day Jews were disappearing without a trace.

He turned to Sophie and gallantly took her hand. His handshake was firm and pleasant, accompanied by a slight tingling in her fingers. Eugen Habicht was a fascinating man.

Soon after, Sophie bade goodbye to the other guests and thanked Annemarie for the evening. She slipped into her fur coat, put on her hat and gloves and left the house. Accompanied only by the sound of her footsteps and the distant hum of the city, she walked through the darkened streets, Habicht's earnest words echoing in her head.

Your voice could make a big difference if you use it properly.

Sophie stopped and looked up at the starlit sky. She thought of the countless people suffering under the regime and decided that she would no longer remain inactive. Even if she didn't have the influence of her father or brothers, she could still do good within her limited scope.

First thing in the morning, she would start exploring ways to help the persecuted.

CHAPTER 4

Despite the cold, Holger had been sitting in the garden all day on pins and needles, eagerly awaiting Frau Lemberg's return. As usual, the adults hadn't let him in on their plans, thinking these matters weren't for children.

They might be right with that opinion when it came to Hans and Hertha, but definitely not in his case. He was aware of his new responsibility as the head of the family and wanted to be treated accordingly. Regrettably, no one else seemed to see it that way.

He scrutinized his siblings: Hans, outwardly unaffected by the events of the past few days, was shaping blocks from the hard snow, which he used to build breathtaking constructions. His little brother was a genius constructor. Where other boys made towers, Hans created airplanes, bridges, ships or construction machines.

On the other side, Hertha was holding a huge spider in her hand, which she had baptized Agatha and had been carrying around since early morning. No matter where Hertha was, she always seemed to find an animal to pet and cuddle.

She adored dogs and cats; once, to her parents' horror, she had petted an SS guard dog. To everyone's surprise, the dog seemed to like it and had nudged her with his snout. Holger got goosebumps just from the memory. Unlike his sister he was afraid of German shepherds – and the SS.

"Do you want to hold Agatha?" Hertha offered generously.

"No, thank you." Holger raised his hands in defense. Naturally, he wasn't afraid of spiders or other creepy-crawlies, he simply preferred to observe them from afar, or better yet, not at all.

"Do you think I can teach her tricks like I did with the rabbits?" Hertha beamed at the mention of the cuddly four-legged friends the siblings had picked up about a year ago. Then a shadow fell over her face. "They're having a good life, aren't they?"

"Of course. Amelie swore they would, with her hand on her heart." Amelie was Frau Goldmann's adult daughter. Back then, when a heinous decree had ordered the Jews to put down their pets, Amelie had devised a rescue plan for the rabbits and taken them to her Aryan aunt in Oranienburg. Since the adults in their three-family household weren't allowed to know about the illegal activity Amelie had sworn the siblings to secrecy.

Finally, Frau Lemberg's tall, lean figure appeared at the rusty, ivy-covered garden gate. When the school had been functioning – before the Nazis decided that Jewish children didn't need an education – this part of the huge premises had been a paradise for the students, where they had played countless adventure games during breaks.

The girls had posed as enchanted princesses and the boys as daring robber knights – separately, of course, because what self-respecting boy wanted to be seen near a girl by his friends? These days the dilapidated gardener's house served as accommodation for the Lembergs, because they had been driven out of their apartment in a wing of the school building.

For some time now, the former school building had housed the transit camp for Jews, which Frau Lemberg had referred to the day before. Holger would have loved to take a peek inside, grasping at the small chance to find his parents waiting there for transport. But he was far too afraid of the SS who patrolled the grounds incessantly to attempt sneaking inside.

Holger jumped up and ran toward Frau Lemberg as soon as she closed the garden gate behind her. At the last moment, he remembered that as the new head of the family, he was practically an adult and should behave accordingly. So he stopped in his tracks and walked the last few meters with measured steps. "Good day, Frau Lemberg."

"Hello, Holger. I hope no one has seen you out here?" Her jaws were clenched tight, which Holger took as a bad sign.

"We were exclusively in the back part, the way you told us," he answered politely, although he was nearly bursting with curiosity. "What's going to happen to us?"

She took a deep breath and smiled at him. Holger immediately recognized that her good mood was only pretend. Her next words confirmed his fear. "We'll talk about that later. First, I'm going to cook dinner."

Adults always postponed unpleasant things until later, while they told good news instantly. It was hard for Holger to hold back the tears forming in his eyes as he nodded.

"I'll call you when dinner is ready. Until then, don't let yourselves be seen, I don't want the SS marching in here asking questions."

"Don't worry, Frau Lemberg." Holger trudged back to his siblings, before he changed his mind and hurried after Frau Lemberg to the house. Taking a detour to the outhouse, he snuck inside and settled on the wooden bench beneath the coat rack in the dark hallway. Pulling his knees to his chest, he leaned against the wall, intently listening to the muffled voices coming from the kitchen.

"How was your visit with the pastor?" Herr Lemberg asked.

A heavy sigh followed. "He turned me away. The Gestapo is watching the parish, so he can't take anyone in for the time being. Especially not for more than a night or two." Frau Lemberg's voice sounded desperate.

"You know we can't keep the children here. It's too dangerous. Sooner or later, someone from the transit camp will notice their presence. Besides, we don't have ration cards for them."

Holger's pulse ratcheted up. Hans and Hertha were playing in the garden, unaware of the uncertainty of their future. They relied on him; he had to be strong for them. If only he could think of something. Anything.

Frau Lemberg spoke again. "We can't send them back, either. They're even less safe at my brother's place than they are here."

Holger wrinkled his nose in thought until he remembered that their landlord Julius Falkenstein was Silvana Lemberg's brother. His wife Edith, like Helga Goldmann, wasn't Jewish, which afforded the entire household a few tiny advantages.

"Do you really think so?" asked Herr Lemberg.

A few seconds of silence followed, during which only the rhythmic chopping of a knife on a cutting board filled the air, before Frau Lemberg answered in a serious tone, "I'm pretty sure that's where the Gestapo will search for the children first. If they find them, they'll be more than happy to arrest the other members of the household as well. No... sending the three back is the worst solution."

Holger had to swallow several times to keep down the rising panic. He didn't want to be responsible for anything bad happening to the nice Goldmanns or the Falkensteins.

"Do you want to keep the children with us?" Herr Lemberg asked.

"Not really, but we can't send them away. If only we could find a family that would agree to take them in and hide them."

Holger pressed himself closer against the wall, straining his ears. He had never suspected that Frau Lemberg, who always seemed so strong and brave, might not have a solution to a problem. The realization shook his belief in the power of adults to its very core.

The Nazis could truly do whatever they wanted with the Jews, and no one – including the adults – had the power to stop them.

"Maybe there's another possibility," Herr Lemberg said after a while. "What about your sister Adriana's summer cottage?"

"She transferred it to the name of her husband's business partner before emigrating so the Nazis weren't able to confiscate it." There was a pause during which Holger anxiously chewed on his fingers. "As far as I know, it was mothballed as soon as the war began. It's not much more than a hut without heating and certainly not suitable for living."

"It would be a possibility during spring and summer. If we hide the children with us until then, they can at least spend the warm months there. And by winter, the war might already be over."

Holger lifted his head. People constantly made contradictory statements. Some believed the war was going to last for a long time, while others announced its imminent end on a daily basis. The Jewish community was certain the Allies would win sooner or later and lift their yoke, while the newspapers proclaimed Germany's grand victory through some kind of wonder weapons in their headlines.

"It's our only option." Frau Lemberg sounded tired.

For a while, it remained quiet, but then footsteps came toward Holger. He jumped up from the bench, fumbling with putting on his gloves. Seconds later Herr Lemberg stepped into the hallway and looked at him inquisitively.

"Is everything alright, Holger?" he asked, trying to sound friendly, but he couldn't fool Holger. The concern in his eyes was frightening.

"Yes, Herr Lemberg, I just came here to get my gloves. I'm going back outside to play with Hans and Hertha," Holger replied, hoping his eavesdropping hadn't been noticed.

Herr Lemberg seemed too preoccupied with his own problems to question Holger's statement. "Dinner will be ready soon. Go get your brother and sister and tell them to wash their hands."

Holger breathed a sigh of relief. He was off the hook. Slipping on his gloves, he hurried outside to fetch his siblings. For now, he wouldn't tell them what he'd found out; they were too young to understand anyway. Better they believed they were safe with the Lembergs.

CHAPTER 5

Baumann sat in a noisy Berlin pub, taking a hearty swig of his beer. The air was heavy with cigarette and pipe smoke, and the more or less muted conversations of other patrons created a busy yet cozy atmosphere. Beside him sat his loyal comrades, Manfred and Reinhard, men he had been friends with for many years and trusted implicitly. They all shared a deep-seated hatred for the Nazi regime.

"The pastor is under Gestapo surveillance," Baumann murmured, leaning forward to ensure his words weren't overheard by unwanted ears. "The cops from the station across the street are on our side. If there's imminent danger, they'll put a watering can in the flower box hanging from their windowsill."

"How's that supposed to help?" Manfred had worked his way up from steel worker to union official. A few years ago, he had joined the Nazi Party to be above suspicion and secretly help his communist friends escape when they got on the wrong side of the authorities.

"Nothing, stupid. When the watering can is there, it's a sign, so everyone knows not to knock on the pastor's door. Otherwise, they'll be snatched up before they know it."

"We need to warn the underground," Reinhard said.

"That's why we're here."

"Oh, and here I thought we were meeting for a beer-drinking session." Manfred raised his glass and drained it in one go.

Baumann suppressed a grin. "One doesn't rule out the other. Spread the information strategically to your contacts, word of mouth will do the rest."

"You can bet on it." Manfred wiped the foam from his mouth with his hand. "Anything else?"

"I have something," Reinhard chimed in. At first glance, the delicate, slender, industrialist's son seemed out of place among the bull-necked working class men, but over the past fifteen years, he had proven to be an excellent ally, first in the class struggle and later in the resistance against the Nazis. Thanks to his father's good connections – who must never learn about his son's anti-Nazi sentiments – he moved in the highest circles of German society and had direct access to many Nazi bigwigs.

"Well, out with it," Baumann urged him.

Reinhard hesitated for a moment before responding in his characteristic, thoughtful manner: "I was invited to a soirée at the home of Baroness Annemarie zu Steinfeld a few days ago."

"Showoff," Manfred muttered good-naturedly.

Ignoring the interruption, Reinhard continued, "There, I met an interesting woman."

"Now you've got me." Manfred's ears perked up with interest, since he was always eager to hear any stories about women.

"My gosh, let Reinhard finish, will you?" Baumann reprimanded him, before signaling the waitress to bring three more beers.

"Thank you." Reinhard nodded in Baumann's direction. "The woman I was introduced to is the Countess Sophie von Borsoi." He shot a dark stare in Manfred's direction for good measure. "Her regime-critical convictions are well-known. At the soirée, I got the impression she's a committed and courageous woman who just hasn't been given the opportunity yet to put her words into action. I think she would be very valuable to our cause if we could win her over."

Baumann and Manfred exchanged skeptical glances.

"A countess?" Manfred raised his eyebrows. "How do we know we can trust her?"

"There's no absolute certainty – with anyone," Reinhard admitted. "My gut feeling tells me she'll follow through on her words if given the chance. Besides, she has connections that could be useful to us."

Baumann scratched behind his ear. "Baroness Steinfeld is known among the illegals in the underground for helping out with food and clothing. If this countess is a friend of hers, that's definitely a good sign."

"Exactly my thought." Reinhard nodded with satisfaction.

"And how are we supposed to convince her to work with us? What would she even do?" Manfred wasn't on board yet.

"A countess doesn't fit in with us, that's true." Baumann rested his head on both hands to think. Just then, the waitress appeared and placed three glasses of beer on the table. Baumann took a big gulp and licked the foam from his lips with relish. "But the pastor... he would be a more innocuous contact. Especially now that the Gestapo is watching him. A countess visiting his parish wouldn't arouse suspicion."

"I hadn't even thought of him." Reinhard looked around the group before raising his glass. "To the countess."

As they toasted Baumann watched in amazement how Reinhard managed to drink his beer without the foam sticking to his lips. *Bloody hell!*

"So, who's going to approach her?" Manfred asked.

"Reinhard, of course." It was clear to Baumann that no one else in their group was in a position to convince the countess. "He's the one who knows her."

"Then it's settled. Reinhard will talk to the countess and introduce her to the pastor," Manfred summarized. "The rest is none of our business; the fewer connections between her and our group, the safer for everyone involved."

Baumann finished his beer and knocked on the table. "I've got to be at work early tomorrow."

"It's better if we leave anyway." Manfred cast a meaningful side glance at a group of SA men who'd just entered through the door. "We'll only get into trouble if we stay."

Unfortunately, that was true. Especially when SA men were drunk, they would pick a fight with anyone who didn't bellow "Heil Hitler" fervently enough or belt out the Horst Wessel Song at the top of their lungs. Sometimes it was rather tedious to pretend to toe the party line when you'd prefer to wring these scumbags' necks.

"See you," Baumann said and left. Outside the pub, a bus was just turning the corner and he quickened his pace to reach the stop in time. As he jumped onto the footboard at the last second and hauled himself inside the bus, he nearly collided with one of his workers from the locomotive workshop.

"Baumann? You here?" David Goldmann, nicknamed Kessel, was leaning right next to the door, quickly covering the empty spot on his jacket with his arm.

"Don't worry, I've known for quite a while." Baumann had no intention of ratting out the boy for once again being out and about without the mandatory yellow star.

"Thanks." The relief was written all over Kessel's face.

"Just make sure you're on time for work tomorrow."

"I will." Whether Kessel had to get off anyway or preferred to make himself scarce, at the next stop he disembarked with a short nod, without saying another word beforehand.

During the remainder of the journey, Baumann pondered whether Kessel would be a good candidate for Pastor Perwe's network, before he dismissed the thought. As a halfbred, Kessel's situation was bad enough; he didn't need to take on more risk pursuing illegal activities.

CHAPTER 6

Countess Sophie von Borsoi was sitting in the cozy living room of her tiny, centrally located apartment, leafing through a book on veterinary medicine when a knock on the door interrupted her studies. Always when an unannounced visitor came, a wave of bile rose in her throat.

So far she had received two visits from the Gestapo, and once they had taken her for interrogation to their headquarters at Prinz-Albrecht-Strasse because someone had denounced her for subversion of the war effort. She only got away with a reprimand because the interrogating officer was an old acquaintance of her father.

Her fingers trembling, she put the book aside and went to the door. When she opened it, Reinhard Busch was standing in front of her.

"Countess Borsoi?" he asked politely. "Reinhard Busch. We met recently at Baroness zu Steinfeld's, do you remember?"

"Of course I do, Herr Busch. What can I do for you?" During the dinner at Annemarie's, Sophie had come to appreciate the serious man, whose father often had business dealings with her family. Reinhard evidently did not share his father's National Socialist beliefs. Nonetheless she decided to exercise caution.

"May I come in for a moment?" Herr Busch asked.

"Certainly, if you'd please follow me." She led him into her living room, although she would have preferred to deal with him at the door. After her friend Annemarie had been denounced to the Gestapo by the cousin of a good old friend for possessing indexed books, Sophie no longer trusted anyone – no matter how close they were to someone in the inner circle. If Herr Busch was here to compromise her, she would show him she had nothing to hide.

"I was studying for an exam," she apologized, pointing at the jumble of notebooks, medical books and lecture notes on the coffee table in the living room.

"Your father must be very proud of you. A skilled veterinarian is a huge benefit for every large estate," said Herr Busch, glancing at the open anatomy book.

Sophie tilted her head for a few seconds, mulling over her response. "On the contrary. My father is deeply saddened, because I don't conform to the traditional role of a woman. He would have preferred me to marry the son of a neighboring estate, like my sisters did."

For a moment, Herr Busch's facial features slipped before he regained control. "Please accept my apologies. I didn't mean to rub salt in old wounds."

"Don't worry. I've gotten used to it." Inwardly, Sophie rolled her eyes and wished he would get to the point, for surely he hadn't taken the effort to visit her to exchange pleasantries.

When he kept silent, she asked him straight out, "What brings you here?"

"It's just...My dog seems to be ill and I had hoped you would be able to offer advice."

Sophie squinted at him. Why didn't he just take his dog to a veterinarian? Herr Busch certainly didn't lack the money. The whole visit stank to high heaven. She decided to put him to the test. "What exactly is wrong with your dog?"

Herr Busch sat down on the sofa – uninvited – and furrowed

his brow as if in deep thought. "He hasn't had an appetite for several days in a row and seems very weak. I don't know what to do."

Sophie made an earnest face, although she had to stifle a laugh at his contrived behavior. The aforementioned dog was certainly not sick, if it even existed.

"Did you bring your dog with you?" she asked, looking around as if searching for an invisible animal.

"No, he's too weak to walk," Herr Busch replied. "I came to ask for your advice."

Sophie's pulse quickened. This was definitely a trap. If his dog was indeed so sick, the logical course of action would have been to rush him to an experienced veterinarian, not to ask a student for advice.

There was only one way to find out. "Do you work for the Gestapo?"

"What? No!" His expression showed genuine shock. "What makes you think so?"

"Firstly, because I'm sure you don't have a sick dog." A smug grin curled her lips. If he had indeed come to spy on her, she certainly wouldn't give him any more hints to help him better deceive his next victim.

With a disarming smile, he raised his hands. "You caught me. The dog was a pretext so you wouldn't send me away immediately."

"Why do you think a made-up dog would make me trust you?"

He answered with a contrite grimace, "Please forgive me, that was a very bad idea on my part. You must think I'm an informer, but I assure you, I don't work for the Gestapo. Quite the opposite." He looked around the room, as if to make sure they were alone in the apartment, before he lowered his voice. "Together with some friends, we help people who have undeservedly fallen on hard times, if you understand what I mean?"

Sophie was still suspicious. "You mean, people persecuted by the regime?"

Again, he looked around the small apartment, then visibly gathered himself and nodded. "Yes. Jews, gypsies, deserters, escaped prisoners of war... we help where we can."

With relief Sophie noted that he had finally laid his cards on the table. If he intended to denounce her, she could do the same to him and claim she had only pretended to go along with his proposal to extract information to give to the police. Slowly, she asked: "And how does that concern me?"

Herr Busch stood up, paced the room and came to a stand within an arm's length. His steel-blue eyes bored into her. "You're known for your opposition to the regime. I know someone who would be delighted to make your acquaintance."

The surprising offer hit Sophie like a punch to the gut. For the second time in a week, she was challenged to put her words into action. Perhaps it was time for her to join the active resistance. However, she kept harboring doubts about the sincerity of Herr Busch's invitation. It could very well be a trap.

"This someone is you, I assume?"

"Not at all." He took a step backward, out of her personal space.

She swallowed down the sarcastic response on the tip of her tongue. For several breaths, silence fell over the living room as Herr Busch and Sophie sized each other up.

Finally, he spoke again, "The person I have in mind is Pastor Perwe from the Swedish Victoria church. Do you know him?"

"Regrettably, I haven't had the pleasure yet."

"You should definitely rectify that. Pay a visit to Pastor Perwe and decide for yourself if his work is worth risking your life for." He handed her a note with the address and mass times of the Swedish church.

"Risk my life? What do you mean by that?" Sophie looked up from the yellow note into his face with its piercing blue eyes and shuddered under the earnestness of his gaze.

"You're a clever woman, Countess Borsoi. You must be aware that you're playing with fire. Due to your family's connections, you might get away with regime-critical remarks, but if the Gestapo finds out you're actively supporting undesirable population groups, they won't turn a blind eye."

Sophie was still uncertain what to make of Herr Busch's visit, so she retreated to a noncommittal response. "Thank you for your concern, Herr Busch. I'll pay the pastor a visit."

"Don't wait too long, Countess." With a slight bow, he took his leave.

As soon as he had left the apartment, Sophie let out a loud groan. She locked the door and leaned against it, her heart wildly pounding. Several minutes later, she returned to the living room and picked up her anatomy book, re-reading the same page several times without understanding the meaning because thoughts were swirling in her head.

She had long hated the Nazis with all her heart, but until now she hadn't entertained the thought of taking action and resisting. She had convinced herself it was pointless, too late, too dangerous, or that she was too insignificant, not in the right position and without enough influence to make a difference. But now an opportunity had been served to her on a silver platter. If she didn't seize it, what did that make of her? A coward? A pretender? A follower?

After several hours of useless brooding, Sophie slammed the book shut with a loud bang. She needed fresh air to think. A walk through the nearby park would provide the perfect setting. Putting on her mink coat and tucking a flashlight into her pocket just in case, she left the house. The cold, crisp winter air brushed her cheeks.

She didn't need the torch, because the snow reflected the moonlight. Despite the general blackout, it was surprisingly light in the park. As she walked, the snow crunched under her shoes and she pushed her hands deeper into the warm pockets of her coat.

In her mind, she went over the meeting with Reinhard Busch time and again. Each time, she was more convinced that he had told the truth. Still, she hesitated to plan a visit to Pastor Perwe.

Just as she was passing a boarded-up fountain, rapid footsteps came up behind her. She turned around and saw a young man in a hurry, constantly looking over his shoulder. He noticed her too and paused, his eyes wide with fear.

"Herr Habicht?" Sophie asked, surprised.

"Countess Borsoi!" he called out breathlessly. "Go away! I'm being followed."

Without hesitation, Sophie grabbed his hand. "Come with me. I live just around the corner."

"I can't. I'd be putting you in danger."

"Don't dawdle." Ignoring his protest, she pulled him along behind her. When they reached her apartment building, she hastily opened the door. After looking over her shoulder to make sure there were no pursuers or passersby in sight she pushed Herr Habicht inside. There, she put a finger to her lips to signal him to be quiet before walking through the hallway, unlocking her apartment door and motioning for him to follow her.

Once inside, they both leaned against the door, breathing heavily, until Sophie regained her composure and whispered, "Don't move."

She walked into the living room, drew the blackout curtains and turned on the radio before calling him inside. "What happened?"

"An SS patrol was on my heels." Herr Habicht wiped sweat from his brow. "I'm afraid I was out a bit too late in the evening." For Jews a curfew was in place after nine o'clock.

"I don't think anyone saw us, but just to be on the safe side, you should stay here until we're certain the coast is clear."

"Countess Borsoi, I'm greatly indebted to you." Eugen Habicht regained his composure. His charming smile made Sophie's knees weak. To distract herself – and him – she quickly asked, "After that shock, I need a drink. Would you like a glass of wine?"

"If it's not too much trouble, I'd love one."

"Please, have a seat. I'll fetch us something." Sophie disappeared into the kitchen, took a bottle of red wine from the shelf and placed it on a tray with two glasses. Just as she was about to carry the tray into the living room, she changed her mind, cut a few slices of bread and cheese and added them to the tray. Heavily laden she returned to the living room.

The instant he noticed her, Herr Habicht jumped up. "That wasn't necessary, Countess." His hungry eyes, however, belied his words.

"Please, it's nothing special, and it would be extremely impolite not to offer a refreshment to a guest."

As they ate bread with cheese and sipped their wine, she enjoyed their splendid conversation. It turned out that Herr Habicht was well-versed in the fine arts. Until the dismissal of all Jewish employees, he had worked as a director for various Berlin theaters and therefore knew most of the classic plays Sophie loved.

"That's wonderful! You must accompany me sometime—" Sophie stopped mid-sentence, chiding herself for her lack of sensitivity as soon as she noticed his sad expression. "Please excuse me, I didn't mean to... I mean..." She became hopelessly tangled in her words and finally shut her mouth to avoid blurting out more ludicrous things.

"Not at all, Countess." Herr Habicht took her hand in his.

The intense look in his dark eyes held her captive, while the warmth from his hand traveled the length of her arm all the way up to her shoulders. Involuntarily, her lips parted as a pleasant tingling made her shiver. Secretly, she wished he would pull her into his arms for a kiss.

"Countess..."

"Call me Sophie." Her gaze was glued to his and even if she

had wanted to, she wouldn't have been able to move. "My name is Sophie."

"Sophie." His mouth caressed her name, pronouncing it softly yet demandingly. "You are a fascinating woman."

She was frozen in place, staring spellbound at his face, on which the most wonderful smile appeared.

"I want to kiss you, Sophie."

Unable to give an answer, she threw herself into his arms and pressed her mouth to his gently curved lips. She kissed him – or did he kiss her? – as if she hadn't drunk a drop of water in days and only he could quench her desperate thirst.

Many minutes passed before they let go of each other. Heat burned hot in her presumably bright red cheeks, while sweet desire spread through her limbs. Despite the sweet sensations, she released him, repeatedly smoothing her skirt. What must he think of her? "Please excuse—"

Eugen placed a finger on her lips to silence her. "Say nothing. I should probably leave now, but if I may, I'd very much like to see you again."

His sincere gaze held Sophie captive, so much that she needed to clear her throat several times before her voice obeyed her again.

"That would be lovely, Eugen."

His beaming expression was proof of his feelings for her.

CHAPTER 7

Nearly a month had passed with the Lembergs, and talk of relocating the three siblings had faded. Secretly, Holger was relieved—he'd grown fond of Herr and Frau Lemberg. But the collection camp for Jews next door kept him on edge, a constant reminder of the looming danger. Day in and day out, the shouting of the SS men filled the air and when he crept close enough to the hedge separating the garden from the campgrounds, he sometimes caught a glimpse of the shuffling, dusty, gray prisoners.

Hertha was more afraid of them than of the SS men, since she believed they were ghosts. Despite Holger's repeated assurances that ghosts didn't exist and those sorry creatures were indeed humans, she didn't fully believe him. He couldn't ask Frau Lemberg for help with this issue, because she had forbidden the siblings from going near the hedge and would scold him for disobeying her.

Nonetheless the three were constantly drawn toward the hedge, for different reasons: Hertha had found little friends in a pair of mice that lived between the roots of the plants; Hans used the branches and needles of the thujas to obtain material for his next building project. Holger, on the other hand, had a much more important reason: He spent hours in hiding, hoping to one day spot his parents among the downtrodden figures.

He hadn't yet decided what he'd do if that moment came, but one thing was clear—he couldn't share his plan with Hans and Hertha. They might thoughtlessly leap up and rush onto the campgrounds just to hug their mother.

Holger grimaced. Sometimes it was quite hard to look after the two little ones. He had no idea how his mother had done it with such effortless ease.

"Quick, come!" Hertha whispered with excitement in her voice. "Look what I found!"

From experience, Holger knew his sister wouldn't stop pestering him until he indulged her, so he left his observation post and crawled on all fours until he reached her, where he asked just as quietly, "What is it?"

She turned her face to him, her cheeks bright red from the cold, her braids smeared with slush, her eyes shining with excitement. "Shh. Otherwise you'll scare him."

Not another animal, Holger thought. The next moment his suspicion was confirmed as she opened her hands, revealing a tiny, skinny hedgehog, completely motionless.

"Is it dead?" Goosebumps appeared on Holger's arms.

"No, he's just scared. Look how cute he is." And indeed, the hedgehog seemed to have become comfortable sitting on a human hand, as it stretched out its snout.

"Where did you find him?"

"Over there under the dry leaves," Hertha answered, as if it were the most natural thing in the world. After a fearful glance at her brother, she added, "I didn't wake him up, honest!"

Although Hertha was the animal expert, even Holger knew that hedgehogs hibernated and that this one had woken up much too early for some reason. It wouldn't surprise him if the reason was that the poor animal could no longer tolerate the SS men's constant shouting and had decided to find a quieter place for its long winter's nap.

"We should carry him to the other side of the garden, he can go back to sleep there," he suggested.

Hertha rolled her eyes. "As if that would work. A hedgehog doesn't just go back to sleep. He needs something to eat first."

By now, their whispered conversation had piqued Hans's curiosity. He came over and hunched down next to them. "What do hedgehogs eat anyway?"

At a loss of ideas, Holger looked questioningly at Hertha.

"They like beetles, snails and worms best." Hertha knew everything about animals.

"Well, we won't find any of those in winter," Holger said.

"I can build a house for him while you look for food," Hans offered.

"Oh, yes!" Hertha cried so loud that all three of them startled at her voice. She quickly clapped her free hand over her mouth and pressed deeper into the hedge.

Holger gave her a reproving glare. His little sister knew that they had to stay absolutely quiet so they wouldn't be discovered. Trembling with nerves, they crouched motionless for several minutes until Holger was confident no one had heard them and gave a hand signal for the all-clear.

"Not another sound," he whispered. "Let's go behind the shed. We can safely talk there."

"And the hedgehog?" Hertha asked.

"We'll take him with us, of course. We'll discuss what to do with him in our headquarters."

In a small procession, Holger in front, Hertha with the hedgehog in the middle and Hans bringing up the rear, they crept as quiet as mice behind the dilapidated former tool shed on the other side of the garden, where they couldn't be overheard by the SS. In fact, Frau Lemberg had ordered them to play exclusively in that area, but it was far too boring to be confined to such a small space.

On the wind-protected side of the shed, they had built their headquarters: a patch of ground, where they had removed the snow and covered the frozen earth with pine branches. There, they settled down to hold a powwow.

"What are we going to do with the hedgehog?" Holger asked.

"He needs a house and something to eat." Hertha gazed tenderly at the shivering bundle in her hand. "Look, the poor fellow is cold."

"I'll build the house." Hans let his eyes roam until they settled on a huge ivy. "I'll make him a cozy den out of ivy branches. In there, he'll be nice and warm."

"I'll take care of his food. Here, hold him for a moment." Hertha pressed the hedgehog into Hans's hand. "First, I'll go and get some water."

Holger managed to grab her arm before she ran off. "Careful. You mustn't be seen."

"I know that." In her annoying manner, she rolled her eyes the way she always did when she believed her brothers were treating her like a baby. Seconds later, she stormed off.

Hans handed the hedgehog to Holger and began expertly building a den out of the ivy branches. A few minutes later, Hertha returned with a bowl of water and a sealed jar full of beetles.

"Yuck! Where did you get those from?" Hans made a disgusted face, for which he earned another eye roll.

"From the potato storage, of course. Prickly will love them."

"Prickly?" Holger shot his sister a questioning look.

"The hedgehog, dummy! Now that he's our pet, he needs to have a name." Hertha shook her head, as if she couldn't believe Holger didn't know that pets needed names.

Sometimes he really didn't have it easy with his younger siblings. His annoyance was instantly forgotten as he watched, spellbound, how she unscrewed the jar, took a beetle between her index finger and thumb and held it out to Prickly.

Cautiously, the hedgehog unrolled itself and sniffed briefly before stretching out its – admittedly – cute snout. Then he greedily devoured the beetle.

"And now let's show Prickly his new home." Hans beamed with excitement.

The three of them watched in awe as the hedgehog took possession of his den, snuggling into a corner.

"Won't he get cold at night?" Hertha worried.

"I stuffed the walls with leaves to properly insulate the den," Hans replied.

"What does insulate mean?"

"It means the walls don't let wind or cold through."

"Are you sure?" Hertha wrinkled her nose in doubt.

"Of course I'm sure!" Hans was in his element and launched into a lengthy explanation of how insulation worked and why leaves, in particular, made such a good insulating layer. Holger could tell from Hertha's expression that she didn't understand a single word, and if he was honest, he had to admit that he couldn't quite follow his brother's explanation either. It was a mystery to him where Hans had picked up so much knowledge about construction topics, since he had only attended elementary school for three years before the Nazis banned Jewish children from getting an education.

After making sure Prickly was comfortable in his den, Holger said, "Let's go inside. It's getting dark."

"I'm cold." Hertha shivered as she rubbed her bare fingers.

"And I'm starving," Hans declared.

Holger nodded sadly. He couldn't remember how it felt not to be hungry. When they'd still lived together with their parents and the other families in the apartment, the adults had used to serve him, Hans and David, the Goldmanns' adult son, an extra helping of food, and yet it had never been enough to still the hunger.

Since they'd come to live with the Lembergs, conditions had become worse: Due to their being illegals, the siblings didn't receive ration cards, which meant the Lembergs had to divide the already meager meals into five portions instead of two.

If the situation worsened any more, one day he might taste a beetle. If Prickly liked the critters, perhaps they weren't so bad. Involuntarily, Holger gagged and decided to test this idea only as an absolute last resort.

CHAPTER 8

Baumann sat in his glass booth, his gaze sweeping across the noisy main hall at the locomotive workshop. Everything seemed to be normal, yet something nagged at the back of his mind. He mentally went through each station. Two men had just entered through the gate carrying an engine block between them, heaving it onto the workbench for repair before they began to meticulously disassemble it.

At the next station, Koloss, a huge, muscle-packed man whose real name was Elmar, put on his safety goggles and thick work gloves before starting to weld a broken spare part. Baumann's eyes wandered further, scanning the workstations one after another until he finally realized what, or rather who, was missing: Kessel.

Once again, the lad had made himself scarce for an astonishingly long time. Which wasn't that surprising, since Kessel supervised the electrical work and helped the mostly unskilled forced laborers with tricky tasks, after practically all trained workers had been drafted into military service.

Only Koloss and Baumann had been granted the status "indispensable" and kept the workshop running, together with Kessel, who was exempt from military service for being a halfbred. Kessel was an excellent worker and Baumann would have promoted him to foreman without hesitation if not for his Jewish blood. As such, he stood only a hair's breadth above full Jews in the Nazi racial pyramid and was officially allowed to do menial work at best.

Lately, however, Kessel had been out on the grounds far too much, often right before his shift ended. Baumann was certain the lad was up to no good.

"I'm not gonna let him pull the wool over my eyes," Baumann muttered before opening the door of his glass booth and stepping into the main hall. Once outside the protective panes, a deafening noise enveloped him, which made it nearly impossible to converse. But after over twenty years of working together, that wasn't necessary. Koloss seemed to sense Baumann approaching his station and looked up from his work as soon as he finished welding the piece he was working on.

Baumann gave him a hand signal indicating he was going to the outdoor area. Koloss nodded briefly and took on the next broken piece.

Once outside, Baumann enjoyed the relative quiet. In the past, when he had toiled nonstop in the hall himself, the noise hadn't bothered him, but the administrative work in the glass booth had softened him.

Like a sniffing dog, he tilted his head until a hunch told him where Kessel might be. So he made his way to the back of the vast grounds, where the perimeter fence met the shunting tracks. On the way, he passed the tool shed and looked inside. The door gave a pitiful squeak as he opened it.

Baumann made a mental note to oil the door when he got the chance, then discarded the idea. First, oil was scarce, and second, the squeak was an excellent theft deterrent. Just as he'd suspected, he found nothing unusual in the shed and closed the door again. The squeaking once again reverberated through the air, startling a sparrow that had settled on a bare tree nearby.

Again, Baumann tilted his head and pondered where Kessel

might be disappearing to every evening, until he saw him walking from the direction of the railway cars parked on the sidings. Without hesitating, he walked toward him.

"Hey, Kessel, got a minute?" Baumann called out.

Kessel raised his head and looked in Baumann's direction. For a second, uncertainty flashed in his eyes before he answered with feigned casualness: "Sure, boss."

"Something wrong with the wagons?" Baumann observed Kessel closely and didn't miss the lad's brief flinch.

"I was just checking which ones we'll fix up tomorrow."

That was certainly a lie, because they always worked on the wagons in the order they were delivered by the Reichsbahn.

Kessel seemed to sense Baumann's skepticism, as he launched into a long-winded explanation: "Instead of working on the wagons in order of their arrival, it would be more efficient to group them by type of repair. For example one day we fix wheels, another day couplings, and so on."

"Newfangled nonsense," Baumann muttered, although he secretly agreed. The current process was impractical and wasted a lot of time. He preferred not to tell Kessel the reason for the cumbersome and inefficient handling of repairs.

Sabotage of war-critical production, which definitely included the repair of Reichsbahn locomotives and wagons, was considered undermining the war effort or treason and could be punishable by death. But an inefficient working method? Let someone try to prove that.

"Don't you think it would help to work through our backlog?" Kessel asked as he walked back to the main hall alongside Baumann.

"Nah, forget it. They'd just increase our workload even more." Baumann waved the suggestion off. "It's enough of a slog as it is."

Understanding flashed in Kessel's eyes. "The work here is hard, but it could be worse."

"You're right about that. They could lock us all up in a concentration camp. So don't do anything stupid."

"I won't, boss."

"Good." By now Baumann was fully convinced that Kessel had done something forbidden. He decided to snoop around the wagons after the shift ended to find out exactly what was going on. Due to the main hall's glass roof, they were not allowed to work after daylight hours because of blackout regulations, except for a few stations that had been fitted with wooden barriers or curtains.

In the evening, when most of the workers had left the workshop, Baumann stayed behind. He put a flashlight in the pocket of his coveralls and, for good measure, grabbed a steel rod before marching to the sidings, which by now lay in almost total darkness.

His surprise was balanced by satisfaction when he searched the fence in the beam of the flashlight and discovered a hole in it: half-hidden by a bush and barely big enough for a person to slip through.

"Aha." Now he just had to find out why someone was secretly entering the grounds. After all, he hadn't noticed any thefts of material lately. He turned around and his gaze fell on one of the wagons, whose blackout curtains were drawn in one compartment.

Cautiously, he approached the wagon, clutching the iron bar tightly. The door was slightly ajar. He pulled on the handle until it slid open. Baumann listened briefly for suspicious sounds, but everything remained quiet.

He climbed in and closed the door behind him. Then he walked through the corridor until he came to the compartment where the blackout curtains were drawn. After making sure no light could escape the train wagon, he turned his flashlight back on and shone it around the compartment.

Surprise caught him unaware: in one corner lay a coarse blanket, which normally served to protect sensitive components from dust, neatly folded into a bundle. Next to it stood a canteen and a bottle of water.

"Clever lad," Baumann whistled through his teeth. Kessel had created a cozy, weather-protected spot for fugitives in search of shelter for the night. He might as well continue doing so. Baumann certainly wouldn't tell anyone about it.

On his way back to the factory hall, he regretted that Kessel wasn't suitable for Pastor Perwe's underground network, because the lad certainly had what it took. However, due to his heritage, it would be irresponsible to expose him to this additional danger.

The next morning, a new group of forced laborers arrived, mainly Jews and prisoners of war.

Baumann cursed at the sight of them. How on earth were these emaciated wretches supposed to carry heavy loads for ten or twelve hours a day? Grimly, he prepared himself for a fastidious discussion with the factory manager. He fully planned to demand extra rations to fatten up the men.

Because under Baumann's care, no one starved. To keep up appearances, it mustn't look like he pitied these people. Therefore he usually argued that workers who collapsed under heavy loads were of no use to the factory. And strong men needed something to sink their teeth into.

A particularly skinny lad caught his eye. He ordered the lad to follow him into the glass booth after he had assigned the others to the various departments.

Baumann closed the door behind them and said, "You can barely stand on your feet, what have they done to you?"

The not-yet-adult boy seemed afraid of being sent away and puffed out his chest. "I'm much stronger than I look, Herr Baumann."

"Just Baumann," he grumbled. "You really think you can lug around a heavy piece like that?" He pointed at a worker who was heaving a rim onto the workbench.

The boy turned pale to the roots of his hair, but nodded bravely. "Certainly."

"What's your name?" Baumann rubbed behind his ear.

"Michael Israel Hammerschmidt."

Baumann rubbed his ear harder, resisting the urge to tell the boy he didn't agree with the legally mandated second names for Jews. Just then, the factory manager, Herr Merkle, walked by with a few important-looking men.

Merkle stopped in front of the glass booth and motioned for Baumann to join them. Baumann ordered Hammerschmidt, "You stay here 'til I get back. Don't you dare move from this spot."

"Yes, Herr Baumann."

"Just Baumann," he growled while leaving the booth. Outside, he was greeted by deafening noise that made normal conversation impossible, so he just nodded briefly to the visitors, joined the group, and followed them to Merkle's office, which was located in the flat administration building next to the main hall.

Once they arrived there, Merkle introduced Baumann to the men, who turned out to be envoys from the Reichsbahn.

"Who was that boy in your office, Baumann?" Merkle asked.

"One of the new workers they sent us today."

Merkle made an exaggerated gesture and said to the Reichsbahn officials, "Did you see him? How are we supposed to meet our quota with subjects like him?" Then he turned toward Baumann. "Make sure the new hires perform, or I'll make sure they disappear."

"I'm on it, Herr Merkle. The little one serves as a runner; he's quick on his feet." Baumann seized the opportunity with both hands. "If these men are supposed to do hard work, they need enough to eat."

"Always the same old tune," Merkle groaned.

"Because otherwise they'll make mistakes and that costs time and money. After all, we want to deliver the best quality to the Reichsbahn."

Under the critical eyes of the railway officials, Merkle couldn't admit that he didn't care about quality as long as the workshop met its quota. Grumpily, he gave in. "Fine. The forced laborers get half the ration of the Germans."

"For lunch and for the afternoon break," clarified Baumann, not wanting to leave any doubt. The factory director's tightly clenched jaws revealed that he hadn't meant for both meals. Baumann was satisfied with that, knowing he couldn't get more out of the penny-pincher who would have preferred only giving the forced laborers nothing but a ladle of watered-down soup a day.

After Baumann reported to the Reichsbahn representatives about the current status of work in the repair shop, he was dismissed from the meeting. Relieved, he left the administration building and marched back to the main hall. In the glass booth, Hammerschmidt was still standing in the same place Baumann had left him.

"My goodness, I completely forgot about him." Baumann looked around for Kessel, who was tasked with training the new hires. He spotted him at the grinding station and waved him over.

"What's up, boss?" Kessel shouted over the noise.

"Come with me." In his glass booth, Baumann pointed to Hammerschmidt. "This is our new runner, take him under your wing."

"Will do." Kessel nodded to the young lad. "Come with me."

Satisfied, Baumann watched the two of them walk away. With Kessel taking the youngster under his wing, he would do good work and thus be allowed to stay. He didn't even want to think about what might happen to the boy otherwise.

CHAPTER 9

Sophie had tossed and turned for most of the night. Reinhard Busch's visit and his suggestion to seek out the Swedish pastor had left her restless. Her reunion with Eugen added to her inner turmoil, upsetting her for so many reasons.

Of course, she knew about the persecution of the Jews and sympathized with them, but it wasn't until she had gazed deep into Eugen's haunted eyes that she had actually felt the torment. He was suffering so terribly — and she with him.

On an impulse, she put on her mink coat, left the apartment and made her way to the Swedish congregation in Wilmersdorf. Her heart pounding wildly, she stood in front of the entrance door, grabbing the knocker.

Shortly after, a slender blonde woman peeked out and scrutinized Sophie carefully. "What can I do for you?"

"Countess Borsoi," Sophie introduced herself. "An acquaintance gave me this card. I want to help." She showed the yellow paper with the mass times.

The woman's expression brightened. "I'm Frau Perwe, the pastor's wife. Please come in, Countess Borsoi, I'll take you to my husband's office."

THREE CHILDREN IN DANGER

Her spine tingling with nerves, Sophie reassured herself that nothing bad would happen to her within the Swedish congregation. Even if the Gestapo had followed her, which was very unlikely, she wasn't doing anything forbidden. One was still allowed to attend mass and pray.

After a long walk through labyrinthine corridors, Frau Perwe knocked on an unmarked door.

"Come in," a deep voice sounded.

"There's a visitor for you, Erik. Her name is Countess Borsoi," Frau Perwe announced.

Sophie took in the unpretentious office. The walls were lined with bookshelves and a large crucifix hung above the desk.

"What brings you to me, Countess?" asked the pastor, a sturdy man with a friendly, yet serious face, after he had offered Sophie a seat.

She got straight to the point. "I want to join the resistance."

A smile appeared on Pastor Perwe's lips. "I certainly didn't expect such an offer. What makes you think our congregation is a place of resistance?"

Sophie bit her lip. She had expected that Reinhard Busch had announced her upcoming visit, which obviously hadn't happened. Or did the pastor want to test her? Was he perhaps in cahoots with the Gestapo and this was a trap? A scrutinizing look at the man sitting in front of her convinced her that he was no collaborator. However, she would refrain from mentioning Reinhard Busch's name just to be safe.

"Someone handed me this piece of paper and mentioned that you help people who have to go into hiding."

"But you aren't here because you need my help?" He was looking at her with a hint of amusement.

"No, I'm here because I want to help you bring persecuted people to safety." She looked him straight in the eyes. "In light of the daily atrocities, I no longer wish to remain inactive."

Pastor Perwe leaned back and inspected her silently. His probing gaze left a tingle in her stomach, but she gritted her teeth and sat motionless until, after what seemed like an eternity, he finally spoke up. "This is not a game, Countess."

"I'm very serious about my offer," Sophie hurried to assure him.

The pastor raised his hand. "Listen to me first, Countess. What we do may sound like a romantic adventure, but it's not."

Inwardly, Sophie seethed with anger. This pastor was no better than the rest of society. He, too, judged her to be a spoiled upper-class girl wanting to alleviate her boredom. Involuntarily, she clenched her fists. If he didn't want her help, she'd spite him by setting up her own resistance network.

"Underground work is dangerous. If the Gestapo finds out about your involvement, it might well cost you your life. Neither your title nor your family's good connections will be of any use to you in that case."

So, he seemed to have heard about her. Apparently, Herr Busch had announced her after all and they had made inquiries. This conclusion gave Sophie courage. "I understand your concern, Pastor. But I can assure you that I'm well aware of the danger. I've been criticizing the Nazis for many years, which is not enough for me anymore. I can't stand by in good conscience and watch people being murdered without doing something when I have the means to help. Please, give me a chance to prove myself."

The pastor folded his hands. "If you're indeed determined to risk your life to help those in need, I might have a task for you. Can you drive a car?"

What an unusual question, Sophie thought, as she answered: "Yes. It's been a while since I've driven the last time. My car was confiscated shortly after the war began, but if you can get me a vehicle, I'll chauffeur you anywhere."

"Not me." Pastor Perwe leaned back. "My sexton Lars will let you know when the time has come. Until then, don't tell anyone about our meeting and for heaven's sake, don't return to our parish."

Disappointment welled up in Sophie. Did the pastor hope to get rid of her by promising a mysterious future assignment? She raised her chin. "Don't keep me waiting too long, Pastor Perwe; I'm not known for my patience."

To her surprise, he laughed heartily. "Indeed, Countess, indeed."

Back at home, Sophie sat on pins and needles for the next few days, starting at every phone call or doorbell in anticipation Lars would finally contact her, but each time she was disappointed.

CHAPTER 10

FEBRUARY 1943

Hertha knelt in the slushy snow, coaxing Prickly out of his burrow with a new supply of beetles and harvestmen she had collected for him in the storage room.

"Let's go inside," whined Hans, whose lips showed a bluish color.

Holger, too, sensed the cold creeping into his limbs. "Come on now, we're cold. Maybe he's returned to his winter sleep."

"But Prickly is way too thin to hibernate." Hertha wasn't ready to give up just yet.

Hans snapped impatiently at his sister: "Hurry up, will you!"

The next moment, he clapped his hand over his mouth, his expression frozen in horror.

Holger had heard the voices too. Carefully, he crawled on all fours a little way along the hedge until he got a glance at what was happening on the other side of the shed. He bit his tongue to keep from screaming out loud, as soon as he noticed the men in black SS uniforms approaching the Lembergs' house from the direction of the collection camp.

His eyes darted frantically between the men, the front door and his position. The SS was much too close. He would never be able to successfully dash into the house and warn the Lembergs of their approach. With a heavy heart, he crawled backward until he was out of sight.

"Hans, Hertha, quick!" he whispered. "The SS is here. We have to hide."

Without a second's hesitation, Hans grabbed Hertha's hand. Together they squeezed into the dense bushes next to Prickly's den. Holger followed and pulled the ivy over the three of them as cover. But he wasn't satisfied with that. Although the siblings huddled close together, anyone who entered this part of the garden would inevitably discover them when taking a closer look.

Shaking violently, he nudged Hans, holding his index finger to his lips. Hans understood immediately. Nodding, he turned away and gave Hertha the same sign. Thank God his sister grasped the situation in a flash and was smart enough not to make a sound. After all, it wasn't the first time they'd had to hide.

Holger remembered all too well the anxious hours they had spent with Roxy in the attic last December. He swallowed hard to suppress the tears welling up. On the evening of that same day, his parents hadn't returned home. To avoid thinking about their disappearance, he focused on the pricking of the twigs in his back.

A short time later, he had regained control and motioned for Hans and Hertha to hide behind Prickly's pile of leaves, whereas he lay flat on the ground and crawled a bit further into a bush.

From there, he no longer managed to see the house, he just heard heavy bootsteps approaching.

"Search the house!" a deep voice bellowed.

Holger held his breath, while pressing himself against the cold earth. Carefully, he turned his head and noted with satisfaction that his siblings had completely disappeared behind the pile of leaves. Even he couldn't guess where the two were hiding.

A wave of loneliness shot through his limbs and his fear became so strong that he bit into his hand to keep from sobbing out loud. Motionless, lying on the ground, he fought the urge to crawl over to join his siblings, since that would put them in danger.

He didn't want that. He mustn't do that.

If the SS men searched this part of the garden, he would stand up and lure them away from Hans and Hertha. Hans would take care of their little sister, he was sure of it. With an uneasy feeling in his stomach, he prayed it wouldn't come to that.

The minutes ticked by. Nothing happened. His left leg itched, but he resisted the urge to scratch. Next, something tickled his nose and he focused all his attention on not sneezing. It was like a curse.

A rustling behind the pile of leaves alerted him. He would have loved to yell over for Hans and Hertha to play dead. But that wasn't possible. So he just shook his head and continued to wait in complete silence.

Then, suddenly, heavy footsteps sounded again.

Holding his breath, he carefully inched forward a few centimeters until he gained a partial view of the path from the Lembergs' house to the former school building. His heart missed a beat at the sight. With rifles at the ready, the SS men were driving Herr and Frau Lemberg in front of them.

Holger closed his eyes, hoping his imagination had conjured up the scene. But even after blinking three times, the figures were still there — until they disappeared behind the school building.

Holger didn't dare move. Agonizing minutes — or hours? — later, loud commands ripped through the air, followed by shouting, metallic clicking and the roaring of engines. Finally silence settled over the garden.

He swallowed hard. What he had heard were the dreaded, inconspicuous delivery vans in which Jews were taken away to the next collection camp or to the train station, never to be seen again. More endless minutes passed, during which Holger didn't dare to move. Only when his feet turned numb from the cold did he crawl toward his siblings and whisper, "I think they're gone."

Together, the three pricked up their ears, but apart from the rushing of his own blood, Holger couldn't hear a thing. After a while a soft rustle sounded and Prickly appeared at the entrance of his leaf den. He stuck his little snout in the air as if to say, "You can come out now, the bad men are gone."

Hertha gently stroked his face with her finger and held a wriggling beetle in front of his snout. "You did well, Prickly. You knew it wasn't safe to come out."

Uncertain of what to do next, Holger let her feed the hedgehog while he conferred with Hans: "The SS took Herr and Frau Lemberg with them."

"What do we do now?" Hans grimaced.

"We have to get out of here."

"But where to?"

"I don't know. First, let's go inside the house and assess the situation." Holger felt very grown-up making this suggestion.

Hans seemed to feel the same way because he looked up at him admiringly. "Good idea. That's what we are going to do."

Holger put his hand on Hertha's shoulder. "We're going to check the situation in the house."

"Isn't that dangerous?" she asked, wrinkling her nose.

"No more dangerous than staying in the garden. But warmer." Holger barely felt his hands and feet anymore and desperately wished to warm up in front of the hot stove.

Hertha crawled out of her hiding place and followed her brothers into the house. As soon as they entered the living room, she gasped. Furniture was overturned, drawers emptied, scattered papers and objects were strewn everywhere.

"We can't stay here. We have to go back to our old apartment.

Frau Falkenstein and Frau Goldmann are both Aryan, they will be able to help us." Holger wasn't nearly as confident as he pretended to be. After all, Frau Goldmann had brought them to the Lembergs precisely because she feared the Gestapo would search for them in their old place. But the little ones didn't need to know that.

"Are you sure?" Hertha's hand slipped into his.

"Of course. I'll make sure nothing happens to us."

"I'll be very good. I promise." Her eyes shone with gratitude as she pressed herself tightly against him. Hans leaned against his other side. Holger could practically smell his brother's fear, though Hans would never admit he was afraid.

It was already getting dark and the thought of sneaking through the city made chills race down Holger's spine.

"We'll wait until tomorrow morning," he decided. "For tonight we're going to stay here. While you sleep, I'm going to keep watch. But first, let's eat something."

In the kitchen, they found the same chaos as in the living room. They picked up cooked potatoes from the floor and retrieved half a loaf of bread from the nearly empty pantry, which they ate with jam. Then they settled in front of the stove, which was still warm, because Frau Lemberg had been cooking dinner when the SS came.

After their meal, Hertha and Hans curled up together on the sofa, where Holger covered them with a thick blanket. He draped a second blanket over his own shoulders, chose a stick from his collection by the entrance and settled in a spot on the windowsill. From there, he could see both the front door and the path to the street through a gap in the blackout curtain.

He passed the time by whittling the end of his stick into a sharp point with a kitchen knife. In the case of an emergency, he needed a weapon to defend his siblings.

Only the ticking of the wall clock and the steady breathing of his siblings filled the silence. The hours passed excruciatingly slowly. Nonetheless, he didn't dare leave his lookout post to

THREE CHILDREN IN DANGER

check the time. At some point, he must have fallen asleep, because he was startled awake by the distant bark of a dog.

The first daylight was seeping through the gap in the curtain. Holger slipped off the windowsill, stretched thoroughly and woke his siblings. "We have to leave."

Contrary to her habit of pulling the blanket over her head and sleepily begging for a few extra minutes, Hertha sat up instantly and shook herself like a wet dog. "I'm ready."

Holger had to smile. In moments like this one, he loved his little sister to bits. Hans, whose head peeked out from under the blanket on the opposite side of the sofa, needed a bit longer to shake off sleep. A few minutes later, the three of them stood fully dressed, with shoes on, in the ravaged kitchen.

Instinctively Holger ducked his head between his shoulders. Both his mother and Frau Lemberg had a strict rule, forbidding anyone to wear shoes inside the house. But given the muddy boot prints the SS men had left all over, it didn't make much of a difference anyway.

They ate the last of the bread and jam and drank water from the tap, because the stove had completely cooled down overnight, so they weren't able to heat water to make tea. Normally, Herr Lemberg got up before dawn to heat the kitchen stove with dry branches from the garden; they hadn't had firewood for the other rooms for a long time.

"Here, take this." Holger pressed a sharpened stick into Hans's hand.

"What about me?" Hertha grumbled.

"You're too little."

"I'm not little. I want a stick too," she hissed at him.

Fearing she would whine the entire journey and draw attention to the small group, he reluctantly gave her one of the sticks from his collection.

"This one isn't sharpened!" she complained.

"Because I didn't have time to whittle it."

Hertha made a face that meant he shouldn't take her for a fool.

"Listen. Either you take that one or none at all. Understood?"

With a dark glare, she snatched the stick and grumbled, "I'm not little."

"Did you pack your things in your satchels?"

Two nodding heads were the answer. Holger looked his siblings up and down before taking Frau Lemberg's thick wool stole from the coat rack and wrapping it around Hertha's shoulders.

"Hey... we can't do that. That's stealing." Hertha wriggled to get rid of the stole.

"Frau Lemberg doesn't need it anymore."

Both Hertha and Hans turned chalk-white, their mouths opening and closing silently. Next, Holger took Herr Lemberg's scarf and gave it to Hans, before slipping into an old holey coat, which had belonged to the gardener — back when the Lembergs lived in the big school building.

"Let's go now. We're going home."

"But..." Hans fell silent immediately when he looked into Holger's serious face.

In reality, Holger wasn't nearly as confident as he appeared. From his brief time at the Lemberg School, he remembered the way home, but in the past he had taken the bus and tram. However, they had no money to buy a ticket, and besides, it was forbidden for Jews, even though they had removed their yellow stars weeks ago on Frau Goldmann's orders.

Therefore, they had to make the long journey on foot and pray they wouldn't encounter any SS patrols along the way.

CHAPTER 11

FEBRUARY 27, 1943

The morning dawned gray and bleak. Baumann turned up his coat collar before stepping off the tram and marching toward the entrance gate of the locomotive workshop. The damp, cold air seeped into his bones and aggravated his bad knee.

Just before the entrance, he ran into Kessel, strolling over from the other direction without the mandatory yellow star on his jacket, as usual. A pang hit Baumann's chest, as he feared it was inevitable that the young man would one day be arrested for his defiant disregard of the rules. And then may the gods have mercy on him.

"Everything all right, Kessel?"

"Sure." Kessel turned away as a coughing fit overtook his senses.

Baumann looked at him with narrowed eyes. "I don't like your cough one bit."

"It's nothing. Just a cold."

"No wonder, in this weather." To make matters worse, Jews had been forced to hand over their winter clothing the previous year, so Kessel was wearing a light jacket, which did nothing to protect him from the biting cold.

"You better start at the welding station," he instructed Kessel. "It's nice and warm."

Kessel gazed at him gratefully with reddened, feverishly shining eyes, while simultaneously sniffling and wiping his nose. "Got it, boss."

When Baumann checked on him half an hour later, he found a shivering Kessel leaning against the workbench. In this condition, the lad would only harm himself and others.

"You better go home," Baumann ordered.

"I can't," Kessel protested, raising his hands. "I have to—"

"You don't have to do anything. Except get into bed and recover."

"But then I won't get paid. I need the money."

Baumann observed the lad, who barely managed to stay upright on his feet. "If you drop dead on me here, that won't help anyone either. I'll sort it out with Merkle. Now get out of here and don't come back until you're recovered."

"Thanks." Without another word, Kessel turned and shuffled to the changing room. Baumann yearned to give him his own padded coat, but he didn't want to take any risks. In his current state, Kessel didn't possess the necessary quick-wittedness to talk his way out of an inspection.

Afterward, Baumann gestured to the welder and shouted, "Take a break, Koloss."

The sturdy man finished his work, put aside the welding equipment, and approached Baumann. "What's up?"

"Kessel's sick. Make sure you keep an eye on the new hires."

"Will do." Koloss grimaced. He preferred to work alone and undisturbed; he possessed little patience for checking on other men's tasks.

Nonetheless, Baumann knew he could rely on him, so he disappeared into his glass booth to check on the deliveries and distribute the necessary repairs among the work groups.

Shortly before lunch break, the noise level decreased. Baumann was just getting ready to sound the break gong when he heard an unusual sound. Seconds later, the hall door flew open and the factory director entered, trailed by a dozen SS men.

"Well, this ought to be fun," Baumann said to himself as he left the glass booth. These were too many uniformed men for a routine inspection.

The news of the SS's arrival spread like wildfire; even before Baumann reached the grim-looking officer, silence fell over the enormous factory hall.

The clicking, rattling, hammering and hissing of the various machines ceased. Dozens of pairs of eyes stared curiously at the men in black uniforms.

"This is the head of our workshop, Philipp Baumann," Herr Merkle introduced him to the SS-Scharführer.

Bile rose in Baumann's throat, and the reason wasn't because he hated being addressed by his full name. Before he had a chance to say anything, the Scharführer barked at him: "We're taking the Jews with us. Send all of them to the yard."

Baumann nearly blacked out as he feared for the fate of the Jewish forced workers toiling in the workshop. "Excuse me, Herr Scharführer, how are we supposed to meet our quota if you remove most of our workers?"

The Scharführer glared at him with cold eyes: "Get replacements. There are plenty of prisoners of war or politicals."

Although the chances of success were slim, Baumann dared one last attempt. "I dislike Jews as much as you do. The reason we employ them, is because they own special skills. If I get a bunch of unskilled workers, it'll take weeks, if not months, to train them."

"That's your problem. Today we're making Berlin free of Jews." The Scharführer clicked his heels and shouted, "Heil Hitler!"

Whether he liked it or not, Baumann had to return the Hitler salute. Out of the corner of his eye, he noticed the Germans in his crew following his example, while the prisoners of war stared straight ahead. The Jewish workers, though, stood there with hanging shoulders, their dejected gaze to the floor, probably wondering what was going to happen to them.

Sighing, Baumann turned around and yelled, "You heard him. All Jews line up in the yard. Leave the factory tools at your station and take your personal belongings with you."

"That won't be necessary," the Scharführer replied.

"Did I misunderstand, and the men are returning to work tomorrow?"

"No," the Scharführer sneered. "But where they're going, they won't need their belongings."

Of course, Baumann knew, or at least suspected, what happened to the Jews when they were picked up. Still, the answer hit him like a punch to the gut.

He had to avert his gaze as the Jewish workers filed into the yard. The stench of mortal fear hung rancid in the air and Baumann hated himself for doing nothing to help. He cast a desperate look at Koloss, who watched with slumped shoulders as young Hammerschmidt was the last one to leave the factory hall.

The seemingly endless rattling off of names wafted through the thin walls. Baumann stood frozen in place, unable to take action. Next he heard shouting, calling, quick footsteps, groaning, screaming. After that, it was quiet. Baumann was about to tell the remaining workers to return to their tasks when the door was torn open a second time and the Scharführer burst in.

"One Jew is missing. David Goldmann."

It took Baumann a few seconds to realize the Scharführer meant Kessel. "I ain't seen him at all today. Maybe he's sick."

"Address?" the Scharführer demanded.

Baumann instantly recognized he had said too much. He absolutely had to send the SS on a false trail and warn Kessel.

"Sorry, I don't know his address." To buy time, he scratched

THREE CHILDREN IN DANGER

behind his ear. "But something just came to mind. Yesterday he asked for permission to go to the employment office."

"These idiots!" the Scharführer cursed. "There will be consequences if a Jew slips through our fingers because those numbskulls are sleeping on the job."

Baumann faked a guilty expression. "If I'd have known you were coming, I wouldn't have given him permission."

"Not your fault." The Scharführer waved it off. "Don't worry. We'll get the little rascal. We won't let a single one of these filthy Jews escape."

Baumann would have loved to laugh heartily because Kessel had escaped Hitler's henchmen, at least for now. As soon as the SS left, he would visit the Goldmanns' apartment to warn him. Then he remembered that he hadn't been lying to the SS after all. He didn't know the address and would have to ask for it in the accounting department under some pretext.

Damn it. To ensure his absence wouldn't be noticed, he was going to inform Koloss about his plan; the man was just returning from the canteen and was about to put on his safety goggles.

"I'm gonna drop by Kessel later. You'll hold down the fort here?"

"Sure, boss." Koloss didn't ask questions. After being friends for such a long time he knew without explanation what Baumann was up to.

Baumann was going to fetch his coat when Herr Merkle's secretary knocked on the glass booth and motioned for him to follow her. Inwardly, Baumann groaned. He kept his coat on, put his papers in his pocket and followed the young woman to the administration building.

After they left the noisy workshop hall she explained, "Herr Merkle needs to speak to you urgently."

Baumann had already guessed that. From experience, he knew that he wouldn't be able to extract further information from the young woman, who was a fervent member of Hitler's

Bund Deutscher Mädel, the League of German Girls, so he didn't even try.

As soon as they arrived in front of Herr Merkle's office, she knocked on the door, announced Baumann and sat down at her desk in the anteroom to type some letters for her boss.

Baumann thoroughly disliked the loyal Nazi woman. He had clashed with her several times because she thought herself better than the factory workers.

"This is a disaster!" Herr Merkle ranted. "The SS has taken two-thirds of our workforce. How are we supposed to meet our quota without them?"

"You should have asked this question of the SS, maybe they would have left us the workers." Baumann's sympathy was limited. Merkle hadn't uttered a peep of protest. On the contrary, the director had countered the Scharführer's anti-Jewish slogans with his own.

Merkle glared at him. "That doesn't help us now."

But it might have helped if you had said something, you cowardly dog. Baumann was careful not to voice his thought and instead nodded submissively, albeit without offering a solution.

Let the jerk figure out how to deal with this mess; someone who didn't give a damn about the fate of Jewish workers didn't deserve Baumann's support.

"Aren't you going to open your mouth?" Merkle barked at him. "What shall we do?"

Baumann rubbed behind his ear for an extra long time, as if thinking hard. "Bring the people back?"

"For heaven's sake! Even you can't be that stupid!"

"I'm just saying." Inwardly, Baumann smirked. Herr Merkle might have attended university, but they both knew the workshop wouldn't run longer than two days without Baumann. So he shrugged and waited for Merkle to calm down, while considering how he might manage to disappear inconspicuously to warn Kessel.

"We need new forced laborers, and fast." Herr Merkle's carotid artery pulsed dangerously.

Personally, Baumann wouldn't shed a tear if the factory director suffered a heart attack and dropped dead on the spot. Regrettably, that wouldn't help anyone, because the Wehrmacht had long been eager to take control of the locomotive workshop. If the place was swarming with soldiers, both Kessel's overnight shelter for the persecuted and the sabotage through inefficient and cumbersome processes would most likely be exposed.

Therefore he adopted a conciliatory tone: "If you organize men with experience, I can whip them into shape in a week or two."

Herr Merkle furrowed his brow and studied Baumann for a few seconds. "That is an excellent idea. You get on the phone right away to make it happen."

"Me?" Baumann raised his hands defensively.

"Who else? You have an overview of all the processes and know what skills are needed for the new workers."

"But I gotta..." he frantically searched for a plausible excuse, "...gotta go to the Reichsbahn."

Merkle made a dismissive gesture. "Call them and explain what happened. They'll understand that our priority is finding new men." Before Baumann could utter another protest, Merkle called his secretary through the intercom on his desk: "Herr Baumann will be coming to you shortly. Help him organize new workers. No one leaves the office until you've arranged for qualified replacements for the Jews."

Baumann bit his tongue. To make matters worse, he had to spend the afternoon with the Nazi woman and couldn't even send Koloss to warn Kessel.

For the next hours, he hung on the phone, begging for qualified forced laborers for the workshop. The Nazi woman didn't let him out of her sight for a second — to her credit, she generously supplied him with Ersatzkaffee, sandwiches and cigarettes throughout the afternoon. Herr Merkle also kept poking his head into the anteroom to check on the progress.

Baumann noted with satisfaction that Merkle was afraid of the consequences if the workshop didn't deliver as usual. For a moment, he was tempted to let the hated factory director fall flat on his face by sitting back and doing nothing. But he had to think of the workers under his supervision, men like Koloss, who secretly did so much good for the resistance. And of the people gone underground, called submarines, who slept in the empty train wagons... so he gritted his teeth and dialed the next number to negotiate with another bureaucrat.

He couldn't do anything to help the Jews taken away this morning, but he could at least ensure that the prisoners of war who had to toil in the workshop were treated decently and got enough to eat.

Angrily, he clenched his fist. Why did he always have to choose between two evils? What brainless idiot had come up with this scenario? The answer was obvious: Hitler. It was a shame that none of the numerous assassination attempts on his life had succeeded.

Finally, when the sun had disappeared behind the horizon, Baumann put the telephone receiver down for the last time and announced, "Done. We'll get replacements tomorrow."

"You did an excellent job," the secretary praised him. If she hadn't been such a diehard Nazi, he might actually have liked her.

"Thanks for the coffee and cigarettes." He put on his coat and returned to the main hall, hoping Koloss was waiting for him. As soon as Baumann entered the glass booth, Koloss, changed into his civilian clothes, rushed toward him.

"You were gone for quite a while. Everything alright?"

"Merkle had me chained to the phone all afternoon to find replacements for the Jews they took." All the strength drained from Baumann's body and he feared he would collapse to the floor. On days like this, he was close to giving up hope that Hitler's reign of terror would ever end.

"You didn't manage to warn Kessel?"

Baumann tiredly shook his head. "I couldn't even look in his file for the address."

"Shit," Koloss grumbled. "What do we do now?"

"Nothing. All we can do is wait and hope for the best."

"Kessel's smart. He'll manage." Koloss gave him an encouraging pat on the shoulder. "Shall we go for a beer? That always helps."

"I could definitely use one or two." Together they left the factory grounds and headed for their regular pub, where Manfred was sitting at their usual table.

"Did they come to your place too and take the Jews?" Manfred asked instead of a greeting.

Koloss nodded. "It all happened so fast. Suddenly, the SS showed up with a dozen men and took everyone."

"Like everywhere," Manfred croaked.

"Was this something big?" An icy shiver ran down Baumann's spine.

"Huge. The Gestapo calls it the Factory Action. Today they combed through every single business in Berlin and took every last Jew."

"Damn..." Koloss grabbed his beer glass and emptied it in one go, before wiping the foam from his mouth with his hand and signaling the waitress to bring another round.

"Why didn't you warn us?" Baumann hissed. It wasn't like Manfred at all to hold back vital information.

"Because I knew nothing. Sure, there were rumors, but the whole thing was top secret. Apparently, the Gestapo was unhappy with the industrialists stonewalling, reluctant to give up their Jews. To avoid resistance they didn't announce the action beforehand. Our office found out this morning along with everyone else."

"Bastards!" Koloss slammed his huge fist on the heavy

wooden table, rattling the glasses. The patrons at the neighboring tables eyed him curiously.

Because informers hid everywhere, Baumann yelled, "The Tommies will pay for this!"

The neighbors turned back to their conversations. Cursing the English arch-enemy was a daily occurrence. Baumann, however, glared at Koloss: "Be a little more careful."

"I'm sorry." Koloss looked genuinely crestfallen. He was a good man, even if he lost his temper at the slightest occasion recently. But in a crisis, Baumann would trust him with his life.

He turned back to Manfred: "Just at work?"

"I think so. By now, all of Berlin knows what happened. The grapevine took care of spreading the news."

Baumann relaxed a little. If the information had reached him in time, Kessel would stand a good chance of escaping.

"It looks like the SS didn't just take full Jews, but also those married to Aryans. They interned them in the Rosenstrasse transit camp. And now imagine what's happening." Manfred leaned forward before continuing in a barely audible voice: "The Aryan wives are gathering in front of the camp, protesting. They're demanding their husbands and children be returned to them."

An image appeared in Baumann's mind of a dozen women with kitchen aprons over their dresses, armed with wooden spoons and carpet beaters, facing off against a hundred SS men with machine guns. "That's ridiculous."

"I'm telling you," Manfred insisted. "They're standing in front of the Rosenstrasse building and refuse to leave. The SS is at a loss as to what action to take, since they don't want to shoot unarmed German housewives."

"How do you know that?"

"Word of mouth." Manfred leaned back.

"Let's go there," said Koloss.

"What do you want to do?"

"Go and blend in with the protesters. If they're really making a ruckus, this is our chance to fight." Koloss's eyes shone with anticipation. "Imagine what might happen if the spark catches on and the people rise up? This might well be the final fight against the Nazi reign."

Baumann pondered the suggestion for a few seconds. It was brilliant. Although he didn't expect the protest to be successful, if it helped to free even one of the captured Jews with an Aryan spouse, they would have already won. And if the SS wanted to crack down on the women, he and his friends might prevent the worst.

"Alright then. Tomorrow after work." Baumann looked at Manfred, who reluctantly agreed. "I'm in."

It was late when Baumann said goodbye. He had to be at the workshop early the next morning to instruct the new recruits, and during lunch break, he planned to stop by Kessel's place.

CHAPTER 12

"How much further?" Hertha whined. Holger had no idea; he wasn't even sure if they had taken the correct turn this time. Back then, with the tram, the journey to school had been so much quicker and easier. For Hertha's benefit however, he put on a confident face: "Ten minutes at most."

"You've said that at least three times," Hans complained.

"This time it really is only ten more minutes."

"I can't walk any longer. Besides, my toes hurt." Through the holes in her inherited shoes, Hertha wiggled her dirt-encrusted toes.

"We have to keep going. If we loiter on the street, we'll soon be picked up by the police." That was Holger's biggest worry. If the police checked their papers, they would arrest them and put them into a collection camp, and who knows what would happen to them after that. "I'll give you my stick if you want. It'll help, because you can lean on it."

"Alright," Hertha said magnanimously, though she couldn't quite hide the gleam in her eyes.

After taking two more wrong turns, they came to an intersection Holger recognized. Turning to Hans, he asked,

THREE CHILDREN IN DANGER

"Over there, isn't that the shop where Father used to buy tobacco?"

"Yes, it is. I recognize it." Hans gave a little jump for joy. "Now it really isn't much further."

"How far?" came Hertha's exhausted little voice.

"Five minutes at most." This time Holger was sure they had finally found their home. Once they arrived at their old apartment, everything would be fine. Frau Goldmann and Frau Falkenstein wouldn't turn them away. Besides, so much time had passed the Gestapo certainly wouldn't be looking for them anymore.

Just before reaching the once-grand, but now run-down townhouse, Holger signaled his siblings to hide in the bushes. Carefully, he peered across the street. Nothing stirred. The front door was slightly ajar. This wasn't unusual, because the locking mechanism had been jammed for a long time, even though David had tried to repair it several times. After the residents of the apartments on the lower floors had been taken away during a raid, David had strung an alarm wire in the stairwell to warn of SS patrols.

"On my signal, we'll walk into the house. Watch out for the wire."

Hans and Hertha nodded.

He waited until he couldn't see any vehicles or pedestrians in either direction, before he said, "Now."

The front door swung open with surprising ease, but the alarm wire was no longer in place. The stairwell was eerily quiet. An uneasy feeling crept into Holger's bones and he was about to turn on his heel, but Hans and Hertha had already stormed up the stairs. With a sinking heart, he followed them.

On every floor the apartment doors had been broken open, revealing devastated rooms. With each step, Holger's heart sank deeper into his pants. On the top landing was the Falkensteins' apartment, where his family had lived.

"Phew," he sighed when he found the door untouched.

Hertha was pressing her finger on the doorbell, which made no sound. Hans knocked repeatedly on the door. Nothing happened. Holger perked up his ears to listen. He stepped forward and pressed his ear against the door, but no sound came from inside. No footsteps. Nothing at all.

After hesitating for at least a minute, he rummaged in his pants pocket for the apartment key. He should have given it to Frau Goldmann when she had dropped them off at the Lembergs'. Now he was glad he had forgotten to do so — and a bit guilty. He felt like a burglar because, strictly speaking, they no longer lived here.

"Come on, what are you waiting for?" asked Hans, who obviously had fewer scruples.

"Wait a second, will you?" The door swung open. He looked into a tidy hallway.

Holger noticed that not a single coat was hanging on the rack, which meant the adults must have gone to work. He should have thought of that. Usually, the adults left early in the morning and didn't return until evening.

He ushered his siblings into the living room, which looked exactly the same way it had a few months prior. Still, he swallowed down the rising fear. Someone else could have moved in by now. Such things happened. Bravely, he pushed his fear aside.

"Let's warm up and have some hot tea." As soon as the words left his mouth, tears threatened to spring. They were a painful echo of his mother's voice—she used to say the same thing every time they came in out of the bitter cold.

The kitchen also looked the same as always. Even the bowl of herbs Amelie had picked and dried last summer stood in the same place. Holger put the kettle on the stove, lit the gas and added some herbs to three cups. Then he waited.

Shortly after, Hertha came rushing into the kitchen: "Someone else is living in our room now. All our things are gone."

An icy shiver ran down Holger's back. It hadn't been right to break into the apartment. They should have waited outside. Right after, he scolded himself. As soon as Frau Goldmann or another adult came home from work, everything would be cleared up.

"Take off your shoes and wipe away the dirty footprints." He cast his sister a disapproving stare.

Hertha rolled her eyes. "You're not my Mutti. You can't order me around."

Holger puffed out his chest. "I'm the oldest, therefore I'm in charge as long as Mutti and Vati aren't here. So you better do what I tell you, or you'll get a thump on the head."

Hertha obediently shuffled away and returned with a rag. She made a show of sulkily wiping the floor. Meanwhile, the kettle whistled. Holger poured three cups of tea, carefully carrying them one by one to the table.

"Where on earth is Hans?"

"He wanted to check the attic to see if Roxy still lives up there."

"Great. Can you please get him? The tea is ready."

"Why always me?" Hertha protested.

"Because I'm busy."

Grumbling, she obeyed his request. Holger slumped into a chair, wrapping his cold hands around one of the tea mugs. The longer he sat there, the more anxious he became. After a few minutes, his two siblings finally entered the kitchen, chattering and laughing. They didn't seem to realize the great danger they were in. For them, all of this seemed to be an exciting game of hide-and-seek.

Hans grabbed his mug and stared into space, the way he often did when his thoughts roamed elsewhere. Then he suddenly said, "Why don't we hide in a train wagon?"

"Where did you get that idea?" Holger often had trouble following his brother's leaps of thought.

"Do you remember how Roxy told us that she used to live in a trailer before the Gestapo deported her clan?"

"And what does that have to do with train wagons?"

"Man, you don't understand a thing." Hans sighed theatrically. "Just like trailers, they have a roof, benches you can lie on, and a toilet."

"Plus, they stand on railway tracks and roll God knows where." Holger couldn't see any merit in the idea.

"Mutti always says you must not misuse God's name." Hertha's know-it-all response was the last straw for Holger.

"Damn it! Mutti is probably dead by now!" No sooner had the harsh words left his mouth than he regretted them. Especially because Hertha burst into heart-wrenching sobs and Hans seemed to be on the verge of crying.

"I'm sorry." Holger stroked his sister's hair. "I didn't mean it like that."

"Do you really believe she's dead?" Her lips trembled so much she barely managed to mumble the words.

"Come here." Holger wrapped Hertha in his arms and rocked her like a baby. "Of course not. I'm sure she and Vati are fine. That's what Frau Goldmann said and she should know, right?"

"I miss them so terribly," Hertha whimpered.

"Me too." Hans had joined them.

The three were hugging each other fiercely, when suddenly a voice sounded. "Hello? Is anyone home?"

They froze in place, not making a sound, until footsteps echoed in the hallway. Holger's eyes frantically searched for an escape route, but it was too late. In the next second a tall man with short dark blond hair entered the room. When he saw the children, he stopped abruptly.

"Sorry, the door was open."

Holger shot Hans an angry look: "Did you forget to close the door again?"

Hans simply shrugged.

"I'm looking for Kessel, uh, I mean David Goldmann."

"He doesn't live here," replied Holger hastily.

"Really?" The man furrowed his brow. "Do you live here?"

Before Holger could prevent the worst, Hertha chattered away cheerfully. "Nope, we don't. We're not Jews either, if you wanna know."

"Not another word," Holger hissed at his sister.

"What are you doing here, if you don't live here?" asked the man. "Are you trying to steal something?"

"No. We... we just made some tea," Holger stammered before regaining his chutzpah. "What are you doing here anyway?"

"I'm a friend of David's."

"Anyone could say that." Holger crossed his arms, as he had often seen adults do.

The man wasn't the least bit impressed by Holger's threatening stance. "Listen up. I don't mean you any harm. By the way, I'm Baumann."

Holger continued to be suspicious, which the stranger seemed to notice.

"I don't particularly like the Nazis either."

"Really?" asked Hans.

"Really. Now tell me the truth, what are you doing here?"

"We lived here until our parents didn't come home one evening. Then Frau Goldmann, David's mother, dropped us off at the Lembergs' place. But they were taken away by the SS yesterday and..." Holger broke off. "...well, we planned to hide here."

"That wasn't such a smart idea." Baumann scratched his head. "This is a Jewish house. The Gestapo probably searches it often. You can't stay here."

"But where else should we go?" asked Hans.

"That's the one-million-Reichsmark question." Baumann bit his lips before continuing. "Best you come with me."

"No way." Holger stood in front of Baumann with his legs hip-width apart, glancing at his sharpened stick, which he had left in the hallway.

CHAPTER 13

A tender romance had blossomed between Sophie and Eugen over the past few weeks. Whenever possible—which was not often—they met. The previous evening, though, he hadn't shown up at their agreed meeting place.

Eventually, she had gone home dejected. When he didn't call from a payphone either that evening or the next morning, a Sunday, she seriously worried about him. It was so unlike Eugen not to give any sign of life. He knew she would be beside herself with fear that something might have happened to him.

All morning she had been debating whether to visit him at his apartment, until she finally couldn't stand the uncertainty anymore. On an impulse, she jumped up, put on her mink coat and hopped on her bicycle.

Since it hadn't snowed during the last few days, the streets were free of ice, though cycling through slush and wind was still unpleasant. She already regretted not taking the bus, but with the bicycle, she traveled considerably faster because she would have had to change twice to get to Eugen's place.

After half an hour of vigorous pedaling, she stopped in front of the run-down apartment building. These days, few Aryans dared to venture into a Jewish neighborhood, let alone a Jewish house. Sophie shrugged; she didn't care about conventions. Let them report her for the crime of visiting a Jew.

As she parked her bicycle, her hands were frozen stiff despite her gloves and she rubbed her fingers vigorously several times to get the blood circulating again. After the burning sensation subsided, she finally managed to move her fingers enough to snap the bike lock shut and remove the key.

With an uneasy feeling, she walked toward the entrance. The front door stood wide open like a giant maw, swallowing everything that approached it.

"You have far too vivid an imagination," she scolded herself, squaring her shoulders. One might be afraid of many things, but an open front door certainly wasn't worth it.

She had never visited Eugen at home before. After that one time when he had sought refuge in her apartment, he had never returned to her place either, even though she had often urged him to. For safety reasons, he had insisted they only meet in parks or cafés.

During their first date, she had asked him if he was afraid of walking on the streets without the mandatory yellow star. At the memory of his answer, her chest tightened.

"I'm more afraid being out and about with the star. It makes me fair game."

A strange unease trickled through her veins as she climbed the stairs to the first floor. In an apartment building like this one, you normally heard noises at any time of the day or night: a crying baby, the toilet flushing in the stairwell, footsteps, a radio.

But here it was eerily quiet. Nothing stirred. Only the echo of her steps reverberated off the walls. She stopped to listen. Nothing. Goosebumps formed on her arms. Despite her discomfort, Sophie continued on, bracing herself for the worst.

She already imagined Eugen lying in a pool of blood on the floor—stabbed because he was a Jew and the perpetrator risked no punishment for his crime.

Just as she approached the apartment on the first floor, the door opened and a boy of about ten years age rushed out. Sophie instinctively jumped back a step.

"Heavens, you scared me," she gasped.

The boy was about to slip past her when she grabbed him by the collar. "What were you doing in the apartment?"

"Nothing," he answered with a protruding lip.

"Do you live here?"

"That's none of your business." He wiggled to get free.

Sophie tightened her grip. It wasn't for nothing that in her childhood she had often—much to her mother's chagrin—wrestled with the boys in her class in a very unladylike fashion.

She adopted a gentler tone: "Listen, I don't mean you any harm. I just want to know what happened to the residents."

The boy snorted derisively. "You don't know? Yesterday the SS picked up everyone while at work. This morning they came back and grabbed the rest."

"Why didn't they take you?" No sooner had the question slipped from her lips than she chided herself for it. He would hardly tell her the truth, and even if he did, what would she learn from it? She wanted to find out about Eugen's fate.

"Because I'm smart."

Sophie suppressed a laugh. "Just tell me one more thing: Eugen Habicht, was he taken too?"

He tilted his head. "Why do you want to know?"

"I'm a friend of his and want to help him."

"Anyone could say that."

Sophie thought about how she could gain the boy's trust. Because nothing came to mind, she said lamely: "Please just tell me if he's alright."

"I don't know. Honestly."

"Alright. You can leave." With a deep sigh, she let go of him. He didn't hesitate for a second before darting away faster than the wind.

Sophie remained on the landing for a while, unable to muster the courage to enter the strange apartment. Eugen had occupied one of the rooms; a married couple, a single older lady and a mother with her child lived in the other three rooms. The child was probably the boy she had just met.

She wished she had questioned him further, but it was too late now.

Finally, she gave herself a push and entered the apartment with a pounding heart. Inside, everything seemed ordinary. In the hallway, a hat hung on the coat rack and several pairs of slippers stood neatly side by side on a mat; in the kitchen, dishes stood on the drying rack. It was as if the residents had left the house to return soon.

A pang in her heart reminded her that this was exactly what had happened: The people had gone to work, expecting to return in the evening. But they hadn't. Completely distraught, she leaned against the kitchen counter and stared out the window.

What had happened to Eugen? Would she ever see him again?

CHAPTER 14

Baumann shook his head with a sigh. When he had set out to warn Kessel, he certainly hadn't expected to find three orphaned children.

If Kessel wasn't here, it meant he had either gone into hiding or had been arrested. No matter what had happened to him, the children couldn't stay at the apartment, because this would be the first place the Gestapo would look for them.

Unless they've already given up the search. After all, the siblings had disappeared months prior. Baumann shook his head again. He couldn't and wouldn't rely on a hunch. Besides, their presence would compromise the other residents of the house.

No, the children had to disappear. He had to find them a safe hiding place, whether they had told him the truth or not. But where? Scratching his chin, he remembered the train wagons Kessel used to prepare in the evening so that Jews in hiding could spend the night with a roof over their head. Without hesitating, he decided to take the children to the locomotive workshop and accommodate them in an empty railway car for a few days. At least until he found a better place for them.

Now he just had to overcome the resistance of Holger, who was adamant about defending himself and his siblings.

"Listen to me. You can't stay here, you know that yourselves."

Holger nodded hesitantly before squaring his shoulders. "But we're not going with you either. We'll find something."

"And what will that be?" Baumann was impressed by the boy, whom he estimated to be twelve or thirteen years old, tall, but very, very skinny. He would grow up to be a good man.

"I'm not about to tell you, so you can go to the Gestapo and rat us out."

Baumann leaned down and locked eyes with Holger. "True. That's a risk. But if I don't help you, the Gestapo will definitely find you. Three kids alone on the street, you're lucky you made it this far."

"We'll manage." Holger wasn't going to give in.

Baumann needed a different approach. He gazed at the other two children and fixed his gaze on the little girl. With outstretched hands, palms up, he said to her, "I promise I'll take you to safety. Kessel, I mean David Goldmann, has found a very good place where the Nazis will never suspect you. You're not the first ones to sleep there for a few nights."

Hertha lowered her gaze, giving Baumann the feeling he had already half won her over. He crouched down to be at eye level with the little girl. "You can leave anytime if you don't like it after all."

"I... don't... know." Her lips trembled. "I'm scared."

"You know, I once had a little daughter, just like you."

"What happened to her?" The second boy chimed in.

"Nothing. She's grown up and lives on her own." Baumann didn't mention that his daughter had been arrested a year ago for making statements undermining the war effort and he didn't know her whereabouts since.

Holger had come to a decision. "Alright. We'll come with you. But if you try anything shady, we disappear in a jiffy."

Baumann suppressed a smile. Glancing at the satchels in the hallway, he asked, "Is that all your belongings?"

The children nodded.

"Good, let's get going. If a patrol stops us, don't say anything. Let me do the talking."

In single file, they trudged down the stairs, and across the street to the bus stop. Baumann asked the children for their names and impressed upon them not to answer if anyone asked them a question. He bought bus tickets for himself and the children, which the conductor punched without a word or even a second glance.

During the entire journey, Baumann racked his brain about ways to walk to the locomotive workshop without meeting police, because he didn't feel half as confident as he pretended to be. If a patrol checked their papers, not only would the children be arrested, but Baumann himself as well. These days, people who helped Jews were punished as severely as those who undermined the war effort. He shrugged; even the smallest offenses were punishable by death — another reason why he hated the Nazi regime so much.

They got lucky and weren't bothered by anyone. Just as they turned the last corner, the gong signaling the end of the lunch break rang out and shortly after, he saw the glass roof structure of the factory hall looming before him. Baumann's pulse ratcheted up as he realized he couldn't simply march onto the factory premises with the children, so he slowed his steps.

"What's wrong?" Holger asked.

"You'll have to sneak inside through a hole in the fence. No one must know you're here."

Holger wrinkled his nose, doubt creeping into his eyes.

"I'll take you to the spot, where you have to wait until I come to get you." Before the guard at the entrance gate could spot them, Baumann turned into a side street circling the factory premises. After another five-minute march, he stopped in front of the hole in the fence.

"Hide among the bushes." He pointed to the vegetation between the fence and the railroad tracks.

"What shall we do if a train passes?" Holger asked with a choked voice.

"That won't happen. These are sidings for repairs. I'm leaving now and I'll return to get you as soon as the sun is setting." Baumann looked at his wristwatch. "In three or four hours. Until then, no one must find you. Hide well."

Then he made his way back to the main gate. Throughout the entire afternoon, an uneasy feeling pooled in his stomach and he was about to leave his workplace at least a dozen times to check on the children. But during the day, there was simply too much activity on the premises. Furthermore several of the workers were staunch Nazis, for whom hidden children would be a perfect opportunity to show their loyalty to the regime.

In the large hall, Koloss was looking for him. Baumann made a hand signal to his old comrade to follow him into the glass booth.

"Where have you been? Merkle's secretary has asked for you a couple of times."

Baumann groaned. "Just what I need. I'll deal with her later. Who's preparing the train wagons for the night?"

"Kessel and Hammerschmidt," Koloss answered, before slapping his forehead with the palm of his hand. "Hammerschmidt is gone. And Kessel?"

"He ain't coming back. Gone underground or arrested." Baumann furrowed his brows. Neither he nor Koloss were able to check daily on the train cars without arousing suspicion. "I'll ask Matze. He's a good one."

"But can he keep his mouth shut?"

"His father is in the Sachsenhausen concentration camp, he won't betray us." Baumann had needed to warn the young lad a few times to think before opening his mouth to criticize the regime, as one was never safe from overzealous Nazi supporters.

"That surely wasn't the reason why you called me over," said Koloss.

"I found three children on the run in Kessel's apartment and brought them with me."

"Jews?" Koloss asked.

"Most certainly." Baumann smirked at the memory of little Hertha telling him unprompted that they weren't Jews. "The parents have been taken away months ago. Yesterday, the SS arrested the people who had been hiding them."

"Lousy sons of bitches." Koloss obviously meant the Nazis. "What are we going to do with the children?"

Baumann reached for the thermos that had been sitting in the same spot on his desk for years and poured himself some lukewarm Ersatzkaffee into a cup. "Hide them in a train wagon until I've found a better place."

Koloss grimaced. "At night that's not a problem, but during the day? There are far too many people milling about the premises."

"I know." That was exactly what worried Baumann. The risk of being discovered during the day was enormous. To prevent arrests, he had spread the word through the grapevine that illegal overnight guests had to be gone by six in the morning. But where should the children disappear to during the day? Especially alone?

"We'll ask the priest," Koloss suggested.

"If he'll take them? A while back, someone inquired about orphaned children, but the church is no place for them all alone. Frau Perwe has her hands full with the parish, she has no time to look after them."

"Asking costs nothing."

"That's true." Baumann finished his coffee. After a brief consideration, he decided, "You go to the Rosenstrasse protests on your own. I'll accommodate the children in a train car and after my shift I'm going to visit the priest to ask if he can give them shelter."

"Alright. Should I ask Matze whether he wants to prepare the train wagons from now on?"

"Yes." If Matze didn't want to take the risk, they had no one else and either Koloss or Baumann himself would have to do it, which would increase the danger of discovery.

"Which one do you want for the children?"

Baumann mentally went through all wagons on the premises. "The one with the broken coupling. Tell Matze to move it all the way to the back on the siding. It can stay there for three or four days."

"Consider it done." Koloss already had his hand on the doorknob when he turned around once more. "Don't worry. We'll save these children."

Baumann nodded gratefully, knowing he could always count on his friend. With anything.

CHAPTER 15

Holger rubbed the sleep from his eyes, after an elbow to his ribs woke him up. It took a second to realize he was sitting behind a bush.

"There's a dog sniffing around," Hans whispered. "What are we going to do now?"

"Don't move." In an instant Holger was wide awake. Terrible rumors circulated about German shepherds trained to tear prisoners limb from limb in the concentration camps. He fervently hoped this dog wasn't one of them.

A few seconds later, he heard rustling. In the twilight, the silhouette of a large, black animal approached them. Holger's heart raced. The dog seemed to be without its owner. Hopefully, it was just a stray animal looking for something to eat. The next moment, an icy chill ran down his spine as he wondered if dogs ate humans if they were hungry enough.

"Oh, aren't you a sweetie." The voice was unmistakably Hertha's; she was hiding a few steps to his right, cooing at the dog. Holger was about to hiss at her to be quiet when Hans pressed his arm and whispered, "Let her be. The dog won't hurt her."

Hertha had a gift for befriending practically any animal, yet

Holger felt uneasy about the situation. He listened intently until she spoke low again.

"You're such a good dog. What's your name?"

Holger flinched as a soft snuffling was the answer. A shrill whistle, followed by a loud call, cut through the air. "Freya, come here! Freya!"

"You better go to your master," Hertha whispered and gave the dog a pat, causing it to bound away toward the man calling for it.

Holger breathed a sigh of relief and carefully crawled over to Hertha. "That was close."

"He was so sweet. He just wanted to be petted."

He couldn't be angry with his sister, especially because she had probably saved them from discovery. After all, because of her petting, the dog hadn't barked, and since it couldn't speak, it wouldn't reveal their hiding place to anyone. "You did well, but please be quieter next time. We must not be heard."

She looked at him with wide eyes, just now realizing the danger they had been in. "I will. Big promise."

Meanwhile darkness had settled. Holger chewed on his fingernails while they waited for Baumann to fetch them. Just as he couldn't stand it anymore and was about to give the order to leave, a hiss came from the other side of the fence. "Over here."

Holger signaled his siblings to stay put, while he crawled to the hole in the fence to make sure it was really Baumann and that he was alone.

"Where are your siblings?" Baumann asked.

"They're coming."

A crooked grin appeared on the man's face. "Still suspicious?"

Holger nodded sheepishly. "A little."

"Better safe than sorry. But now, be quick and come inside. I'll wait next to that wagon over there." Baumann pointed to a dark outline at the very end of the yard and disappeared into the darkness.

Holger waved to Hans and Hertha. They crawled to him and the three squeezed through the hole in the fence one after another. They passed so many railway cars that he wondered why on earth Baumann had chosen the one furthest away. By now it had grown completely dark and he had to concentrate hard not to stumble on the uneven ground.

"Stop," a voice suddenly whispered. "Here's your shelter. I'll help you get up." At the same moment, Holger was lifted about a meter high into the air and set down inside the wagon. Hans and Hertha followed. Baumann climbed up last, locking the door from the inside, which made Holger feel like a rabbit in a trap.

He strained his eyes to watch and memorize how to unlock the door, but Baumann didn't linger. Instead, he marched ahead, down the aisle, until he stopped in front of a compartment, opened the sliding door and ushered the children inside. After making sure the blackout curtains were drawn, he switched on a flashlight.

For a moment, Holger was blinded. When his eyes had adapted to the light, he discovered that the wooden benches were outfitted with coarse wool blankets and even a pillow. Moreover, he spotted a canteen, a bottle of water and a quarter loaf of bread on the floor.

"It's cozy in here," he blurted out.

Baumann smiled with content. "I can't let you starve, now can I? But you must promise me never to leave the wagon."

"We can't go outside?" Hertha asked with a hint of panic in her voice.

"No. It's too dangerous. During the day, this place is crawling with people, which means you must be absolutely quiet."

"And at night?" The idea of being locked in the wagon, no matter how comfortably furnished, for weeks or even months, didn't sit well with Holger.

"At night, there usually aren't workers on the premises. But if you make a noise, someone might call the police."

"If we're very quiet, are we allowed to go outside?" Holger didn't warm up to the idea of being prisoners.

"No. Sometimes the night watchman makes his rounds. He's a loyal Nazi. Besides," Baumann inspected Hans and Hertha, "you probably won't be able to climb back up onto the platform."

He might be right about that, Holger had to admit. Still, he didn't want to give up yet. "How long do we have to stay in here?"

"A few days at most," Baumann reassured him. "I'm looking for a family for you. A much nicer place than this wagon."

Holger was relieved. "Thank you."

"I have to leave. Take care. Tomorrow morning, a young lad named Matze will bring you something to eat."

"What about you?" Hertha asked.

"I won't return until I've found a better hiding place for you. Remember, don't go outside and always keep the blackout curtains drawn." Baumann tipped his cap and disappeared into the aisle.

Holger stared after him into the darkness. He hoped they hadn't just jumped out of the frying pan into the fire.

"What do we do now?" Hertha's fearful expression tugged at his heart strings.

"First, we eat," decided Hans, who was always hungry.

Eating wasn't a bad idea, since their last meal had been in the early morning. After they finished, they lay down on the benches and chatted until eventually first Hertha and then Hans fell asleep.

Despite his fatigue, Holger stayed wide awake. Inside his head a thousand thoughts kept spinning in circles. Above all, he feared what would happen if they were discovered.

Since his siblings were asleep there was no need to appear strong for them, so the tears started flowing. At first just a few, then more and more, until he was sobbing uncontrollably into his blanket.

At some point, a small hand touched his shoulder and Hertha whispered into his ear, "Don't cry. Everything will turn out just fine."

He didn't want to show weakness in front of his little sister, but his energy was spent, so he had no choice but to turn toward her and hold her tight. "I miss Mutti and Vati so much."

"Me too. Terribly so."

They lay together for a while, tightly embracing, until his tears dried up and he finally fell asleep.

CHAPTER 16

The hidden children in the locomotive workshop weighed heavily on Baumann's mind. He couldn't bear to think of what would happen if they were discovered. No one would believe they'd gotten inside on their own, and under Gestapo interrogation, the children would break —they would give him away.

His stomach clenched painfully as he imagined the three undergoing an "intensified interrogation", as the Gestapo liked to call their torture sessions. He had to prevent that from happening at all costs. The children needed to leave the factory premises sooner rather than later.

He finished work early, claiming he needed to run an errand for spare parts, and boarded the S-Bahn to Wilmersdorf. Before knocking on the door of the Swedish parish, he checked for the watering can in the flower box of the police station across the street, relieved when it wasn't there.

Although in theory he had nothing to fear from the Gestapo, it was better if the police knew nothing about his connection to Pastor Perwe. For this reason, they had agreed Baumann would only visit the parish when he received a message requesting him

THREE CHILDREN IN DANGER

to do so. Today was not such a case, but his concern couldn't wait.

"What brings you to me?" asked Pastor Perwe.

"Today I come with a request."

"I thought as much." The pastor's kind eyes rested on Baumann. When he hesitated, the pastor added, "Feel free to speak. What is troubling you?"

"I've found three Jewish children. Their parents were deported long ago and recently, during the factory action, the family who'd been hiding them was taken, too."

The pastor rested his chin on his folded hands. "We don't have the facilities to shelter children."

"The three are currently hiding in a train wagon on the workshop grounds." Baumann gazed at the pastor imploringly. He didn't want to appear calculating, but he felt it appropriate to point out that it wasn't just about the children's welfare. "It's far too dangerous. If they're found, our entire network might be exposed."

Perwe gave a resigned sigh. "How old are the children?"

"Uh. I didn't ask them." Baumann rubbed behind his ear. "I'd guess, the two boys are about ten and thirteen, the girl six or seven."

The pastor shook his head back and forth. "It's not ideal. Not at all. We have no one who can take care of them, and with so many people passing through our parish, you can never be sure that everyone will follow the rules. The children would be prime targets for exploitation."

Baumann considered the pastor's words. People in the underground often committed morally questionable acts in their quest to survive. It was absolutely possible that someone might harm the children if they thought it would give them an advantage. "The oldest, Holger, is big for his age and pretty smart; he will protect the three of them. Besides, he'd surely be a good help for you."

"I see you're not going to give me a choice." The pastor

smiled. "All right, we'll take the children. I already know who to task with bringing them here."

Baumann had been in this business long enough not to ask their identity.

"How urgent is it?" the pastor asked.

"The sooner, the better. They can stay in the workshop for a few more days at most." With each passing day, the danger grew that the children would act carelessly and be discovered because they couldn't stand being confined in the wagon any longer. On the other hand, the pastor needed time to organize the handover, because it wasn't possible for Baumann to take the siblings by their hands and march across Berlin to Wilmersdorf with them.

"Good. I'll organize the transfer. You'll receive word from Lars where and when the handover will take place."

"A thousand thanks." Baumann stood up and bade his goodbye. In the pastor's care, the children would be safe and he could finally sleep again.

On the way back, he made a detour to a hardware wholesaler, where he bought the clamps and cables he'd used as an excuse for his errand, before returning to the workshop. It was unlikely anyone would ask about them, but it was better to be safe than sorry.

At the locomotive workshop, Koloss informed him they were going to meet with Reinhard, Manfred and Manfred's wife at Rosenstrasse after their shift.

"Alright. I'll come along. Just let me put away these spare parts." Baumann waved his purchases so that any spy in the workshop would understand why he had been absent for such a long time.

At the S-Bahn station Börse, they were already expected, not only by their friends but also by dozens of protesters, mainly women.

"Incredible," Baumann called out over the roaring chants. The narrow alley was packed with people, not a patch of asphalt visible. Baumann fought his way through the crowd until he bumped into a living wall: about a dozen women stood with linked arms, shouting, "Give us back our husbands! Give us back our children!"

Without hesitation, he joined them. To his left, he linked arms with Reinhard and with Manfred's wife to his right. It didn't matter that he had neither family nor friends in the collection camp. This protest was about something bigger. Finally, he had the chance to publicly protest against the regime — and live to tell the tale.

"Man, I never thought people would actually protest," he said to Reinhard during a lull in the noise.

"The people have awakened!" Reinhard declaimed enthusiastically. "They rise against the tyrant! The twilight of the gods has begun."

"What nonsense," grumbled Baumann, who had little patience for such grandiose talk.

"Just because you don't understand it, that doesn't mean it's nonsense." Reinhard shook his head, visibly disappointed, before launching into a lesson on theater history. "Richard Wagner was a genius. His operas are magnificent, especially *Götterdämmerung*. It's a shame Hitler for once shows great taste."

"What's that got to do with anything?" asked Manfred from the other side.

"A great deal. For years I haven't been to the Wagner Festival in Bayreuth because I despise the way Winifred Wagner sucks up to Hitler. And because I don't want to risk running into His Holiness, the almighty ruler over life and death of all Germans, our godlike savior." Reinhard's voice dripped with sarcasm, while his shoulders shuddered.

"That would be a prime opportunity to blow him to kingdom come." Koloss made a hand gesture of cutting a throat.

"The only reason you're saying that is because you've never been to Bayreuth. The security measures are overwhelming. Anyhow, in July 1940, shortly after the French campaign, His Holiness said to Winifred after the performance of

Götterdämmerung: 'I hear the wings of the goddess of victory rustling!'"

"That's a mere legend," Manfred remarked.

"Not at all. My father was there and heard it with his own ears." Reinhard's face twisted in disgust. His father's unconditional glorification of Nazi ideology weighed heavily on his conscience.

"Götterdämmerung or not, something's happening here." Baumann pointed to the steady influx of protestors streaming into the small alley.

Suddenly, a guard stepped out of the building and made a few half-hearted attempts to disperse the crowd. A group of women approached him, shouting and gesticulating, causing him to quickly disappear into the building once more.

"They're pretty scared. By the way, I haven't seen the SS yet," remarked Koloss, who towered over most of the others by almost a head.

No sooner had he finished speaking than a topless Kübelwagen raced around the corner. An SS man stood in the back seat, clutching a megaphone. "Go home. There's nothing to see here! I repeat: Clear this area!"

But the crowd didn't back down. On the contrary, one of the women took a few steps toward the vehicle and yelled, "Murderers! You're murderers! You should be ashamed of yourselves!"

Baumann stilled. Around him, a deathly silence fell over the street. In the face of this incredible provocation, everyone seemed to be waiting with bated breath for the SS man's reaction. The silence stretched on. Baumann's lungs were about to burst by the time he finally remembered to breathe and slowly exhaled through his nose before inhaling again.

Still, no one moved.

After an endless tension the SS man lowered his megaphone and the Kübelwagen reversed out of the street.

"What, that's it? I don't believe it," Manfred commented in awe.

"They just drove away," gasped Baumann. He didn't quite trust the peace, yet a heavy weight lifted from his chest and he could breathe freely again. No shots had been fired. No one had been harmed. It was at least a partial victory. If only the population would wake up and realize they could rid themselves of the Nazi regime if enough individuals stood together.

"They'll be back. You can bet on it." Koloss wasn't easily impressed; he'd been through too many skirmishes with the brownshirts.

"So what? You don't win a war with one battle." Reinhard craned his neck to see better.

Meanwhile, the crowd had resumed their battle cries. "We want our men back! We want our children back!"

A few minutes later, Koloss announced: "Look, the wimps are back."

Indeed, the open-roofed Kübelwagen rolled around the corner a second time. This time, the SS man didn't have a megaphone in his hand. Instead, machine guns were mounted on the back seat.

One of the men aimed his weapon at the nearest woman and bellowed, "Move along immediately or we're going to shoot!"

Instinctively, Baumann ducked his head between his shoulders. His legs were about to start moving when he noticed that the threatened woman didn't budge. If she wasn't going to be intimidated, neither would he.

Despite the adrenaline pumping through his veins, he remained rooted to the spot, observing the scene unfolding.

"You are murderers!" the woman with pitch-black hair hurled at the SS man.

Baumann couldn't hear his response. It was drowned out by the angry shouts of the crowd: "That's what you are! Murderers!

A disgrace to our country! Give us back our men! Give us back our children!"

The people standing to Baumann's right and left joined in the battle cries, and automatically, without making a conscious decision, Baumann added his voice to theirs. He yelled and screamed, demanding the release of the arrested people. The shouts echoed in the narrow alley, soaring up to the sky. Surely the tumult could be heard all over Berlin.

After a while silence fell over the narrow street again. Protesters and SS faced each other. No one moved. The tension multiplied, until something happened that made Baumann's heart leap with joy: The soldiers lowered their rifles. The Kübelwagen turned away and disappeared around the corner.

"That was something. Such a brave woman." Baumann was full of admiration for the unknown black-haired woman. To his shame, he had to admit that he wouldn't have dared to hurl these accusations to an SS man's face.

After two or three hours, Koloss said, "I have to go home."

"I'll come with you." With a final glance at the considerable crowd, Baumann suggested, "Let's return tomorrow after work."

CHAPTER 17

Sophie found a folded note in her mailbox. Her heart immediately started racing, expecting a message from Eugen.

A few days after his disappearance, he had rung her doorbell late one evening to let her know that on that fateful February 27th, he had narrowly escaped the clutches of the SS and Gestapo.

She gently ran her finger over the note and smiled, remembering their brief encounter.

"Eugen! What are you doing here? I thought you..." The shock overshadowed her joy at seeing him again.

"Aren't you going to invite me in?" His charming smile was the same one she had fallen in love with, but she noticed the hard lines around his mouth for the first time.

"Of course, yes." She stepped aside to let him in. Then she locked the door and gestured for him to wait in the hallway while she walked into the living room to make sure the blackout curtains were closed, before she beckoned him to follow her.

He took off his hat and nervously turned it in his hands. "I had to go underground, that's why I couldn't earlier—"

She didn't give him a chance to finish the sentence. Instead, she threw herself into his arms and silenced him with a passionate kiss. When she came up for air minutes later, she said, "I'm so relieved you're alive."

"Me too." He smiled sadly. Then he lifted her into his arms and carried her to the bedroom. For the rest of the night, they made love without speaking a single word. Neither of them dared to address the issue that stood between them until the alarm clock rang at the crack of dawn.

When Eugen had dressed, he turned toward her. "We can't keep seeing each other, it's too dangerous."

"But..." Sophie's brain knew it was better this way, but her heart refused to accept the truth.

He approached her and stroked her cheek with his finger. "It has to be this way. I don't want to put you in danger."

The way he worried about her was touching, especially because he was the one facing arrest and deportation. "Can I at least help you somehow? With ration cards? Clothing? Money?"

Eugen tried to appear nonchalant, but she had seen his eyes light up at the word money. Life underground was expensive; people had to be bribed, accommodations had to be paid for and food had to be bought on the black market.

"Please, let me help you," she pleaded.

"Fine." He furrowed his brow. "Every two weeks, I'll leave a note in your mailbox with instructions where and when we can meet. None of these random meetings can last longer than a few minutes."

Although it would never be enough, she agreed. One or two stolen minutes were better than nothing. At least she would catch a glimpse of him every now and then to assure herself that he was still alive.

When he kissed her one last time before disappearing, Sophie's heart broke a little.

In the days that followed, Sophie clung to the memory of their last kiss, replaying every moment, every look. She carried that sliver of hope with her, checking the mailbox more often than she'd like to admit. Each day, she yearned for a sign—a simple slip of paper that would mean he was safe. So when she finally spotted an envelope waiting for her, her heart leapt. Cheerfully, she carried it into the living room, holding the paper close as if it might reveal his presence beside her.

As she unfolded it, she stared in confusion at a list of church mass times. She was about to crumple up the paper in disappointment when it dawned on her: The sender was Pastor Perwe from the Swedish parish.

Adrenaline pulsed through her veins, dispelling her disappointment. Finally, the time had come. After weeks of waiting, Pastor Perwe needed her help.

She feverishly pondered what to wear. Was she supposed to spy on a high-ranking Nazi and wear elegant clothing for the occasion? Or did the mission involve retrieving objects from a hiding place, requiring sturdy clothing and solid shoes? Her imagination ran wild as she conjured up countless exciting adventures.

In the end, she opted to stay in the dark blue dress with a narrow white belt she had worn to work. To go with it, she chose flat shoes, comfortable enough to run away if necessary, but still elegant enough to match the dress. To spruce up her outfit, she wrapped a silk scarf around her neck, a gift from her mother for her coming of age. Hidden under her coat, it was unpretentious, but skillfully displayed. It would lend her simple dress the necessary finesse, if required.

"How nice of you to come so quickly," Pastor Perwe greeted her.

"What am I supposed to do?" she asked, still out of breath from cycling so fast.

"Easy does it," said the pastor. "Nothing today."

He must have seen her disappointment, for he added, "But tomorrow evening. Someone from the network has found three Jewish children who urgently need to be taken to a safe place.

Therefore, they will be living with us in the parish for the time being."

Sophie couldn't contain her curiosity and asked, "Who are these children and where are they now?"

The pastor gave her an earnest gaze. "Countess Borsoi, I understand your eagerness to do good, but too much knowledge is dangerous. Please understand that I must tell you strictly what is necessary for your assignment and refrain from answering further questions."

Sophie could have slapped herself. She wanted to show Pastor Perwe that she was a good candidate for his underground network, not an overzealous woman. "I apologize, that was indeed very unwise of me. The enemy has ears everywhere."

Now Pastor Perwe smiled. "Indeed. We can't be too careful. The Gestapo keeps trying to infiltrate our parish with informants. Fortunately, we've always managed to unmask and neutralize them so far."

Sophie squinted at the friendly gentleman in his mid-thirties. Surely he didn't mean that the informants...

Perwe seemed to have guessed her thoughts. "Don't worry. We use different methods than the Nazis. No one gets hurt with us. Even though sometimes I wish God would punish criminals in this life already instead of waiting for the Last Judgment."

She could understand his opinion well. "So, what should I do?"

"Tomorrow evening, you're going to pick up the children and drive them here." He explained the details of how the operation should proceed and told her the meeting point — an underground tunnel used for storing important documents — where she should pick up the children.

"Do they know where I'm bringing them?"

"Yes and no. They know they're being moved to another hiding place, but they don't know the location. Introduce yourself as midwife Theresia and take this with you." He held out a small, worn stuffed dog. "The dog's name is Rufus. His job is to protect the children."

"That's a lovely idea." Sophie remembered her childhood. Her parents had owned several hunting dogs and Sophie had whined until she got her own dog for her eighth birthday. He had become her constant companion, making her feel safe and loved. He had comforted her when no one else had and he'd adored her just as she had loved him.

The pastor held out a key. "The vehicle will be parked in the parking lot next to Anhalter Bahnhof tomorrow evening. Be punctual."

"Don't worry. I'll transfer the children safely to your parish." A mixture of anticipation and fear flowed through Sophie's veins as she tucked the car key into her handbag.

Time crawled by, but finally, Sophie could leave on her mission. During the day, temperatures were still pleasant, but as soon as the March sun disappeared behind the horizon, it became bitterly cold. Therefore Sophie wrapped a cozy wool stole over her winter coat before setting off on foot to Anhalter Bahnhof. Earlier in the morning, she had explored the route from the station via the tunnel entrance to the Swedish parish by bicycle, memorizing every intersection so that nothing would go wrong at night when she had to drive in almost complete darkness.

She had even mapped two alternative routes in case a street was impassable. Afterward, she had locked her bicycle to a lamppost in front of the Swedish church so she could disappear as quickly as possible after the operation.

Upon arriving at the parking lot in front of Anhalter Bahnhof, she found the car without difficulty thanks to the pastor's description. As soon as she settled behind the wheel, she felt transported years back in time, to when she owned her own car.

Back then, she — like probably every young adult — had looked expectantly into the future, dreaming of great things.

Since Hitler had come to power, these dreams had been destroyed bit by bit, and the ongoing war had demolished what was left. Sophie didn't want to pity herself, because she was well aware that she fared much better compared to others, especially Jews like Eugen. The thought of her lover stabbed her heart. After he had gone into hiding, they had seen each other only once.

However, she had expected more from life than an assignment in the post office, snooping around in strangers' personal lives, reading their most intimate thoughts in their letters.

If these thoughts were not only intimate but also important to the war effort or critical of the regime, she had to blacken the sentences and, if necessary, report it to her superior so that the sender could be punished.

Reading other people's secrets, especially in matters of love, was unpleasant enough, and censoring text felt like a betrayal of both the writer and the recipient, but the critical passages were the worst. Every time, Sophie struggled with herself until she finally refrained from reporting the sender. Her negligence had been discovered twice so far, which had gotten her into serious trouble. A third time, she wouldn't be able to talk her way out of it.

She pushed away thoughts of her work and focused on the task at hand. Before driving off, she checked her handbag for the stuffed animal Rufus and the permit for private car trips: She was the midwife Theresia on her way to a woman in labor.

Sophie had never attended a human birth, although on her parents' estate she had often witnessed when cows or horses had calved or foaled. This experience would have to suffice to feign profound knowledge of the midwifery to an SS man during an interrogation.

Preferably, she wouldn't be stopped at all.

It had been over a year since she'd last sat behind the wheel of a car. Gripping the steering wheel tightly, she leaned forward to make out the street in the weak light of the front headlights equipped with blackout inserts. She found the exit of the parking lot and cursed because she was a hair away from running over a pedestrian dressed in black.

At the last moment, she hit the brakes while he simultaneously got himself out of the danger zone with a bold jump to the side. Normally, she would have stepped out and apologized, but politeness had to take a back seat today. She had a mission to accomplish.

After the near-accident, her heart was pounding in her throat as she steered the car onto the main road and crept toward her destination in the almost absolute darkness. It took several minutes until she got used to driving. Then the tension eased up.

Sophie moved her stiff shoulders and turned her neck left and right, but her hands continued to grip the steering wheel far too tightly. She was grateful that she had not only memorized the route using a city map beforehand but had also cycled it, as she recognized every intersection and didn't have to decipher street signs in the darkness.

At least the war-related confiscation of private cars had one advantage: There was virtually no traffic on the streets, especially not after nightfall. After what seemed like an endless drive, she reached the agreed meeting point where she was supposed to pick up the children.

Following to the letter the instructions Lars had given her, she parked the car at the entrance to the tunnel, made sure no one had followed her, unlocked the trunk and knocked three times on the iron door.

Seconds later, the door swung open and a man dressed in black stepped out. "Who are you?"

"Theresia, the midwife. I've been called. It's urgent."

"It's about time, the birth is already underway." She could hear the relief in his voice as he responded with the agreed-upon code. "The children are with me. I'll send them out. You've never seen me. You picked them up from the roadside."

"I understand." Sophie had memorized the instructions.

The door closed with a creaking sound that evoked finality as the man disappeared behind into the tunnel. A cold shiver ran down her back and she double-checked that not a living soul was loitering nearby.

If she were caught in this instant, she'd be done for. Even the fake pass as a midwife, which the pastor had procured, wouldn't help her in such a compromising situation.

During several anxious moments, Sophie stared at the metal door until it opened again, revealing the dark maw of the tunnel. Shortly after, three children stepped out in single file.

"Quickly. You must climb in the trunk," Sophie whispered. It occurred to her with a jolt that the children might not be able to breathe in the trunk. She sent up a quick prayer that Pastor Perwe had considered this detail, as she absolutely could not leave the lid open even a crack.

The two boys nimbly climbed in, whereas the girl hesitated. "I'm scared," she whispered.

"You don't need to be afraid. I'll drive you to a safe place." Sophie lifted the little one and gently placed her in the trunk with the others. "Lie down, and no matter what happens, you mustn't make a sound."

The oldest squeezed the little girl's hand and nodded. "We won't."

Sophie remembered the stuffed dog. "Just a moment." She hurried to the driver's door, rummaged Rufus out of her handbag and handed him over to the girl. "Here, this is Rufus. He'll look after you."

"Oh, how sweet." As soon as the little one cuddled the stuffed animal, her features relaxed.

Sophie inwardly thanked the pastor for having such foresight. Squaring her shoulders she got back behind the wheel

THREE CHILDREN IN DANGER

and drove off. If everything went well, they should arrive at the Swedish parish in less than twenty minutes.

Just as she was driving at a moderate pace along the road, she noticed the dark outlines of a car blocking the road ahead and stepped on the brake. From the trunk, she heard a thud and a muffled cry. But there was no time to check if one of the children had been hurt, as two black figures approached her.

When they reached the front of the car Sophie recognized the SS uniforms. In that instant, she wished it were an ordinary criminal confronting her; she would have offered him her golden bracelet to leave her and her forbidden cargo alone.

"Pull yourself together!" she encouraged herself, rolled down the window and smiled at the two young men. "Good evening."

One of them directed a flashlight at her face.

"Where are you headed so late?" he asked with furrowed, very bushy, eyebrows.

"I'm a midwife on my way to a birth," Sophie answered so calmly it surprised even herself.

"Papers."

She rummaged in her handbag while fervently praying the children were as quiet as mice. With a steady hand, she handed the SS man her identity card, driver's license, and the permit for civilian car trips as a midwife, which Pastor Perwe had procured.

The young man passed the documents to his colleague while shining the flashlight into the vehicle's interior. On the back seat stood an oversized black bag Pastor Perwe had placed there in case she ran into an inspection.

"What's that?" asked the SS man.

"My midwife bag."

"Open it."

"Gladly. May I step out of the car to do so?" she asked politely, even though her voice almost failed her due to panic.

He thought for a moment before nodding. "Please."

"Then you'll need to step back so I can open the driver's

door." Sophie was regaining her composure. She could handle the two young men.

He looked at her, bewildered, until he finally stepped aside.

With deliberately slow movements, Sophie got out of the car and tilted the driver's seat forward to reach for the midwife bag. The thing was incredibly heavy. She heaved the bag out and placed it on the hood, so the SS man wouldn't even think of walking toward the trunk.

After she unsnapped the bag's locks, the policeman took a look inside. On top lay an elongated wooden object, which looked somewhat like a vase.

He reached for it. "What's this?"

"This is an ear trumpet for listening to the baby's heartbeat."

"That's supposed to work?" he asked doubtfully.

"Yes, it functions similarly to a stethoscope. However, it takes a lot of practice to locate the unborn child in the womb. You can only hear the heartbeat if you find the precise spot." Sophie improvised a bit, as she wasn't entirely sure about the details.

"Interesting. My wife is pregnant."

She hadn't expected that. It was a good thing he couldn't see the blood draining from her face in the darkness. "My heartfelt congratulations."

"Thank you. The child is due at the end of summer. If it's a boy, we want to name him Adolf."

"What an honor for the child and what joy for our Führer." Sophie had mastered the art of politeness. After all, she had endured years of training in the customs of high society. His dreamy expression encouraged her to ask, "May I please continue on my way? You want a healthy and lively child to be born for our Führer tonight, don't you?"

"Of course." He stepped aside, startled as he realized he was keeping a woman in labor waiting for the much-needed help. "Please excuse the inconvenience, but you have no idea what kind of shady characters are out at night. Jews, gypsies and other vermin."

Meanwhile, his colleague had finished examining her documents and handed them back to her. "Everything's in order. You may proceed."

"Thank you for ensuring the safety of the Reich." Sophie could hardly wait to rush off. In a flash, she stowed the ear trumpet in the midwife's bag, placed it on the rear seat and got behind the wheel.

But it wasn't until she had left the roadblock far behind that she dared to take a deep breath. Shortly after, the white church tower of the Swedish parish appeared in the sky before her.

"Thank God," she whispered in relief.

They must have been waiting for her, because as she approached the entrance gate, it opened as if by magic.

Inside, she was greeted by the sexton, Lars, who took charge of the car with the precious cargo before he promptly escorted Sophie to the exit. She would have loved to see the children in the light, talk to them and ask questions about their origins. But she knew that any unnecessary information meant danger, so she reluctantly said goodbye to Lars and walked the few meters to where she had locked her bicycle.

After the tension of the car ride, her knees threatened to give way beneath her, which made her doubly relieved to sit on her bicycle and pedal home.

Once there, she poured herself a glass of schnapps, which she direly needed after the excitement.

CHAPTER 18

The car stopped, and Holger's stomach clenched. They had stopped once before. He and his siblings had lain stock-still for what seemed like an eternity, barely daring to breathe, until Theresia had driven on. With all his willpower, he suppressed the rising panic and forced himself not to make a sound.

Still, he involuntarily squeaked when the trunk lid opened. Except for the faint beam of a flashlight directed at the ground, it was pitch dark. Holger wasn't able to make out more than the vague outlines of buildings. Upon closer inspection, he noticed a man standing next to the trunk, reaching out a hand toward him.

"Welcome to the Swedish Victoria Parish. You're safe with us," said a tall man with a shock of white-blond hair that seemed to glow in the darkness. "I'm Lars, the sexton."

"Are you Swedish?" Hans asked.

"Of course I am. Can't you tell?" Lars laughed.

Holger had never met a Swede before, though he knew from the racial studies at school that Swedes belonged to the Nordic race and were typically blond, blue-eyed, slim and tall. They stood at the top of the Nazis' racial pyramid, followed by the Falic and Dinaric races.

THREE CHILDREN IN DANGER

Lars looked exactly like the people in the pictures in Holger's racial studies textbook. And yet he gave him a kind gaze, unlike most Aryans who considered themselves better than Jews.

"Theresia, the midwife, where is she?" Holger asked, half-fearing she might have been arrested and this was a trap.

"She had to leave. It's better if she doesn't see you too clearly. Then she can't give anything away if she's arrested."

"What happens to her if she's caught?" Hans asked, always wanting to know such things in detail.

"Well, let's not imagine that. It won't be pleasant. Now, out you come." Lars put the flashlight in his mouth, grabbed Hertha under her arms and lifted her out of the trunk with apparent ease, before he repeated the same action with Hans.

When he made to reach for him, Holger shook his head indignantly, "I can climb out on my own. I'm twelve already."

Lars grinned and took the flashlight back in his hand. "Sure thing. Show me then."

After lying motionless for so long, it wasn't easy to coordinate his arms and legs, but after two attempts, Holger managed and climbed out of the trunk – admittedly a bit clumsily.

"Is this luggage all you have?" Lars asked after glancing into the trunk.

"Yes, that's all we have." After their third escape in just a few months, they owned nothing more than the things they carried in their satchels. Everything else had been left behind.

"I'll bring this up to the attic for you later. First you need to warm up."

As Lars spoke, Holger realized how much he was freezing in the cold night air. Next to him, Hertha clung to Rufus, which she had immediately taken to her heart. She had been grief-stricken about having to leave Prickly in the Lemberg's garden. It had taken Holger quite a bit of effort to convince her the hedgehog was better off staying behind, because he would miss his freedom and his pile of leaves if they took him along. In the end, she had reluctantly agreed.

"Come with me." Lars led them to a low building next to the church, with its whitewashed tower rising high into the sky. Inside, Lars checked the blackout curtains before turning on the light. "We don't want to give the police a reason to pay us a visit. Sit by the stove while I get your luggage."

Lars turned on his heel and disappeared. The huge, tiled stove radiated a cozy warmth. While Hans and Hertha huddled against it, Holger seized the opportunity to inspect the room. He couldn't make sense of what this room was used for. It seemed to be a bit of everything: Several tables and chairs stood in the middle, a blackboard hung on the wall, in one corner stood a glass cabinet with dishes, in another corner lay a spread-out blanket with building blocks and a doll on it.

Soon after, Lars returned with their satchels. He was followed by a plump middle-aged woman carrying a tray with steaming cups and sliced bread.

"I'm Svenja," she introduced herself. "You must be hungry, right?"

At the sight of the thick, cheese-covered slices of bread, Holger's eyes nearly popped out of the sockets. He hadn't seen, let alone eaten, such amounts of yummy food in ages.

"I'm starving." Hans was, as usual, the first to grab for a piece of bread, but Svenja moved the tray out of his reach and pointed to a door. "Wash your hands first."

Holger glanced at his soot-stained hands, which he had probably dirtied in the trunk. "Will do, Frau Svenja."

"Just Svenja," she said good-naturedly. "We Swedes usually drop the Herr and Frau, except for the pastor and his wife."

On the sink in the bathroom lay a piece of real soap, nothing like the coarse laundry soap they had been using for years. Even that was only thanks to Frau Goldmann, who'd sometimes brought home a few flakes from her work as a cleaning lady. She always claimed they had stuck to her apron, but Holger knew that wasn't true. She'd pilfered the soap scraps so the household members could wash themselves.

Hertha held the soap to her nose and smelled it. "This smells so good. It can't be soap."

Before Holger managed to stop her, she took a bite, whereupon she made a disgusted face. "Yuck. How gross!"

He sighed. "Do you now believe it's soap?"

After washing their hands, they sat at one of the tables where Svenja had set places for them. In no time at all, they devoured their food to the last crumbs.

"Can I have some more?" Hans asked.

Holger elbowed him in the ribs and hissed, "Don't be rude."

But Svenja laughed. "I'll get some more. Another slice for each of you?"

"Yes, please," Holger replied politely and nudged his brother a second time, until Hans followed his example. Hertha, though, shook her head. "No, thank you. I'm full."

As soon as Svenja had disappeared with the empty tray, Hans hissed at his sister, "Next time, don't turn down an offer of food. I'll eat your portion."

The warmth and the full stomach made Holger tired. Since they had left the Lemberg's house over a week ago, he hadn't slept properly, because he was constantly worried. His two younger siblings might have experienced the stay in the railway car as an adventure, but he had been aware of the danger every single minute. Each night he had kept watch, ready to defend their lives if necessary.

"Lars will show you where you'll sleep. Although our parish is Swedish territory and the Gestapo can't just walk in, you mustn't leave the attic during the day. Every now and then informants sneak onto the premises and we don't want to give them any reason to report us."

"Will you be arrested otherwise?" Hertha asked, her mouth forming an O.

"Probably not. I'm a Swedish citizen. But Pastor Perwe has

enough trouble with the authorities. They might close the church and send us all home if they have reason to believe we're hiding fugitives in here."

"What's so bad about being sent home?" Hertha's eyes widened in disbelief.

Svenja stroked her head. "For me, it would be nice to return and see my family, but people like you who find shelter in our church would be arrested as soon as we're all gone. And that would be terrible."

Hertha wrinkled her nose. "Yes, I believe that too. The SS is evil. And the Gestapo is even more evil."

"That's true, but you don't have to worry about them anymore. You're safe in our parish. However, because many other people continue to seek refuge, no one must know that you're here."

Holger could tell from Hertha's furrowed brow that she didn't understand the connection. Nevertheless, she nodded. "We'll be very good. We hid in a railway car for many days before we came here. There we had to be very quiet and were never allowed out."

"You'll see. You'll have much more space in the attic. Besides, in the evenings, when the big gate is closed and just the permanent residents remain on the premises, you are allowed to come downstairs."

"What about Rufus?" Hertha made a horrified face. "He needs exercise."

Holger was about to reprimand her for her childish behavior, but then fell silent when Svenja didn't bat an eye. On the contrary, she examined the stuffed dog closely and said with a wrinkled forehead, "I think you can take him for walks in the attic during the day. In the evening, though, he can run around the garden. Would that be okay?"

Hertha had a brief conversation with Rufus. Whenever it was his turn to answer, she woofed once or twice for him. Then she announced, "He agrees. He definitely won't bark either."

"Tell Rufus we're very happy to have him here."

Again, Hertha had a short chat with the stuffed animal and translated, "He's very happy too and will guard the attic well."

After their meal Lars led them down a long hallway and up a staircase until he stopped beneath a trapdoor, where he unfolded a narrow ladder Holger hadn't noticed before. He climbed into the attic first, and then helped the children up. Amidst countless boxes stood a large bed with a thick down comforter. Their lodging bore some resemblance to the attic in their old apartment building. Roxi had lived up there without anyone knowing, just as they would do here now.

This thought gave Holger confidence. He had seen Roxi just once, yet she had made a huge impression on him. She'd seemed so strong and independent, coming and going as she pleased, climbing up to the attic through the roof hatch. He wanted to be able to do that when he grew up.

"Get some sleep. Tomorrow morning I'll bring your breakfast up here." Lars disappeared down the ladder and closed the trapdoor from below. Normally, Holger would have explored an escape route; tonight, though, he was much too tired. That would have to wait until tomorrow. Besides, Svenja had explained the Gestapo wasn't allowed to enter the parish because it was Swedish territory.

Holger didn't understand how that was possible in the middle of Germany, but he would rack his brain about the issue in the morning. For now, he was looking forward to sleeping in a real bed for the first time after many months. They took their pajamas out of their satchels and snuggled together under the warm down blanket.

Holger listened for a few minutes to the steady breathing of his siblings along with the sounds of the house: The wind rattled the shutters. The old wooden beams creaked. Before long, he too fell into a deep slumber.

CHAPTER 19

Baumann and Koloss heaved a heavy crate into the railway wagon, which was already filled with wardrobes, dressers, tables and numerous man-sized boxes.

"How much stuff do these people own?" Koloss shook his head, cracked his knuckles and walked a few steps to the delivery truck parked next to the tracks.

"Over the years, a family accumulates quite a bit." Baumann followed his comrade's lead and together they tackled the last crate.

"That's done." He wiped the sweat from his brow and surveyed their work. The entire belongings of a Swedish family were gathered in this railway wagon, waiting to be shipped to their homeland.

He could hardly blame the family for being fed up with war-torn Nazi Germany and returning to neutral Sweden.

"Now we just have to wait for the customs guy." Koloss leaned against the wagon and lit a cigarette before offering one to Baumann.

"He should be here any minute. The pastor scheduled him for six o'clock." Baumann took a long drag on the cigarette.

THREE CHILDREN IN DANGER

A few weeks ago, Pastor Perwe had asked Baumann if he might be able to arrange a railway car for the Nilsson family and help load their household effects. Baumann hadn't needed to think twice. Apart from being happy to help, it was the perfect opportunity to give his frequent visits to the Swedish parish a legal cover.

The customs officer appeared a few minutes later together with Herr Nilsson. The officer held a list in his hand detailing every single household item. He meticulously checked not only the furniture pieces and the number of wooden crates but requested Baumann and Koloss to open each crate, so he could compare the contents item by item with his list.

Once the officer had ensured that only the items on the list were packed into the crates, he gave Koloss the order to nail the crates shut.

Afterward, the customs officer signed the list, stamped it countless times and finally sealed the wagon door. This very evening, it would be coupled to a train bound for Swinemünde. Once at the port, it was going to be loaded onto a ship to Stockholm.

As soon as the customs officer left, Herr Nilsson thanked them warmly and, as a farewell gift, gave them each a bottle of Swedish vodka along with the remainder of his food ration cards.

"All the best back home," Baumann wished the man farewell, watching Herr Nilsson leave with a wistful eye. Secretly, he often dreamed of turning his back on the Nazis and emigrating to a neutral country.

"Shall we share these with the others?" Koloss asked with a nod toward the vodka bottles.

"Good idea." They put on their coats and made their way to their regular pub, where Manfred and Reinhard were already waiting for them.

"Did everything go smoothly?" asked Manfred, who had

arranged the export permits to ensure the move went without a hitch.

Baumann nodded. "The wagon stands on the track and will be picked up tonight." With an air of importance, he pulled the vodka bottle from his coat pocket and placed it on the table. "To celebrate the day."

Reinhard waved to the waitress, who turned a blind eye because they were regulars and placed four empty shot glasses on the table alongside their ordered round of beers.

"Thanks, sweetheart," said Manfred.

"Always for you boys." The resolute woman had a soft spot for the union leader, who tended to tip generously.

After the second glass of vodka, Manfred rubbed his nose. "I have an idea."

"You and your ideas." Baumann groaned. Usually, this meant extra work for the others while Manfred reaped the glory.

Manfred ignored his interjection. "You loaded the furniture and it's on its way to Stockholm, right?"

Baumann shrugged. His comrade had organized the formalities, after all. "You know that. The Nilsson family couldn't stand it here anymore and is moving back home."

"Exactly." Manfred beamed from ear to ear as if hearing about it for the first time. "And all that junk was packed in big crates, wasn't it?"

"Why are you asking all this nonsense?" Koloss poured another round of vodka.

"Because I have a brilliant idea." Manfred downed his glass in one go and peered expectantly around his friends. "Don't you want to know my idea?"

"I'm on tenterhooks, please enlighten us," Reinhard hastened to assure him, although it was unnecessary, as Manfred would tell them either way.

Manfred leaned forward and beckoned the others closer so no one could overhear. "Imagine if instead of furniture, there were people in those crates?"

Baumann shook his head. "How's that supposed to work?"

Koloss said, "Impossible. The customs guy checked every single crate. After looking inside and comparing the contents with his list, he ordered me to nail the crates shut. Then he locked and sealed the wagon. Until that wagon reaches Stockholm, not even a mouse will get in or out, let alone a person."

Reinhard leaned back, his brows furrowed in deep thought. He was the quietest in the group and probably the most intelligent. At least he was the only one who had attended a higher school and gone to university. He stared at his empty shot glass until he finally picked it up and turned it back and forth as if the answer lay hidden within.

"It might work," Reinhard finally said. Three pairs of eyes turned to him.

"See, I told you so." Manfred puffed out his chest.

"Let him explain, will you?" Baumann was willing to listen, because when Reinhard said something, it usually had substance.

"Let's assume," Reinhard tapped his fingers on the table, "the train with the sealed wagon has to stop briefly en route. Let's further assume we just happen to be standing in that exact place. We break the seal and throw the furniture out of the crates. The people climb in, we nail the crates shut, close the wagon, and boom! Done. The entire action takes less than five minutes. The train continues its journey and no one is ever the wiser."

"We just need to be quick enough." Koloss was visibly excited.

"Hold on!" Baumann interjected. "It's not that simple. Have you forgotten about the seal? If it's not intact, the container won't be allowed onto the ship. Or it'll be inspected again beforehand."

"That's right, the seal is the crux of the matter," Reinhard pondered.

Manfred puffed himself up. "Leave the seal to me. If you get me a photo of it, I'll have one made."

"You want to forge it?" Baumann preferred not to know through which shady channels Manfred was able to procure forged seals.

"Well, not exactly forge it, but let's just say: We'll be putting one over on the Gestapo."

"Count me in." Koloss whistled through his teeth. When it came to getting even with the Nazis, one could always count on him. "I'll return to the wagon tonight before it's coupled with the train. I'll just need a camera."

"I'll lend you mine," Reinhard offered. "Or better yet, you show me where the wagon stands and I'll take the photo myself. I'll develop it in the morning at home in my darkroom."

By now, Baumann had come to believe this daring idea might actually work. At least it was worth a try. "Alright. I'm in. We need a watertight plan."

Reinhard pulled a notepad and pen from his jacket pocket. "First, we need a photo of the seal. Koloss and I will take care of that. Second, someone needs to make a new one based on this model; Manfred will organize that part. Third, we need a Swedish family who's moving and willing to sacrifice their furniture for a good cause." He scratched his head with the pen. "That might be the toughest task."

Baumann raised his hand. "I'll do that, the pastor surely knows someone."

"Good, point three goes to you." Reinhard made a note before continuing: "Fourth, someone needs to arrange with the comrades from the Reichsbahn when and where they'll stop the train so we can switch out the contents." Reinhard looked around the group. "Who can do that?"

Koloss nodded slowly. "We know enough people at the Reichsbahn who aren't Nazis. There are definitely some good lads among them."

"Oskar, for example," Baumann chimed in. He knew for

certain that the veteran locomotive driver, who had been arrested twice for regime-critical statements, would participate in the operation, even if it was dangerous.

"Right, Oskar's one of the good ones. I'll talk to him." The offer came from Koloss.

"And I'll make sure the crates are big enough and properly prepared to let enough air inside during the trip. Baumann will discuss with the pastor which hidden people are suitable for the mission." Reinhard summarized the plan so everyone knew what task they had to tackle.

Manfred grinned. "I told you it was a brilliant idea."

For once, Baumann had to agree. He clapped his friend on the shoulder. "You're right, you really came up with something great. Now we just have to pull it off."

"We'll do it with our eyes closed." Koloss looked around the group. "But what do we do with the furniture?"

"What furniture?" Reinhard had stowed the notebook in his pocket and lit a cigarette.

"The stuff in the crates." Koloss shook his head.

"Right." Manfred rested his chin on his folded hands. "It needs to disappear. Otherwise, the entire mission might be discovered."

"Burn it." Koloss made a hand gesture meant to suggest an explosion.

"No, that's too conspicuous," said Reinhard. "We can't have smoke developing."

"Unless we wait for an air raid," Manfred joked.

"Too unpredictable. We don't know when and where the Allies will attack." Baumann scrutinized Manfred's face. "Or do you know more than we do?"

Manfred had to shake his head to that, as he didn't possess secret Allied information either.

"We need to wait with a delivery van nearby the railway track, load the furniture, and drive it somewhere the Gestapo can't find it," Koloss suggested.

Baumann furrowed his brow as he thought hard. "To the pastor. He can store it for later use or burn it as firewood. Yeah, that's how we'll do it: We'll build a duplicate of each crate, drive them to the rendezvous point in the van and switch them there. Six, seven strong guys and the whole action won't take more than five minutes, before the train can continue on its way."

"And the passengers?"

"Well, them..." Baumann looked triumphantly around the group. "They're already inside the crates. Quick in, quick out. And whoosh, they're on their way to freedom."

"That's exactly how we'll do it." Reinhard put his notebook away once more. "Does everyone know what they need to do?"

Everyone nodded.

On his way home, Baumann considered how many people and, more importantly, who they would send on the transport. He definitely wanted to include the three children.

CHAPTER 20

The days in the attic of the Swedish parish dragged on like sticky honey, because they had to remain absolutely quiet during daytime. Only in the evenings, when the gates of the parish were closed, were they allowed to come down to the big room for dinner and to play in the garden for a while. Holger yearned for these hours of freedom throughout the entire day.

Hertha, on the other hand, didn't seem to notice that they were essentially imprisoned. She played with Rufus for hours, whispering to him about the many adventures they would experience together once Hitler was defeated. Hans had also adapted quickly to living in the attic. Each evening, during their playtime in the big garden, he collected sticks and stones, which he then used to build architectural masterpieces. But Holger was bored to tears.

The kind Svenja had given him all the available German books from the parish library, which unfortunately weren't many. By now, he had read each of them several times. In his desperation, he had even tried to read a Swedish book, but had given up after the first page, because he didn't understand a single word.

Occasionally, they were allowed to enter the empty church and listen to Lars practice playing the organ. This was the absolute highlight of their otherwise boring lives and made Holger forget the endless boredom. He didn't want to appear ungrateful, yet he wished they were allowed to move around freely.

After all, both Baumann and Lars had insisted the Gestapo wasn't allowed to enter the premises. So, what could possibly happen?

One evening, Pastor Perwe joined them during dinner in the big room. Holger liked the pastor, even though he rarely laughed and rather looked as if he had to carry the weight of the entire world on his shoulders – a bit like Atlas in Greek mythology.

The pastor gazed first at Hertha, then at Hans and Holger. "I bring good news. There's a family willing to take in Hertha."

Holger's heart skipped a beat. "Just Hertha?" he asked in disbelief. "What about us?"

The pastor rubbed his chin with a sigh. "It's very difficult to find a family that can host three children. Times are tough and most people have very little. This family will take good care of Hertha. They have a little daughter of their own, about Hertha's age. Her name is Mala."

Hertha immediately clung to Holger's arm. "No! I'm not going anywhere without my brothers."

"We're staying together," Holger agreed, pulling his little sister protectively close. Although she oftentimes grated on his nerves, he would never abandon her to her fate. The strange family might treat her well, but that didn't change the fact that the siblings had sworn never to separate. Otherwise, they might not find each other again. Holger squared his shoulders. No, he would not allow the pastor to take away Hertha.

Even Hans, who normally remained unperturbed by most events, grimaced. "We're not letting Hertha go. She's our sister."

"I understand your feelings, but you must think of Hertha's

well-being. She would be in good hands with the family," the pastor tried to convince them.

"My well-being is here." Hertha's fingers dug so hard into Holger's arm he had to suppress a cry of pain. "I'm not going anywhere alone."

"The family doesn't live far from here. In Mala, you'd have a playmate your own age. I'm sure you'd like it with them."

"I'm sure I wouldn't," Hertha insisted, pushing out her lower lip.

Holger became anxious at the prospect of soon being just with Hans, or even alone if the pastor found someone for his brother as well. What would he do all day up in the attic without his siblings? And at night? He would never admit it, because he played the protector for his siblings, but without them, he would be terribly afraid and unable to fall asleep.

No, no, and no again. The pastor couldn't tear them apart. Holger swallowed the lump in his throat before he managed to speak. "Please, Pastor. We need to stay together. Otherwise, we might never see each other again."

The pastor sighed deeply. "I don't want to do anything against your will. But I want you to think about it."

Later, when they were lying in their big bed in the attic, the three of them deliberated on what to do.

Hertha clung to Holger. "You must promise that you won't give me away. I don't want to be alone!"

"The pastor said the family will take good care of you. Maybe it's better this way." Hans, as usual, was swayed by practical arguments.

"You can't be serious," Hertha hissed at him.

Holger feared the two would start an argument, so he tried to calm the tempers. "Please don't fight. Let's think about what we should do instead."

"Please, promise that you won't give me away. I'll always be very good and do everything you say."

Moved, Holger noticed how Hertha's voice trembled as if she was about to start crying. He hadn't expected his little sister to be so attached to him. Usually she hid her affection very well, while constantly pestering him and Hans.

Hans grumbled something before moving closer and putting his arm around Hertha from the other side. "Don't worry, little sister, we'll take care of you."

"Exactly! One for all, all for one – like the Three Musketeers." This book, which he had discovered in the parish library, had greatly impressed Holger.

"What will we do if the pastor insists on handing me over to that family?" Hertha asked with a small voice.

That was a difficult question. Holger rubbed his chin, as he had often seen his father do when thinking hard. After a while, he answered: "Then we'll run away."

"Run away?" Hertha squeaked.

"That's not such a good idea," said Hans.

"I know that myself. But it's the lesser evil. Together, we can manage. Besides, the war can't last forever. It has to end sometime and then our parents will return and we'll all live together again." Holger was giving himself courage with his words.

"Oh yes, I'm looking forward to that." The joy in Hertha's voice was palpable. A few seconds later, her steady breathing signaled she had fallen asleep.

Into the silence Hans asked, "Do you really believe our parents will find us?"

"Absolutely," Holger replied, although he feared they had died many weeks ago. But he refused to voice that thought, especially to Hans, who didn't seem to consider this possibility at all. "The most important thing is for us to stay together."

"True," Hans mumbled and soon after fell asleep as well.

Holger, however, lay awake for a long time, mulling over how to convince the pastor not to give Hertha away. Finally, he decided to speak with the pastor in private the next day – adult to adult.

Then he, too, dozed off. In his dreams, his mother appeared, wrapped him in her arms and hugged him tightly. A warm feeling of happiness spread through his limbs, and he finally fell into a deep sleep.

CHAPTER 21

A few days after the conversation in the pub, Koloss knocked on Baumann's glass booth after lunch. "Can I talk to you for a moment?"

"Sure."

"Not here."

Realizing the conversation would most likely be about Operation Swedish Furniture, as they had dubbed the enterprise, Baumann said, "Alright. Meet me in fifteen minutes by the shed with the spare parts."

Baumann didn't give Koloss another glance and retreated to his glass booth. When it was time, he grabbed a clipboard with a list and said to one of the foremen: "I'm gonna check the sheds to see if we have enough cables."

No sooner had he opened the creaking shed door than Koloss appeared in the outdoor area and called out, "Hey, boss, I need a new saw blade."

"Come on in. We should still have some." Baumann switched on the light and pulled the door shut behind him.

"Why don't you fix that squeaking? It's killing my eardrums," Koloss complained.

"Because that way I can hear right away if someone's sneaking in here trying to nick stuff."

"Clever."

"But that's not the reason why we're here. What's up?"

"I drank a beer with Oskar."

Now he had Baumann's full attention. "Let's hear about it."

"He's all fired up. His work has been giving him stomach aches for quite some time."

"Understandable." Oskar not only transported materials and soldiers to the Eastern Front, but his trains often carried Jews who were deported to the camps in former Poland.

"Well, he said it's no problem at all to stop the train somewhere for several minutes. It happens quite often. Sometimes he has to disembark and clear an obstacle before he can continue."

"Brilliant." Baumann considered how they could best accomplish a forced stop. "We might place a tree trunk across the tracks, so he can truthfully explain why he had to stop."

"That's exactly what Oskar said and he even suggested a location."

"Where?"

"In the forest just past Weissensee. There's no road there, just a forest path leading up to the tracks."

Baumann mulled over it. He didn't know the place. They would need to get the delivery van as close to the tracks as possible to lug the heavy crates with the hidden people to the train and exchange them for the furniture crates. "We need to scope out the area beforehand."

"We mustn't draw attention to ourselves."

"We won't. I have a fabulous idea. My cousin's friend is a forester, so we can explore the woods in his company without arousing suspicion."

"Great. That's what we'll do." Koloss grabbed a saw blade and marched off.

Baumann followed him shortly after, taking a detour to check the hole in the fence. When he marched past the wagons standing on the siding waiting for repair, the full impact of the operation hit him square in the chest.

So far, they had procured food stamps, hidden accommodations and even fake papers, but this operation, would enable them for the first time to completely remove persecuted people from the Nazis' sphere of influence to a neutral country.

The next day, directly after work, Baumann made his way to the Swedish church in Wilmersdorf. The pastor greeted him with a tired face. Despite being well below forty years old, the first gray hairs were showing on his head and countless worry lines furrowed his brow.

Baumann wondered often why the pastor didn't return to Sweden, or at least send his wife back home. Helping other people was all well and good, but if Baumann had the opportunity to emigrate to a country without war, he wouldn't hesitate for a minute.

"Pastor Perwe, why do you put yourself through this?" Baumann asked.

The pastor folded his hands, leaned back and studied Baumann. "My wife often asks me the same question. There are certainly easier posts, but God has chosen me for this one. As long as I am able to, I will continue my work and help people in need."

Although Baumann didn't believe in God, he admired the pastor for his attitude. "The people in Berlin can be grateful that you're here for them."

"Without the help of so many, including you and your friends, my hands would be tied." The pastor leaned forward. "But I assume you didn't come all the way here to inquire about my well-being."

"That's right." Baumann couldn't hide a grin.

"Would you like something to drink? Just yesterday we received a shipment of real coffee beans from Sweden."

"I won't say no to such a tempting offer." It had been so long since he'd drunk real coffee he hardly remembered its taste.

Pastor Perwe called his wife and asked her to brew two cups of strong coffee. After she had served it, she left the two men alone to continue their conversation. Once she'd closed the door behind herself, Baumann gathered his courage and said, "My comrades and I have been thinking about some things. I want to make a proposal."

"You're making me curious." The pastor poured a spoonful of sugar into his cup and stirred before offering Baumann the sugar bowl. "Would you like some?"

"No, thank you. It's been so long since I've had real coffee I want to savor the taste without sweetening it."

"Understandable." The pastor looked at him attentively, as if urging him to state his business.

"So here's the thing: You recently asked me to help with the move back home of a Swedish family, right?"

"I remember." Perwe sipped his coffee. "The Nilssons have arrived safely in Stockholm and have retrieved their furniture from customs without a problem. They asked me to pass on their heartfelt thanks to you."

"Well... when we were loading the train wagon, we had an idea." Then Baumann described to the pastor what he and his comrades had discussed and concluded with the words: "It'll work for sure. We just need a family who's leaving the country and is willing to give up some of their furniture for the good cause."

Pastor Perwe put down his coffee cup and said nothing for quite a while. With each passing second, Baumann's stomach clenched tighter, until he could barely stand it. This wasn't the reaction he had hoped for.

Finally Perwe answered: "It's risky, very risky indeed. But I agree with you. It might work. And I know the perfect family for this operation. They've been wanting to move home to Sweden for a while now."

"Sounds fantastic." Beaming with joy, Baumann emptied his coffee cup. "When can we start?"

"Not that quick." The pastor shook his head. "You know German bureaucracy."

Baumann groaned. "Of course I know it, since I fight with it every day."

"We need to list every single household good and obtain the necessary permits. That alone is difficult enough, but this time we have the second, secret side of the operation. The people who are going to escape must be carefully selected. No outsider must get a hint of suspicion."

Pondering, Baumann replied: "We don't even know yet how many people will fit into the crates. And the crates need to be prepared for such a long journey."

"You see, all of this and much more needs to be considered. After all, we don't want to send these people to their deaths by trying to save them."

An icy shiver ran down Baumann's spine. He definitely didn't want to have the refugees' deaths on his conscience just because he had overlooked an important detail in his haste to get them out of the country sooner rather than later.

"I think it's best not to tell anyone for now, especially not the people we'll be helping to escape. This way, no one can accidentally let something slip."

"Or intentionally." Baumann felt bile rising in his throat. They had recently lost an illegal to a catcher, a Jew who worked for the Gestapo and had betrayed his own kind.

"What makes you say that?" The pastor rubbed his chin.

"Just saying. There are always people who want to infiltrate our network." Even to the pastor, whom he trusted with his life, Baumann had no intention of revealing unnecessary details.

"If you mean the Gestapo informants, you're right. A mere two nights ago, a woman knocked on the door pretending to be Jewish. Luckily, Lars and Svenja have developed an unerring instinct for who is authentic and who is just pretending to be in danger."

"That's true." Baumann nodded. It was hard to explain, but he usually could tell if a person was indeed being persecuted. Even if the Jewish person who had gone underground appeared outwardly calm, they had a hunted aura about them that never completely disappeared.

Then he ventured a request. "I have one favor to ask. It's about the three children I brought here. Can they be included in the operation?"

Perwe was silent for a while, shaking his head back and forth. "Normally, I would say no. The journey to Swinemünde takes many hours. The customs clearance may be delayed. Up to twenty-four hours of traveling is not unrealistic. During the entire time, the children are locked in wooden crates and must remain absolutely quiet. Especially during the customs inspection, a cough or a whisper can betray their presence as well as that of the other participants."

Baumann didn't understand why the pastor's rejection hit him so hard. The three siblings were children like countless others persecuted by the Nazis. He didn't know them particularly well, had only seen them a few times, yet he wished so much for their safety. Somehow, they'd found their way straight into his heart. Holger in particular had impressed him greatly, reminding Baumann of himself at that age.

Before he could protest, the pastor continued: "In this specific case, though, I would be willing to take the risk." He gazed at his folded hands. "We found a family who was willing to take in the little girl. But the three of them resisted tooth and nail because they didn't want to be separated. They even threatened to run away if they weren't allowed to stay together."

Baumann couldn't suppress a grin, since the pastor's description sounded very much like Holger. "They're something special, those three."

"I've been very worried about them for a while now. It's

getting more dangerous in our parish by the day; several times a week Gestapo informants try to infiltrate us. It's only a matter of time, until one of them succeeds."

"Dirty bas..." Baumann muttered and immediately bit his tongue. Swear words might be justified for the Nazis, though not in the presence of the pastor. "It's beyond my imagination. Why don't the Nazis just let the Jews leave the country if they despise them so much?"

"That's a very good question." Pastor Perwe sighed heavily. "Have you read Hitler's book *Mein Kampf*?"

"Me? No way." Baumann raised his hands defensively.

"Well, I have read it. I'm probably one of the few who has studied it intensively. The content is enlightening – in a negative way. The book describes exactly what Hitler intends to do. Back then, it was a look into the future that no one took seriously. Today we know he has implemented, step by step, all the terrible things he put to paper in his pamphlet, or is about to implement them."

Baumann didn't quite understand what the pastor was talking about, as he wasn't an intellectual. So he patiently waited for the conclusion.

"Hitler considers the Jews to be the worst affliction on the civilized world since the beginning of time, which is why he intends to exterminate their entire race."

"But... but..." Over the years, Baumann had heard and seen many things, toughening him up, yet this bold statement left him speechless. The shock of the monstrosity of such a plan pooled in his gut and froze his tongue, even as his mind tried to make sense of the pastor's words. "... but that's not possible. You can't just kill millions of people."

"Hitler seems intent on doing just that." Perwe locked eyes with Baumann. "Therefore we must do everything in our power to save as many Jews as possible. Every single person who escapes Hitler's killing spree is a tender seedling that will contribute to the resurrection of the Jewish people in a better time, when this reign of terror is over."

"You've said this beautifully." Baumann swallowed hard. He knew about the deportations, the horrific conditions in the concentration camps, the rumors of mass shootings, torture and miserable starvation. Nonetheless, it was as if Pastor Perwe's words had lifted a veil from his eyes. Suddenly he saw clearly what he had merely suspected before.

The effect didn't take long to set in. His hands and feet began to shake uncontrollably. Terrible images of the piles of corpses of murdered people assaulted him and choked off his breath. Several times he gasped for air like a fish out of water. His vision was swimming when finally his instincts kicked in and filled his lungs with fresh oxygen.

"It's hard to bear, once you've comprehended Hitler's perfidious plan."

Baumann gave a weak nod.

"That's the main reason why I'm staying in Berlin as long as the German government allows me to. I can't return to my comfortable life while knowing about the genocide happening right under everyone's noses." The pastor's face contorted into a grimace. "Long story short: I will definitely consider sending the three children on the journey."

"Operation Swedish Furniture." Baumann was still in shock.

"I beg your pardon?"

"That's the name my comrades and I have given the operation."

"A very fitting name, if I may say so."

A small worry continued to nag at the back of Baumann's mind. "I've got one more question."

"Go ahead, speak your mind."

"Do you believe Hitler will eventually invade Sweden too, like he did with the Low Countries and Norway, which were also neutral, or with the Soviet Union, which was his ally?"

The pastor shook his head. "That won't happen. You see,

Baumann, while the Swedish government loudly proclaims its neutrality, that stance doesn't stop them from eagerly supplying the German Reich with war-essential goods and raw materials, iron ore above all."

Baumann scratched behind his ear. He had never looked at it that way before. International politics seemed to be nothing more than the bartering of goods, or disgustingly, the lives of people. "What do the Swedes get in return?"

"Usually gold stolen from the occupied countries, sometimes valuables like jewels, artwork, or antiques." The pastor made a sad face. "My government certainly doesn't accept devalued Reichsmarks as payment."

"That's... unbelievable."

"Unbelievable, but true. It gets even worse. You'll surely believe me when I tell you that I don't always agree with my government's actions, despite their justification by claiming to pursue the welfare of our Swedish citizens. In their preemptive obedience, they have allowed Hitler to transport troops and materials through our territory from the German Reich and Norway on one side to the Soviet Union on the other."

"Unbelievable." Baumann felt as if his jaw had dropped to the floor.

"There's one good thing about it: Hitler has many more pressing problems than occupying such a benevolent neighbor, when he's already fighting on at least three fronts." The pastor leaned back. "If it ever comes to the point where my country is next in line to be invaded, the end of the world is near."

"Let's hope that never happens."

The pastor stood up. "I'm sorry, I'm expecting visitors and it would be better if you didn't meet them. You'll hear from me."

Baumann was experienced enough not to ask questions, even though the hint had piqued his curiosity. So he made his way to his regular pub to inform the others he had gotten the green light for their plan.

CHAPTER 22

One evening, as they were having dinner in the big room, Pastor Perwe joined the siblings at their table. Holger startled when he saw how the friendly man walked hunched over as if carrying a sack of cement on his shoulders.

"May I join you?" Pastor Perwe asked.

"Of course, Herr Pastor." Holger nudged Hans to move aside and make room. No sooner had the pastor sat down than Svenja hurried over with a plate and cutlery.

"Shall I serve you?"

"Yes, please."

While she walked to the huge soup pot in the corner of the room, the pastor asked, "How are you doing?"

As a precaution, Holger kicked his siblings' shins under the table to keep them from complaining. After all, anything was better than being sent away.

"We like it here."

The pastor looked into his eyes, surprised. "Is that so? I had a different impression."

While Holger was hesitating, Hans spoke up. "The bombs at

night are terrible. I can barely sleep from fear. Besides, it's awfully hot in the attic."

"That's quite understandable." The pastor didn't seem to hold it against Hans for voicing his distress. "And you, Hertha, are you scared too?"

She shook her head. "Sometimes. Mostly I sleep through the noise and never hear anything. Also, Rufus looks after me." She pointed to the stuffed dog lying on her lap. It was clearly visible that she dragged the dog everywhere: its original beige-brown fur had taken on a dirty grayish-brown color.

"I knew Rufus would take his task very seriously. After all, that's what he was trained for." The pastor stroked the stuffed dog and then looked back at Holger. "The nightly attacks are becoming more frequent and are lasting longer. It's getting too dangerous for you to spend the nights in the attic."

Panic constricted Holger's throat. His voice came out as a croak: "You're not going to send us away, are you? Please don't!"

"Actually..." The pastor bit his lip and seemed to consider something before continuing. "No, I'm not sending you away. But you'll have to move to the potato cellar."

"But why?" Once again, panic coursed through Holger's veins. He hated cellars due to all the creatures crawling around down there: spiders, beetles, ants and who knew what else.

"So far we've been lucky and the church hasn't been hit by a bomb, but we can't rely on our luck to last forever. It's better if you sleep in the cellar. Lars will help you carry your things down."

"I don't want to go to the cellar. It's dark and scary down there," Hans whispered, voicing Holger's thoughts.

"You're not scared, are you?" Hertha glared at her older brothers.

"Of course I'm not scared," Holger hurried to assure her, although the opposite was true.

"There are spiders and daddy longlegs down there." Hans cast Hertha a challenging gaze. "They're gross."

"They are not. Spiders are very smart animals, by the way."

"That's true." Pastor Perwe chimed in. "Spiders are God's creatures, like all animals. There are no poisonous spiders in Germany, so you don't need to worry, the little creatures won't harm you."

Behind Perwe's back, Hertha stuck out her tongue at them and whispered, "See?"

"I'll ask Lars to go up to the attic with you later and help you move."

"Today?" Holger had hoped it would take a few more days before they had to move to the cellar.

"The sooner, the better." The pastor looked at his wristwatch. "I'm afraid I have to get on with my work."

As soon as he stood up, Hans hissed, "I don't want to sleep in the cellar."

But unfortunately, no one asked their opinion on the accommodations. When evening came around, a mattress along with pillows and blankets lay in the potato cellar, which was to be their bedroom from now on.

During the night Holger woke up and stared into the darkness. Unlike the attic, where a bit of light always shone through the cracks, down here it was pitch black. His pulse quickened. Though he couldn't see anything, he had a feeling that something was amiss.

Carefully, he felt for the flashlight at the head of the mattress. But even before his fingers found it, he sensed what was wrong: only Hertha lay beside him, clutching Rufus to her chest. Hans's spot was empty.

Curious, Holger got up and crept out of the cellar. Outside, pale moonlight enveloped him. He peered into the garden and listened intently for sounds. Apart from the rustling of branches and the call of an owl in the distance, nothing could be heard. *Where on earth is Hans?*

He didn't have to ponder for long before he got an inkling where he would find his brother. Carefully, he climbed the creaking stairs to the attic. Relieved, he found Hans was indeed there, stretched out on the floor amidst his collection of rocks and sticks. Holger lay down beside him.

Hans stirred. "What are you doing here?"

"Looking for you."

"I couldn't sleep. The cellar is so creepy. It's much better up here."

Holger agreed. "No one needs to know. We just have to get up early in the morning and return before anyone else wakes up."

"That's not hard. I'm always the first one awake anyway."

Holger let out a relieved breath. "Good. We'll sleep up here every night and won't tell anyone."

"Yes." Hans dozed off and Holger snuggled close to him, because he was just a tiny bit afraid of the bombs.

When they snuck back into the cellar Hertha was wide awake already. She sat on the mattress with her arms crossed, glaring at the two of them: "Where have you been?"

"We couldn't sleep," Hans tried to excuse himself.

"Nonsense. You weren't here all night. I'm not stupid." She tilted her head until her eyes suddenly lit up. "You slept in the attic! Admit it!"

"Yes, we did." There was no point in hiding the fact from her.

"You're mean!"

"Didn't you say you weren't scared in the cellar?" Hans challenged her.

"I'm not." Hertha's lower lip trembled suspiciously. "But it's boring alone. If you're sleeping in the attic, I'm doing it too."

Holger knew she would whine until they allowed her to tag along, so he shrugged. "Fine by me. But no one can know about it."

She rolled her eyes indignantly. "You think I would tell anyone? I'm not a baby."

It was decided from then on, they would wait every evening

THREE CHILDREN IN DANGER

until the others went to bed, before they sneaked up to the attic. It would be a wonderful adventure.

This went on for close to two weeks until one morning, Lars visited them in the cellar, minutes after they had settled back in. "I need to discuss something with you."

Holger's breath hitched. Lars must have noticed their nightly escapades. Drawing out the word, he answered, "Yeeess."

Lars closed the door to the potato cellar, making it pitch black. A second later, he turned on his flashlight.

"We didn't do anything wrong," Hans assured him hastily.

The sexton didn't acknowledge his protest. Instead, he sat down on the mattress and motioned for the children to do the same.

"I have good news for you." Lars looked at them expectantly. "Soon, you'll be done with the boring game of hiding."

"Really?" Hertha cheered. Holger hadn't believed she was also suffering from boredom, since she played non-stop with Rufus or whatever living animal she found.

"Yes, really. It seems there's a way to get you to safety. Then you won't have to sleep in the potato cellar anymore." Lars nodded knowingly, which gave Holger the impression he knew about the two boys' aversion to the creepy room.

Hopefully, he didn't suspect their nightly trips to the attic, because he would surely scold them. Holger brushed the thought aside and asked, "All three of us together?"

Lars nodded, smiling.

"Where to?" Hans wanted to know.

"I can't give you details, just this much: You're traveling to Sweden. You know, my home country. There's no war there, no Hitler and no bombs falling."

Hans's eyes widened. "That's like paradise."

Hertha, on the other hand, hugged Rufus tighter. "Where is this Sweden anyway?"

"Do you know where the Baltic Sea is?"

"Sort of." Holger had studied geography in school, whereas

Hertha had never gone to school and their father had put more emphasis on her learning to read, write and do math than on geography.

"Sweden is on the other side of the Baltic Sea." Lars drew a map on the floor with his finger.

"We're going by ship?" Hans was all fired up.

"I've never been on a ship before. Do you think it might capsize?" There was fear in Hertha's voice. Holger knew where she got the idea from, since she had recently read a picture book where a boat had broken apart in a storm and the man had been washed up on a deserted island.

"No, that won't happen," Lars reassured her. "Before I tell you more, you must promise not to tell a soul about the plan."

"We don't see anyone except you, Svenja, and Herr and Frau Perwe anyway." Holger wondered about the reason for the secrecy.

"That's true." Lars rubbed his chin. "It's just a precaution in case a stranger happens to stumble onto our premises."

After they gave their solemn word of honor, the sexton outlined the plan in broad strokes: The children would have to hide in wooden crates, which were loaded into a train wagon and later onto the ship. During the whole time, they had to keep complete silence. "Can you manage that?"

"Will we even fit in the crates?" Holger asked.

"Of course. They're huge, even a grown man can fit in there."

"And will we get enough oxygen inside?" Hans wrinkled his nose as if mentally calculating the volume of the crate and how long the air would last for the three of them.

"We've thought of that too," Lars reassured them. "Air holes will be drilled into the wooden walls. Plus, you'll each get a bottle of water and something to eat for the journey."

The three looked at each other, then nodded simultaneously.

"Of course we can do it." Holger spoke for himself and his siblings.

"Wonderful, I'll let you know when it's time to leave." Lars was about to stand up when Hertha held him by the arm.

"What if I need to sneeze?"

"Then you hold your nose." Holger demonstrated how to do it by pinching his nose and sneezing against his fingers.

"Or cough?"

"Well, that is indeed a problem." Lars rubbed the back of his neck. "I'll think of something."

"When do we leave?" Holger finally asked.

"Soon. Until then, not a word to anyone."

After Lars left, the siblings excitedly discussed the new turn of events. Even though Holger was afraid of not being in Berlin if their parents returned from the camp, he realized they couldn't hide in the Swedish parish forever.

A life in a country without war, where they were allowed to play outside like other children, seemed very appealing to him.

CHAPTER 23

It was hot and stuffy in Pastor Perwe's office. Sweat ran down Baumann's back and he was on the verge of standing up to open a window for the umpteenth time. Instead, he placed his hands under his thighs and forced himself to sit still. No outsider could be allowed to overhear a word that was spoken in this room.

Too many strangers frequented the Swedish parish to risk being overheard through an open window.

Everyone involved in Operation Swedish Furniture had gathered in the pastor's office to finalize the last details. A risk, certainly. But a smooth execution was essential for the operation to succeed. The meeting, disguised as an event to raise funds for the poor, served as their ruse.

After surveying the area next to the train tracks, Koloss had discovered that the ground was too soft for their original plan. If they carried the heavy crates with people inside –which they called packages – over the forest path, the footprints might remain visible for days.

Therefore they had been forced to change strategies. They divided the helpers into packers and carriers. The packers had practiced for hours, pulling nails out of the crates at record speed, taking out the furniture and handing it to the carriers, who would run the approximately thirty meters to the delivery van, load up and return.

Lars, who was in charge of the overall coordination, said, "After exactly three minutes, I'll give a signal. Then you drop everything, two of the packers jump out of the wagon and help the packages get inside, the remaining two lift the packages into the crates. Nail everything back up, make sure there are no traces to be found and close the wagon door. Manfred stays behind to attach the new seal, the others run to the delivery van. On the way, check that you're not leaving deep footprints and smudge them if necessary. You have another three minutes for that part."

The seven men present nodded.

"What shall we do if we can't unload a furniture crate quickly enough?" Koloss asked.

"Don't waste time. If you have problems with a crate, move immediately to the next one."

From the faces of the other conspirators, Baumann could tell they knew what that meant: If they didn't manage to unload one or more crates in time, packages would have to stay behind and go back to their hiding places. This was extremely dangerous.

Lars gazed in satisfaction at his audience, before he turned toward the only woman in the room. "Countess, you wait here with the packages." He used a pointer to indicate a spot on the sketch he'd made on the blackboard. "It's approximately two hundred meters before the planned stop of the train. Make sure every package is equipped with cough syrup, a bottle of water and a sealable container for important needs."

The Countess, a woman who appeared both elegant and robust, nodded. "Will do."

It was the first time Baumann had dealt with a member of nobility and he was pleasantly surprised. The Countess wasn't snobbish or fussy at all and she didn't seem to think it beneath her to march several miles through the forest with the packages in tow.

"If everything goes smoothly, the operation won't take longer than six minutes. Manfred will whistle as soon as he's attached the seal. This will be the signal for the locomotive driver to start moving."

Six minutes – that was one minute over the duration they had aimed for, but they simply hadn't managed any faster no matter how hard they had tried.

"Remember, no one outside this room must be privy to the operation, neither before nor after the execution. Most importantly, the packages are to be kept in the dark about exactly how and where they're going, in case someone gets caught on the way to the meeting point." Lars looked around the room.

Although he had a burning question, Baumann didn't raise his hand and neither did anyone else.

"If there are no questions, I'm going to end the meeting. Please take a fundraising appeal at the exit, in case you're asked where you were on your way home."

Baumann deliberately dawdled so he could intercept the sexton after the others had left the room.

"A word?"

Lars's furrowed brow clearly showed what he thought of Baumann's request.

"Sorry, I didn't want the others to know. What about the children?"

The sexton's expression relaxed. "I'll take them to the location personally. It's better if they don't walk with the others."

"Good." Baumann was relieved.

Now the only thing to do was to wait until the time to act came. On his way home, he went over every single detail of Operation Swedish Furniture in his head until he was reassured they had thought of everything.

CHAPTER 24

It had been one of those swelteringly hot summer days. After the sun had been beating down on the roof all day, it was oppressively hot and almost unbearable in the attic.

"Shouldn't we go down to the cellar instead? At least it's cool there," asked Hans, who was suffering the most from the heat.

The mere thought of spending the night in that musty, damp, dark room made Holger shudder. So he said to his brother, "Don't be such a wimp. As soon as it gets dark, we'll open the windows on the side and it'll cool down in no time at all."

Hertha lay down with Rufus on the thin blanket they were using as a mattress and instantly fell asleep, while her brothers talked for a long time about their upcoming escape to Sweden.

"Do you think it's nice there?" Hans asked.

"Definitely. A lot better than here."

"We don't even speak the language."

"We can learn it. I asked Svenja if she can teach us."

Hans stretched his arms over his head. "She's always so busy, where will she find the time?"

That was true. Svenja was the heart and soul of the parish, taking care of everything and everyone. Among other things, she prepared meals for the many people who visited in search of help.

A dull rumbling buzzed through the air.

"The English bombers are at it again. I wish they'd finally kill all the Nazis and leave us alone." Hans covered his ears.

So far, the Swedish parish had been spared, which couldn't be said for the houses on the streets to the left and right of the church. Many of the buildings had suffered considerable damage.

At least according to the pastor, as the children hadn't left the premises since their arrival weeks – or was it months? – ago. However, Pastor Perwe had also said they couldn't rely solely on God's protective hand, so he'd arranged for them to move to the potato cellar, where they'd be safer in case of a bomb strike.

The bombers seemed to be turning away; the rumbling grew fainter. When Holger looked over at his brother after a while, Hans was fast asleep. He must have been having a nice dream because his face was relaxed and he was smiling. Next to him Hertha tossed and turned in her sleep, nearly crushing poor Rufus beneath her.

Holger pricked up his ears and listened. Apart from the steady droning in the distance and the echo of detonations at regular intervals, he didn't hear a thing. Eventually, Holger fell asleep too.

He woke up in broad daylight and rubbed his eyes in wonder. Normally Hans, who woke up first, roused his siblings so they could slip into the cellar unnoticed. But Hans was still sound asleep, which was very unusual.

The light flickered. Eerie shadows danced on the wall. A second later Holger shouted in horror, "Wake up! Quick! Fire!"

Hans snapped awake in an instant, but Hertha seemed to notice neither the fire nor his screams. His mother had always jokingly claimed that Hertha was such a heavy sleeper not even a bomb going off right next to her head would wake her.

"Oh my God, please don't let it be true." Holger's eyes

darted feverishly between the flickering flames and his sleeping sister. For the duration of a few breaths, he froze into inaction, overwhelmed by the events. Finally he regained control of himself.

"That was an incendiary bomb! Hans, run downstairs and get help! We need to put out the fire!"

"What about you?" Hans stood rooted to the spot, his gaze fixed on the licking flames.

"I'll go downstairs with Hertha. Now leave. Run!"

At last Hans started moving. In no time, he had reached the trapdoor, opened it, and lowered the attic ladder.

"Hertha, wake up!" Holger shook her shoulders. Out of the corner of his eye, he observed a spark jumping onto her blanket.

Panic drove every thought from his mind except that he had to save his sister. He let go of her and jumped with his bare feet onto the edge of the blanket, trampling out the sparks before they could ignite the fabric.

He barely felt the sizzling on his soles; his fear was too great. Quickly, he pulled the blanket with Hertha on it away from the fire. Around him, the heat intensified. Sweat ran down his back.

Just get out of here! Despite his horror, he knelt beside Hertha and shook her: "Wake up! There's a fire!"

She opened her eyes to slits, but her mind seemed to still be asleep, because she mumbled, "What is it? I'm tired."

"There's a fire," he yelled at her. "We have to get out of here."

At long last she seemed to understand what he was saying. She tore her eyes wide open. As soon as she grasped the situation, she shrieked like a banshee.

"Come on, get up."

While Hertha struggled to her feet, the fire jumped onto the blanket. Desperately, he grabbed his sister by her arm and pulled. Literally at the last moment, he yanked her off the blanket, which was greedily devoured by the flames within seconds. By now, the attic was full of smoke and Holger had to orient himself to figure out the direction of the trapdoor. They absolutely couldn't risk falling through the hole.

Meanwhile the flames licked at Holger's stick collection, the old furniture and the many boxes stored up here. Even the wooden beams holding up the roof were gradually turning black.

Holger's pulse ratcheted up as terror consumed him over the possibility the roof might collapse over them. Coughing, he made his way to the trapdoor. Right in front of him, a tile crashed to the floor. Holger stopped abruptly, causing Hertha to bump into him.

The smoke was getting thicker and thicker. Holger's eyes burned and he coughed constantly. With the fire assaulting all his senses, he had completely lost his orientation. Behind him, Hertha stumbled in one direction, whereas he pulled in the other. A gust of wind rushed through the open window and further fueled the fire, while at the same time driving the smoke away, allowing Holger to glimpse the outline of the trapdoor in the floor.

"Over there," he shouted over the loud crackling.

Hertha turned toward him, standing rooted to the spot. With a soot-smeared face, she stared at him in terror. Then it happened. With a deafening crash, another tile fell down.

A high-pitched shriek pierced Holger's eardrums. An instant later his sister collapsed like a felled tree. He threw himself down beside her and yelled, "Come on, get up. We have to get out of here."

But she didn't move. A thick gash on her forehead indicated where the roof tile had hit her.

"Oh my God! What shall I do?" Holger patted her cheeks, first gently, then harder, but she didn't stir. In school, they had learned that in such cases, you should elevate the unconscious person's legs – and get smelling salts.

He had time for neither. He needed to get Hertha out of the attic before the entire place went up in flames. Filled with desperation, he hoisted her limp body onto his shoulder, as he had seen firefighters do in a book. But she slipped away each time he tried to stand up.

Finally, he gave up. As the fire raged fiercely, it threatened to cut off their path to the trapdoor. Unceremoniously, he grabbed Hertha under her arms and dragged her toward the opening. It was surprisingly easy. A renewed sense of hope filled his soul.

But as soon as he reached the trapdoor, he swallowed hard. The ladder presented an insurmountable obstacle. To climb down, he needed both hands to hold on. There was no way he would manage to climb and carry his unconscious sister at the same time. As he realized the consequences of his conclusion, tears streamed down his cheeks.

Looking around, he estimated the fire would reach them within a few minutes, judging by the speed the flames were consuming the wood. Again, he screamed, yelled, begged and shook his sister. Hertha coughed. A surge of hope rushed through his veins. He shook her shoulders harder. But she didn't open her eyes.

"Please, Hertha, wake up! Please, you have to climb down the ladder. I can't carry you."

Driven by desperation, he somehow managed to shoulder her, but couldn't grasp the ladder's handle. He simply couldn't do it. He was too weak. The tears flowed as he considered his options. Only with the help of an adult would his sister be saved.

"Where's Hans? Why isn't he back yet? What about the others?" he muttered.

With a sinking heart, he left Hertha lying in place, slid down the ladder more than climbed and raced along the corridor as fast as his legs would carry him, hollering, "Help! Fire! There's a fire! Help!"

He stumbled, fell, picked himself up. Then he finally heard footsteps.

"Over here!" he shouted at the top of his lungs. Relief washed over him when he recognized Lars.

"What are you doing here?"

"Hertha." Holger panted heavily. "Hertha. She's up there. I couldn't carry her down the ladder."

"Where's Hertha?" Lars didn't seem to understand.

"In the attic. Next to the trapdoor. Please, please, you have to save her." Tears filled Holger's eyes as he thought of his little sister lying unconscious up there, exposed to the raging fire.

"Understood." Lars darted away, faster than Holger had ever seen anyone run.

"Please, dear God, don't let Hertha die," Holger pleaded, bent over, while waiting for the stitch in his side to subside.

Throughout the next minutes, more and more men and women rushed past him, some with buckets of water in their hands, others with buckets filled with sand. Most of them he had never seen before and could only guess they were illegals, like him and his siblings, hiding in the Swedish parish.

Everyone gathered to help. After what seemed like an eternity, Hans appeared with the pastor and his wife in tow.

Pastor Perwe glanced at Holger and bent down to him. "Are you alright?"

Up until now, Holger hadn't noticed that his bare feet were covered in blisters and black spots. "It's nothing. But Hertha—"

"Where's Hertha?"

"In the attic. She's unconscious."

The pastor muttered a curse beneath his breath and was about to run off when Holger hastened to add, "Lars has gone up there. Please save my sister."

"We'll try." Even as he spoke, the pastor raced away.

Holger began to shake uncontrollably.

Frau Perwe stood by his side and asked in a gentle voice, "Can you walk?"

"Yes, it's nothing." Meanwhile the worst of the shock had

worn off and his feet were burning like hell, but he didn't want to admit it.

"It's good that your brother alerted us. You'd better come with me now."

Hans looked disappointed. "Can't we help with putting out the fire?"

Frau Perwe shook her head. "No, you would only get in the adults' way. Besides, we need to take care of Holger's feet. It's best if you two wait in the big room. Hans, go fetch a bowl of cold water for your brother's burns."

"And Hertha?" The guilt weighed heavily on Holger's shoulders. First, he had put his little sister in danger by allowing her to sleep in the attic with them and then he had left her alone up there. If she died, it was exclusively his fault and he would never forgive himself.

"I'll tell you as soon as we find her. Don't you worry." Frau Perwe's expression clearly showed that she was indeed worried, and very much so.

Hans helped Holger limp to the big room, where he sat down and waited for his brother to bring a bowl filled with water as instructed. After the heat in the attic, he suddenly felt chilly. A violent shiver seized his limbs and he all but slid off the chair.

It didn't take long for Hans to return with the water bowl, placing it in front of him. It was a blessing to put his hellishly burning feet into the cool water. As the burning subsided, his strength returned and the shivering stopped. But the emotional relief eluded him. If Hertha died, it was his fault and his fault alone.

"She wouldn't have been up there if I hadn't been afraid to sleep in the cellar," Hans murmured, apparently plagued by the same feelings of guilt.

"It's just as much my fault. I didn't want to sleep in the cellar either."

"She was always afraid of the bombs."

"We shouldn't have let her sleep in the attic with us." Holger could have slapped himself for allowing it.

"But she was even more afraid of being alone."

"We should have stayed with her in the basement." Holger began to sob, so terrible was the thought of losing his little sister. All of this had happened just because he was afraid of spiders.

"Don't cry." Helplessly, Hans stroked his brother's hair.

After an endless wait, Lars carried the motionless Hertha past the open door.

"What's wrong with her? Is she dead?" Hans and Holger jumped up simultaneously and ran to the corridor, almost colliding in the doorway.

"No. But she's inhaled a lot of smoke in addition to her head injury. The pastor has already sent for the doctor."

"Where are you taking her?"

"To the pastor's private quarters."

Frau Perwe waited at the door, kindly but firmly sending the brothers away. "You return to the big room and try to get some sleep. I'll send Svenja over later."

"And Hertha?"

"She needs medical attention. And then rest."

"Will she die?" Holger forced the words out of his dry throat.

"I can't say. We have to wait for the doctor."

"Will you let us know as soon as he's seen her?" Holger looked at her imploringly.

"Of course. But now go."

Holger sighed deeply and took Hans's hand, desperately needing comfort to endure the uncertainty.

CHAPTER 25

Word of mouth spread the news of the direct hit on the Swedish parish like wildfire. In the afternoon Manfred called Baumann at the locomotive workshop.

"Have you heard?" he asked.

"You mean the direct hit?"

"Yes."

"Course I have." Baumann let his gaze sweep across the workshop. He was pretty sure his phone wasn't tapped, yet he exercised caution. "I was planning to stop by this evening and ask if I could help with anything."

"Good. Unfortunately, I won't be able to make it. We have an important meeting. Ever since those damned Allies landed in Sicily, all hell's broken loose." If there was even the slightest chance of being overheard, Manfred diligently played the role of loyal Nazi. Sometimes he overdid it, which grated on Baumann's nerves.

"We've got our hands full too," Baumann grumbled. "It never ends. One locomotive is repaired and two new ones come in."

"You'll keep me posted?"

"Of course." Baumann hung up. It was probably better if he visited the Swedish parish alone anyway. In case something went wrong, his comrades wouldn't be compromised and would be able to continue the underground work without him.

The thought gave him goosebumps. Baumann was afraid of few things, but an interrogation by the Gestapo definitely ranked near the top. He took a deep breath, waited until the wave of panic subsided and left his glass booth to ask Matze if everything was alright with the fence, by which he actually meant the hole in the fence.

The young lad beamed from ear to ear. He was barely twenty and would have been drafted long ago if he didn't have to wear glasses with lenses thicker than a thumb. They were so heavy permanent pressure marks were stamped on Matze's nose, but without glasses, he couldn't distinguish friend from foe, even if they stood an arm's length away.

"Yes, boss. All checked."

"Good work," Baumann praised him, causing the lad's face to light up like a lighthouse during the night. Following a sudden impulse, Baumann asked him, "Are you free tonight? Some friends of mine need help cleaning up after a bomb hit."

"I'd gladly help. When and where?" The eagerness shone from Matze's eyes. He hated the regime too, after most of his former classmates had been killed: some in concentration camps, others at the front.

"I'll take you with me after work." Baumann gave no further explanations. Pastor Perwe always needed helpers for all sorts of things, but if one of them was caught, it was better if he knew nothing about other participants.

Baumann was horrified about the possibility he might betray his comrades during an interrogation. Like most everyone in the resistance, he lived in constant danger of being caught and he wasn't arrogant enough to believe he was a hero who could withstand torture for long. Therefore he had devised a strategy just in case: He would only betray those who had already been arrested – and there were quite a few – in the hope of protecting those who still roamed freely. How effective might this plan be? Hopefully, he would never have to find out firsthand.

Baumann shook his head and got back to work. At the end of the shift, he collected Matze. Together they took the S-Bahn to Wilmersdorf, where Baumann introduced the lad to Pastor Perwe. Then he sought Lars to ask how and where he could best help.

"Thanks for asking." Lars looked at him with bloodshot eyes, his face smeared with soot.

"Been up all night?"

"And all day. We had a lot of help from our illegals at night, but as soon as the sun dawned, they disappeared like vampires."

"I'm sorry that I couldn't come earlier."

"Better late than never." Lars was laughing again. "You've come at just the right time, I need a strong man to help me prop up the roof."

Upon reaching the attic, Baumann gasped. "It looks like a right mess."

"Let me tell you, it was a lot worse. The women have swept and carried down the debris. But all our spare furniture burned." Lars pointed to charred wood remains in a corner. "We'll use whatever is left to make supports for the roof."

They immediately set to work. After a while Baumann asked, "How are the children?"

A deep sigh came from Lars' chest. "Not good. The three of them were secretly sleeping up here."

"What? They weren't in the cellar?" Baumann's insides painfully contracted. He had personally helped to reinforce the walls of the potato cellar to make it suitable as a bunker. "Are they…?"

"The two boys are fine, but the girl has bad burns and

inhaled quite a bit of smoke. She got knocked unconscious when a tile fell on her forehead." Lars bit his lip. "She can't go to the hospital, so Pastor Perwe sent for the doctor. She's getting oxygen from a bottle, and has to wear a mask over her mouth and nose."

Baumann shrugged helplessly. "If there's anything I can do..."

Lars shook his head. "We can only pray and wait."

He wasn't much for praying, but he nodded anyway. Several minutes later a jolt seized his bones, as it the consequences occurred to him. "What about the transport to Sweden?"

"It's planned sometime next week. I'm afraid the little one won't be back on her feet by then."

"Damn shame." Baumann felt the weight of the statement as if he were personally affected. He so desperately wanted the siblings to be safe. They truly deserved it. He would have preferred to postpone the operation, but that wasn't possible. The meticulous preparations of weeks couldn't be thrown away just because one participant fell ill. That would be unfair to the others who walked the thin line between life and death on a daily basis and urgently needed to be smuggled out of the country.

"I think so too, but we can't let personal sympathies guide our actions. If everything works out, we'll organize another shipment in no time at all. And next time, it will be even safer because we'll have worked out the kinks." Lars wiped the sweat from his forehead and smeared his dirty hands on his coveralls. He didn't look anything like a sexton.

And if it doesn't work out, we'll think of something else. Baumann didn't voice his doubts, but the closer Day X approached, the more nervous he became. So much could go wrong...

"Come on, let's eat something. I'm starving."

"Me too." Baumann had rushed over right after his shift ended and his stomach painfully reminded him of the skipped dinner.

THREE CHILDREN IN DANGER

In the big room, he met Holger and Hans. Baumann had planned to scold them for disobeying the rules by sleeping in the attic, especially during an air raid alarm, but seeing their gloomy faces, he couldn't bring himself to do so.

Holger's feet were wrapped in damp rags and he sported a nasty scratch on his forehead, while Hans looked unharmed.

"Baumann, have you heard about the direct hit?" Hans asked.

"That's why I'm here. I helped Lars shore up the roof." Baumann ladled himself a portion of stew from the field kitchen in the corner and sat down next to the two boys. "How's your sister doing?"

"The pastor says we need to pray a lot." Holger didn't raise his head while talking. "We're not allowed to see her."

Apparently the little one's condition was more serious than Lars had indicated.

"It's our fault," Hans stated.

Baumann's heart bled for the boy. "How can it be your fault? The Tommies dropped the bomb because Hitler started the war. You can't be blamed for any of it."

"Yes, we can. We didn't want to sleep in the cellar and Hertha didn't want to stay alone down there. So it is our fault." Holger's expression conveyed so much grief Baumann couldn't help but wrap his arm around the boy's shoulders.

"You were foolish, but what happened ain't your fault."

"And what if she dies?" Hans's lips trembled.

Although Baumann didn't know Hertha's chances, he tried to reassure the brothers. "She'll get better in a hurry. Your sister is tough. Lars said the doctor has visited to treat her."

"To get the proper treatment, she'd need to go to the hospital, but she can't because she doesn't have papers," Holger said in a grave voice.

"How do you know that?"

"Just because."

That sounded very suspicious, so he eyed the boys sternly. "Out with it!"

Holger pressed his lips tightly together, but Hans didn't withstand the stern gaze for longer than a few seconds before he whispered: "We eavesdropped."

Eavesdropping, not following rules, secretly leaving the bunker. Perhaps it was luck instead of misfortune that the children couldn't go on the transport to Sweden. Sympathy aside, Baumann had to drum into them the damage they had caused with their disobedience.

"If you don't follow the rules, that's very bad."

Crestfallen, the boys looked at their plates. "We know that."

"Not because you're to blame for your sister being injured, but because you put yourselves and others in danger when you don't do what Pastor Perwe says. Do you understand that?"

"Yes, Herr Baumann," came the whispered reply.

"Let's say there was a chance to get you out of the country—"

"You mean the transport to Sweden?" Holger whispered so quietly it was barely audible.

Baumann had assumed the children hadn't been informed yet. "Did you eavesdrop on that too?"

"No. I promise, we didn't." Holger held his hands up in defense. "Lars told us. He explained that we'd have to sit still for many hours and not make a sound."

"Exactly." Inwardly, Baumann chuckled. Now he knew how to convey the importance of obedience to them. "What do you think will happen if you're disobedient during the journey and chat with each other?"

For a second or two, the boys looked puzzled, then it dawned on them.

"We'll get caught," Hans whispered.

"Not just you. Everyone else in the wagon too. Perhaps everyone who helped make the escape possible. Pastor Perwe, his wife, Lars, Svenja, I..." Baumann let his words hang in the air.

Nothing more was needed, as he observed from the chalk-white faces of the boys.

"It won't happen again. Big promise!"

"I'm counting on you." Baumann finished his plate and said goodbye. "Keep your chin up. And no more disobedience!"

"Definitely not, Herr Baumann."

CHAPTER 26

As Sophie read letters from strangers and blacked out inappropriate passages with a thick black marker, her thoughts kept drifting to the upcoming transport to Sweden – and to Eugen.

After Pastor Perwe had informed her that a spot had suddenly opened because the children wouldn't participate after all, Sophie had sent an urgent message to Eugen.

Two days had passed and she still hadn't received a response. He must have received her letter, as the dead drop they used to stay in touch was empty. But he hadn't left an answer, nor had he contacted her in any other way. The fear creeping into her soul told her there could be only one reason why she hadn't heard from him. By the time her shift ended, she had convinced herself that Eugen must have been arrested.

He eyes pricking with tears, she walked to her bicycle, which she had parked at the corner of the building. Just as she was bending down to unlock it, Eugen's familiar voice startled her.

"Don't look. We'll meet in fifteen minutes at the Charlottenburg Palace gardens."

"Alright." Sophie's heart fluttered. He was alive and well. It took her some effort to mount her bicycle and pedal away as if nothing had happened. Less than five minutes later she reached the meeting spot, every cell in her body screaming with joy. There, she sat on a bench, waiting for Eugen with a happily pounding heart.

On foot, he was considerably slower than her, which gave her time to gather her thoughts. However, when he finally stood in front of her, everything she had planned to say vanished.

With a glance around, Eugen checked no one was within earshot before sitting down next to her and pressing a passionate kiss on her lips.

"Thank goodness you're safe. I've missed you terribly." Sophie snuggled up to him.

"I had to take some precautions," he apologized. "Life underground is getting more difficult every day."

That was her cue. Finally her brain started working again. "You need to leave the country."

"I'd sooner die laughing." His fingers caressed her bare arm.

"No, I'm serious." Just in case, she looked over her shoulder once more and lowered her voice to a barely audible whisper. "There's a chance to get on a transport to Stockholm tomorrow evening."

Eugen leaned back, studying her carefully. "How and why?"

"I'm not allowed to tell you." She bit her lower lip.

"Don't you trust me?" He raised his eyebrows mockingly.

"Of course I do, but..." When she noticed his amused expression, she stopped mid-sentence. "You know exactly how things work in the underground."

"So you're working with someone?"

"Maybe, or maybe not." She took a deep breath and leaned against his shoulder. "It's a once in a lifetime opportunity. Someone got sick, so a spot opened up at the last minute. The P..." She bit her tongue. "I was asked if I knew a candidate needing to leave the country."

"Of course I'd love to, but..." The unconditional love and

longing in his gaze warmed her heart. "We might never see each other again."

"You mustn't think that way," she admonished him, pushing aside her own feelings. If he stayed in Berlin and was caught, they certainly wouldn't see each other again.

"To be honest, I'm scared. The chances of success for such an escape are slim, whereas here in Berlin, I know my way around."

"You just said yourself that it's getting harder every day," she chided him.

"Yes, but..." He sighed deeply. "To Sweden? I don't even speak Swedish."

"Is that the only reason?"

"No. I don't want to abandon my mother."

"You have a mother?" Sophie's eyes widened with surprise. It was the first time he'd mentioned his mother. She had never asked about his family, assuming they had long been deported and not wanting to rub salt into open wounds.

"Everyone has a mother." Finally, some lightness crept back into his expression.

"Why have you never mentioned her?"

"Because I thought it safer. She's hiding with acquaintances, pretending to be Aryan."

Sophie nodded. "Do you visit her sometimes?"

Eugen shook his head. "No, that would be too dangerous."

"And yet you don't want to leave the country because of her?"

"I'd feel shabby." He shrugged helplessly. "I couldn't even let her know."

"I could do that for you," Sophie offered.

"Hm."

They sat side by side in silence for a while until Sophie spoke again. "Please, do it for me. I'd feel much better knowing you are safe."

"Even if we might not see each other in years?" He held her tightly.

"Even then." She kissed him long and intensely. "I can bear anything as long as I know you've escaped the Nazis."

He furrowed his brow in thought. "Alright. On one condition."

"And that would be?"

"We get married as soon as the war is over."

"Gladly." Her heart swelled with emotion. If interracial marriages were allowed, she would have dragged him to the registry office on the spot.

"Then it's settled." Eugen sealed her answer to his proposal with a passionate kiss before holding her at arm's length and gazing at her. "I need to memorize your face so I can dream about you every night until we are reunited."

Incredibly relieved, Sophie explained the details of the meeting point for the escape to Sweden. They also agreed on several locations for when and where they would wait for each other after the war.

CHAPTER 27

It took three whole days before Holger and Hans were finally allowed to visit Hertha. She lay deathly pale on a large bed, ugly red burn wounds on her face. Despite her miserable condition, Holger fought against tears of relief.

"Your sister has been very lucky. If Lars had arrived just one minute later..." Svenja didn't finish her sentence.

"Can we sit by her bed?"

"If you're very careful. She shouldn't move so that the wounds may heal without leaving ugly scars."

"We're so sorry, Hertha. We're so glad you didn't die." Secretly, Holger expected his sister to give him the scolding he deserved.

But she whispered, "Me too, because I want to go to Sweden with you."

A stab in the heart took Holger's breath away. Hertha didn't know yet that they weren't going to participate, since the operation was most likely to happen tonight. As always, no one had informed them, but the signs were unmistakable: The entire parish was in an unusual hustle and bustle. People were rushing back and forth, boxes were being carried, orders shouted.

"That will have to wait. First, you need to get well again."

THREE CHILDREN IN DANGER

"Where's Rufus, by the way?" Hans asked.

Hertha broke out into sobs. "Poor Rufus burned to death."

"I'm so sorry." Once again, a lump in Holger's throat threatened to choke him. He definitely needed to get a better grip on himself.

"What have you been up to?" Hertha asked after wiping away her tears.

"Nothing special. We were allowed to help with the cleanup. It looked horrible," Holger recounted.

Hans puffed out his chest. "The pastor asked me to stack the charred wood pieces into a pile for firewood."

"Hans did a great job," Holger praised. "Even Lars said so. Nothing will fall over, thus the stack can stay that way until the wood is needed in winter."

Hertha's attempt to smile ended in a pain-contorted grimace. "It's so boring alone in bed."

"I'll bring you books," Holger offered.

"You'll have to read them to me because reading myself is so tiring. And I'm supposed to rest." A tiny grin pulled at the corners of her mouth.

"I'll do that if I'm allowed to." He glanced over at Svenja, who was busy dusting. "May I, Svenja?"

"Yes. But only for short periods, otherwise it's too exhausting for Hertha." Svenja looked toward the bed. "That's enough for today. Say goodbye."

"See you tomorrow, Hertha. I'll bring a book with me and read to you." Holger lightly touched her hand.

Hans added with a serious expression: "Rest up. We need you to get well soon."

At that, all three of them smiled wistfully, because that's what their mother had used to say, when one of them had been sick.

The joy didn't last long, though. Seconds later tears welled up in Hertha's eyes. "Do you miss Mutti and Vati as much as I do?"

Both her brothers nodded, desperately trying not to join in her crying.

"I dreamed that Mutti took me by the hand. She looked so beautiful, almost like an angel. She kissed me and promised to watch over me. Then I woke up and was lying here in bed."

"Oh, Hertha." Holger quickly turned around and fled from the room so his little sister wouldn't see the tears streaming down his face.

"Surely Hertha will be recovered by the time the next transport is taking place and we can go along," Hans tried to comfort him.

"Yes, surely. Go on ahead, I'll get a book to read." Holger needed to be alone.

"I'll ask Lars if there's anything else I can clean up."

Hans wouldn't understand, since he firmly believed their parents would return as soon as the war was over. Holger, however, had long had doubts about that, and Hertha's dream – if it had been a dream – had destroyed his last hope. By now he'd become absolutely certain his parents had perished – murdered by the Nazis.

He grabbed a book from the parish library, which consisted of a single shelf, and retreated to a corner where he let his tears flow freely.

He hated Hitler, hated the Nazis, hated the SS, the Gestapo, and so many others. Sobbing, he leaned against the wall and wished that he could travel back in time, when life hadn't been so bleak. He yearned to return to a past when the five family members had lived in their own apartment and hadn't been forced to wear the cursed yellow star. A past when he was allowed to attend school and play with other children. When he didn't have to hide day and night, always in fear of being discovered. When he hadn't woken up several times per night whimpering because he suffered from nightmares.

When his shirt was completely soaked, the sobs subsided and

he wiped the tears from his cheeks. He yearned so much for someone to hug and comfort him, like his Mutti had always done.

On days like this one, it was pretty hard to be strong.

CHAPTER 28

Stomach cramps plagued Sophie throughout the entire day. Something was gnawing at her that she couldn't put into words. Tonight, Operation Swedish Furniture was scheduled to take place and she was a bundle of nerves, especially because the farewell from Eugen weighed heavily on her.

On the one hand, she wanted him to escape to Sweden, but on the other hand, every cell in her body demanded she beg him to stay with her. He was her ray of sunshine during these dark days, her support when it seemed to be too difficult to cope with life.

It was a remarkable feat that despite his precarious situation, he never complained or was in a bad mood. He constantly exuded optimism and gave Sophie the strength to carry on with her resistance work. Soon he would be gone, and she'd be so horribly lonely.

Time and again, she reached for the phone receiver to beg Pastor Perwe to cancel the operation. But she never followed through. This wasn't her decision; she was only a small cog in the machine. Her task was to bring the twelve people desperate to escape to the meeting point in the forest behind Weissensee.

THREE CHILDREN IN DANGER

For this purpose, she had explored the area twice, walking a friend's dog. Both times, she hadn't encountered a single soul. It truly was the ideal location for a secret operation.

However, she grew more nervous with each passing minute. When her shift at the post office finally ended, she let out a sigh of relief and cycled home as fast as her legs allowed. Once there, she didn't take time to eat – she wouldn't have been able to keep anything down anyway – and walked straight into her bedroom.

There, she exchanged her sleeveless dress with the white blouse for black cotton pants paired with a dark blue blouse. Despite the warm temperatures, she opted for long sleeves to protect her skin in case she needed to hide in the bushes.

She pushed her chin-length brown hair behind her ears and completed her outfit with dark socks and sturdy shoes. Although it wasn't forbidden to go for an evening stroll in the woods, she wanted to make it difficult for potential observers to spot her from a distance, since it stayed light very late during this time of year.

Maybe that's what bothers me so much, she thought. Under the cover of darkness, it would be much easier to walk unseen to the meeting point. On the other hand, a patrol, which one always had to be prepared for, could ask what she was doing wandering about after nightfall.

It is what it is. Make the best of it, she encouraged herself, while she applied mascara to her eyelashes and painted her lips with a coral-red lipstick. From experience she knew an attractive woman had a better chance of getting away unscathed during an inspection, especially if she flirted with the usually young policemen.

The Nazis were narrow-minded enough to believe a pretty young lady couldn't be up to anything bad. If only they knew! Sophie was looking forward to putting one over on them and smuggling a dozen Jews out of the country right under their noses.

She cast a final scrutinizing look in the mirror, blew herself a kiss, raised her chin, and banished all thoughts of potential dangers from her mind. From this minute on, she had to function like an automaton. Nothing must go wrong. She shouldn't deviate from the plan even by a hair, if the operation stood a chance of being successfully completed.

Grabbing her bicycle, she cycled briskly to Weissensee, locked it up and casually strolled to the forest clearing where she was supposed to pick up the packages, as they called the escapees, including Eugen. Her heart fluttered at the thought of him. They had said goodbye last night, because there would be no opportunity for it tonight. Besides, she didn't want the other packages to know that she and Eugen were a couple.

Lars had clearly watched too many spy movies, since he had built in several precautionary measures in case one or more of the participants were caught along the way.

One of those measures dictated that the illegals shouldn't know exactly where and how the operation was taking place. They had been told to show up at the clearing with a bottle of water and a sealable urine container. Once they arrived, Sophie was going to explain the details to them and distribute the cough syrup she had procured from a friendly doctor and divided into a dozen ampules. A tingling sensation seized her. Once again longing gnawed at her heart. She would miss Eugen very much.

"The war can't last much longer, and once it's over you'll see him again," she whispered, comforting herself.

After the introduction the trickiest part of her task would begin: She was supposed to lead the group of twelve to a spot about two hundred meters' distance from the train's planned stopping point. It was an exposed spot, the only hiding place being some bushes along the tracks. Thus the duration of the wait there had to be kept as short as possible. On the other hand, she couldn't arrive late with the packages, since the locomotive driver would continue his journey without the packages if they weren't at the designated spot on time.

When she arrived at the meeting place with the group, she

THREE CHILDREN IN DANGER

had to whistle two times like a cuckoo; upon which Baumann would open the wagon door and unload the crates. This task was supposed to take three minutes, during which her group had to wait for Baumann's signal to sprint toward the wagon. If they were surprised by a passerby or a patrol during this time span, there would be no excuse. For anyone.

Sophie checked her wristwatch for the umpteenth time. She was too early. Thus, she slowed her steps and strolled more leisurely. She absolutely had to arrive at the clearing after all the packages had assembled. Her stay at the location needed to be as brief as possible. Shortly before reaching the clearing, she would tie an orange ribbon in her hair, so the packages recognized her as a participant in the operation. Another precautionary measure Lars had invented.

Her nerves strung tight, she marched toward the clearing. Here and there, a rustling sound wafted over from the forest, probably a squirrel or a bird; otherwise it was quiet.

The sun poured golden evening light over the countryside. It would take hours before it completely sank behind the horizon and darkness finally settled over the land. This was both an advantage and a disadvantage. Sophie shook herself. It was too late to ponder over the procedure or make changes to it.

Now and then she stopped and listened with pricked ears, seemingly lost in the beauty of the wildflowers along the wayside. No unusual sound reached her ears, until the rattling of a train wafted over from the distance.

Her blood ran cold. Was this the train with the furniture crates? Had she gotten the time wrong? Was she too late? Or was the train too early?

Once again, she checked her wristwatch. No, she was perfectly on time. She prayed to God it was a different train. Otherwise they would be forced to abort the operation, since the locomotive driver couldn't stop for longer than the agreed-upon six minutes, or risk raising suspicion.

Half a minute later a slow-moving freight train appeared in

the distance, drawing closer until it rattled past her without slowing down. Relieved, she took a deep breath and loosened her cramped fingers, the nails painfully digging into her palms. She wondered where the train might be headed to and who or what it was transporting.

As time drew near, she couldn't dawdle any longer if she wanted to arrive punctually. It was a brisk ten-minute march from the clearing to the designated point, where they had to wait for Baumann and his comrades to unload the furniture. At his signal, the packages were to run the last two hundred meters, while Sophie returned to her bicycle.

They had rehearsed the process a dozen times until Lars had been satisfied everyone knew what to do. The great unknown was the participants who would be doing this for the first and hopefully only time. Baumann and his helpers would assist the people into the crates and nail them shut. In exactly three minutes.

Sophie nervously fumbled for the ampules with cough syrup in her handbag, which she was going to distribute, so no one would make a sound during the journey, especially during the customs inspection. They were safely stored in the hidden compartment under the bottom of her bag. Sophie resisted the temptation to lift the false bottom. This she would do once she was on site, handing out one ampule to each package.

About four minutes before she reached the clearing, footsteps sounded behind her. Despite the goosebumps spreading from head to toes, she forced herself not to turn around and to keep walking as if she hadn't a care in the world.

The footsteps drew closer. She racked her brain considering the available options. Under no circumstances could she be seen with the illegals who must have arrived at the clearing by now, waiting for the woman with the orange hair ribbon.

Praying that the footsteps behind her belonged to an innocent hiker, she slowed down until the saving inspiration came to her.

She stopped in front of a beautiful yellow buttercup and examined it closely.

Just before the stranger caught up with her, she plucked the flower, along with some purple knapweeds and bright white daisies, which she arranged into a bouquet. As soon as she finished, she strolled a few steps further and picked some blades of grass, arranging them around the flowers in the hope that the man – a quick glance at his trouser legs and boots had confirmed it was a man – would pass her by in the meantime.

Secretly, she was grateful to her mother for the many, awfully boring hours she forced her to spend in etiquette classes, where Sophie had learned, among other things, how to arrange flower bouquets for table decorations.

She grinned at the horrified expression her mother would make if she knew Sophie was using her social skills not for a glittering gala dinner, but for an escape attempt of illegal Jews.

"What are you doing here?" The harsh voice startled her.

As if caught, she flinched and turned toward the voice belonging to a man in SS uniform. She didn't have to fake her shock and instinctively held the bouquet up to his nose.

"I... I was just picking flowers for my injured friend."

Confusion flickered across his eyes before he asked, "Where are the others?"

"What others?" Sophie forced herself to banish the trembling from her voice. "I'm alone."

"You're not on your way to the meeting at the clearing?"

For long seconds, black stars danced before her eyes. The SS knew about the operation. Someone must have betrayed them. Terror swarmed her senses as she strategized the best way to talk herself out of the situation, while at the same time warn the others.

"I don't know anything about a meeting. Here? In the middle of nowhere?" She looked at him with what she hoped was an innocent wide-eyed expression.

He didn't answer; he silently looked her up and down until her skin tingled as if thousands of ants were crawling over it. When she couldn't withstand his scrutiny any longer, she asked, "May I leave?"

"Where are you going?" The suspicion in his voice intensified.

"Home. I'm finished." Following a sudden inspiration, she looked at him with trusting eyes. "How do you like the bouquet? Do you think my friend will cherish it? Or should I take a few more flowers, maybe some of that light purple cuckooflower over there?" She took a cautious step away from him to test his reaction.

"Hold on, Fräulein, not so fast." He didn't seem to know what to make of her. "Who are the flowers for?"

"For a friend. She was badly injured recently in one of the cowardly ambushes by the English air pirates."

The SS man didn't respond. Instead he craned his head in all directions. For a split-second Sophie considered making a run for it, but a glance at the weapon on his belt taught her better.

"You sure you are alone?"

"Yes." She shrugged, forcing herself to widen her eyes in shock. "You don't think it's dangerous to walk alone in the forest, do you?"

"Only for enemies of the Reich." The young man stepped so close, his warm breath touched her skin. "Are you one of them, Fräulein?"

Since her innocent act clearly wasn't impressing him, she opted for authority. In the arrogant tone her mother used with servants, she said, "Certainly not. I am Countess Sophie von Borsoi. My family is close friends with Himmler."

"That may be true, or it may not."

"Now listen to me!" Righteous indignation took possession of Sophie. Here she was, using her family's fame for once, just to find out it made no difference.

THREE CHILDREN IN DANGER

The SS man ignored her objection. "Did you meet anyone on your way? Or notice anything unusual?"

Sophie's insides burned like fire as she realized she wouldn't get an opportunity to warn the others, including Eugen. Her only chance was to at least save herself and trust in the safety measures Lars had installed. Inwardly, she felt like the vilest traitor for giving up her beloved, while on the surface she remained calm.

"Except for you, I haven't seen a living soul." Her pulse raced wildly. An oppressive pressure weighed on her soul. She hoped her nervousness wouldn't expose her. She consoled herself with the thought that the SS man must be used to civilians terrified by his presence.

"So, you're alone and you don't know anything about a conspiratorial meeting. Also, you didn't encounter anyone on your way," he summarized her statements.

"Correct. That's exactly what I told you. I'm really sorry I can't be of more help." Again, she held the bouquet up to his nose. "I just wanted to pick flowers for my injured friend."

Once more, he observed her every movement for a long time, probably trying to determine if she was telling the truth. Despite the tingling sensation on her skin, Sophie stood completely still, except for slowly lowering her hands with the flowers.

"Your papers, Fräulein," he demanded.

"Countess," she corrected him. "Countess von Borsoi."

"Your papers, Countess." At last, he seemed to have understood he couldn't push her around like a common criminal. Normally Sophie hated the arrogance of the nobility; today though, it suited her purpose.

As nonchalantly as her fear allowed, she reached into her handbag to rummage for her identification card. Her fingers brushed against a bump in the bottom: the vials with cough syrup. An icy wave rolled down her back, followed by cold sweat running down her spine.

She had to prevent the SS man from searching her handbag at all costs – or quickly come up with a credible explanation.

"Here you are." Sophie held out the document and closed her bag with her other hand.

He took the identification card from her, studying it closely. "So you really are a countess," he muttered.

"Did you think I was lying to you?" Sophie gradually regained her composure. For good measure, she mentioned the family connection once more. "My father, the Count of Borsoi, is a close friend of Himmler."

By now, two more men in uniform had joined them from different directions. And if she could trust her ears, others were marching toward the clearing where she was supposed to meet the packages.

My God, I still have the orange ribbon in my jacket pocket. If the operation had been betrayed, the Gestapo probably knew about the recognition sign. She urgently needed to get rid of it. Again, she felt guilty for thinking about her own safety when Eugen and the others were probably being arrested right now.

Inwardly, she apologized to Lars for complaining about the many precautions he had devised. Except for Eugen, who would never betray her, none of the illegals knew her identity. They had been told to wait for a woman wearing an orange ribbon in her hair who would introduce herself as Theresia.

"Is there a problem?" asked the officer wearing shoulder straps of an Oberscharführer.

"I'm not sure," responded the man who had checked Sophie's papers.

"I'm so very sorry." Sophie gave the newcomer a charming smile. "I didn't mean to inconvenience you. If I had known a secret operation was taking place here, I would have picked my bouquet of flowers elsewhere."

"Her papers say she's a countess." The man held out the identification card to his superior. "If they're genuine."

"What are you implying?" Sophie took a step forward,

indignation radiating from her face. "Of course my papers are genuine. No one would be foolish enough to pretend to be a countess if it weren't true. I'm well-known in society. You're welcome to call my father, the Count of Borsoi, who happens to be the NSDAP chairman in Helbing, to verify my identity. Or Reichsführer Himmler." She wasn't sure if Himmler would remember the girl he had last met close to a decade prior, but she hoped to make enough of an impression with the famous name that they would let her go.

The seconds ticked away. The train was going to show up any minute. She fought the urge to look at her wristwatch, while a wave of nausea swept up her throat. She swallowed the bile down. From her position it was a ten-minute walk to the planned stopping point, though it would be prudent to guide the SS in the opposite direction.

"What are you doing here, all alone in the woods? Shouldn't you be at one of those elegant evening events the high society likes to organize?" the Oberscharführer asked sarcastically. Apparently he didn't believe her story either.

Sophie rolled her eyes theatrically. "I've already explained that to your subordinate. I wanted to pick flowers for my friend who was severely injured in a bombing raid by the Tommies."

"We'll check the story later," the Oberscharführer said to the other man, "after we've caught the Jews."

"May I leave?" Sophie asked.

"No, not so fast, Fräulein."

"Countess."

"Fine, Countess." The Oberscharführer eyed her appraisingly. "You're coming with us to the police station."

"But why? I haven't done anything wrong!" Sophie racked her brain, trying to find a way to extricate herself from this situation. The risk of being identified by one of the packages was minimal, yet it was better not to face them at all. Besides, she didn't want to encounter Eugen under any circumstances, fearing her love for him might be written all over her face.

"You were apprehended near a crime scene. There's suspicion that you're guilty of aiding Jews."

"Ridiculous," she hissed, pondering whether one of her acquaintances had recently been injured in a bomb attack and would confirm her alibi.

"We'll see about that." The officer was unyielding. He nodded to his subordinate. "You take her to the vehicle, we'll continue searching for the Jews."

Like it or not, Sophie complied and walked alongside her guard until they reached the street where a police car and several nondescript vans had parked right next to her bicycle.

Damn it. A hot flash of fear reminded her that she urgently needed to get rid of the orange ribbon in her jacket. Just before they emerged from the forest path, she reached for the ribbon, stumbled and let herself fall to the ground. In the two seconds the SS man needed to turn his head, she shoved the incriminating item behind a bush.

"I tripped." She made a show of getting up and dusting off her clothes.

Wordlessly, he motioned for her to keep walking. As they arrived at the police car, he ordered her to climb inside. Then he closed the door, leaned against the hood and lit a cigarette.

An unquenchable desire overcame Sophie. A cigarette would be the perfect means to calm her nerves. She yearned to ask him for a smoke, but didn't want to risk further scrutiny. As she waited, she thought of how best to deal with the situation. If she wasn't on site to whistle to Baumann, he would abort the operation and signal the train driver not to stop.

Her heart bled for Eugen and the others, who would certainly be arrested. Defiantly, she pushed aside all sympathy. Now was the time to act in cold blood. She had to concentrate on her cover story, to make sure nobody else was endangered, especially Baumann and his collaborators, the locomotive driver and Pastor Perwe.

Although the pastor was personally protected by his

diplomatic status, if the operation was traced back to the Swedish parish, he would most likely be put under surveillance and have great difficulty continuing his underground work.

About thirty minutes later, just when Sophie had dared to hope, a group of poorly dressed individuals appeared, being herded along at gunpoint by the SS men.

CHAPTER 29

A tingle coursed through Baumann's veins. At last the big day had arrived: Today Operation Swedish Furniture was being carried out. The journey in the delivery van along the forest road had gone without a hiccup. Fifty meters away from the tracks, they waited for the train and the packages to arrive.

Lars sat in the driver's seat, drumming his fingers incessantly against the steering wheel. He had been doing this since the minute they left the Swedish parish. Even while driving, his fingers had been fidgeting non-stop. Baumann was about to lose his mind.

"I'll take up my position by the train tracks," Baumann said.

"Go ahead." Lars stared straight ahead, as if he could summon the arrival of the packages through sheer willpower. In the back of the van sat the helpers, including Koloss, Matze, Manfred and Reinhard.

Baumann opened the passenger door and circled the van, peering in all directions. It was unlikely that anyone had followed them, but he wanted to be absolutely sure they were alone before opening the back door.

"Everything alright, boss?" Even Koloss, who was rarely

fazed, gripped the handle of the claw hammer tightly in his massive paws.

"You'll break the handle if you squeeze any harder," Baumann joked with a pointed gaze at his comrade's white knuckles.

"Better we start soon."

"Stay calm. We've practiced this a dozen times." Baumann wondered who he was trying to fool; after all, he was a bundle of nerves himself. "Everyone knows what to do?"

They all nodded. Space inside the train wagon was limited, so Koloss and Matze had been assigned to pull the nails out of the crates, while Baumann and Reinhard would stay outside and help the refugees onto the platform. Manfred would keep watch between the van and the train car and apply the forged seal after the operation was completed.

They had deliberately not hammered the nails in all the way, so that the claw of the hammer could easily be slid underneath to pull out the nail.

"I'm going to the tracks. As soon as Lars gives you the signal, you run."

"Understood," the four said in unison. Tension wafted through the van. The next few minutes would determine whether twelve Jews would travel to freedom – or not.

Baumann inhaled a deep breath, forcing himself to push aside all troubling thoughts and to focus solely on the task ahead. He marched to the spot from where he could see both the railway line and the path on which the Countess would arrive with the Jews.

No one was in sight.

He glanced at his watch. Seven minutes to go.

To combat his nerves, he lit a cigarette and leaned against a tree, attentively observing the surroundings.

Hopefully, the train will arrive on time. Lars had decreed they would wait a maximum of fifteen minutes. Although something could always come up, like a fallen tree or bomb damage to the tracks, a delay might also mean that the operation had been discovered.

In case Oskar had company in his locomotive, they had agreed he would continue his course without stopping.

The minutes crawled by. Baumann turned around and stared at the delivery van. Even from that distance, he noticed the Swede drumming on the steering wheel. He even imagined sensing a slight vibration in the ground.

Lars raised his hand as a sign he had seen him and was waiting for the agreed signal to start the operation. As soon as Baumann waved, Lars would notify the men in the back of the van to jump out, run to the train and empty the crates.

Nothing must go wrong. Baumann's pulse was beating so hard the rushing blood in his ears drowned out other sounds. After taking several greedy drags on his cigarette, he flicked it away and stamped it out.

"Where on earth is the Countess?" he grumbled.

They hadn't been able to rehearse this part of the operation. Sure, the Countess had been on site twice to familiarize herself with the surroundings. Today though, she wasn't alone, she had twelve people with her who were here for the first time.

That many people couldn't hide behind a bush. *Damn it!* If they had arrived at the meeting point, he would see them. A tingle made him shudder.

Then came the rattling of a train. Instantly, he forgot about the Countess and her group and focused solely on the sound. It wasn't long before a plume of smoke and the locomotive chugged into view.

He bit his lips in anticipation. Oskar was a reliable man. Nonetheless, a thousand things could go wrong. The train roared toward Baumann at undiminished speed. He was about to curse loudly when it finally slowed down.

Almost in slow motion the locomotive passed. In the driver's cab stood Oskar, raising his fist to show everything was going according to plan. Baumann counted the wagons.

Number eleven, recognizable by the seal, contained the household goods of a Swedish family. It stopped exactly in front of him.

"Precision work," Baumann said appreciatively, though no one was within earshot. He raised his hand to signal to Oskar that the wagon was in the correct spot.

Meanwhile it was high time for the Countess to show up. He took a few steps in the direction of the meeting point, whistled at the top of his lungs and listened. The Countess was supposed to whistle back, before he was allowed to give Lars the signal to send the others. But it remained quiet.

Why wasn't she responding? Hadn't she noticed the arrival of the train? He cursed himself for being a fool. It was impossible not to have heard or seen the rattling freight train.

"Damn it all to hell." His fingers itched to walk over and check for himself, but he had to stay put. No deviation from the plan was allowed.

He counted to thirty. Then he whistled once more. Again, he received no answer.

There was nothing else for him to do. The operation had to be aborted. He couldn't keep Oskar waiting any longer. With a burning ache in his bones Baumann marched the few meters to his original position, raised his hand toward the locomotive and waved three times to signal the abort.

Again, the seconds ticked by. Nothing happened. Car number eleven stood directly in front of him, not moving a single millimeter. Had Oskar not seen him? Or was a Gestapo agent standing next to him and the entire setup was a trap?

Cold sweat ran down Baumann's back and forehead, even into his eyes. He resisted the urge to wipe his eyes, fearing Oskar or Lars might misinterpret it as a signal.

He stood stock-still and waited. And waited. And waited.

Just when he had given up hope of coming out of the operation alive, the train finally started moving. At first slowly, then faster and faster, one car after another rolled past until the track lay empty before him, with nothing to remind Baumann of the drama that had played out in his mind.

With shaking knees, he dragged himself to the delivery van, slammed the rear doors shut, opened the passenger door and climbed inside next to Lars.

"What happened?" The fear and disappointment were not only visible on Lars's face, Baumann could practically smell it.

"Drive."

Lars put the van in gear and drove back the same way they had come. "Now tell me."

"Something went wrong, but I don't know what." Baumann turned his head to the side and spoke extra loudly so the men in the back could listen. "The train was on time, stopped perfectly."

"I saw that."

"But the Countess wasn't there, none of the packages were there. I couldn't do nothin' else, I had to signal Oskar to keep goin'." As Baumann spoke, the tension released and he began to shake terribly.

"Damn. Damn. Damn," Lars muttered.

"What do we do now?"

For a long time it was quiet inside the van. When they turned on the main road Lars looked at Baumann. "Nothing. We drive back to the parish and act as if we had never been at the meeting point."

"How do we find out what went wrong?" Baumann still couldn't believe they'd failed. "You think the Countess got cold feet?"

"No." Lars shook his head. "She's reliable. And cold-blooded."

Baumann had seen the Countess on a handful of occasions at most and hadn't exchanged much more than "Hello" and "Goodbye" with her. She was a noble, none of whom he held in high esteem. They were spoiled, arrogant people who believed themselves better than the commoners and had never worked a single day in their lives.

THREE CHILDREN IN DANGER

Although Countess Sophie seemed to be different. Frau Perwe had told him that she sometimes helped out in the kitchen and wasn't above peeling potatoes. Baumann turned his attention to the road. The mission's failure could have been due to many things; it didn't have to be the Countess's fault.

When they arrived at the Swedish community, Pastor Perwe was waiting for them.

"How..." The pastor glanced at the expressions on Lars's and Baumann's faces and knew. "...I'm sorry."

"I have no idea what went wrong," Lars explained.

"The Countess wasn't there, so we had to abort." With an urgent need to smash something, Baumann clenched his fists.

"Let's free the other helpers first." Pastor Perwe opened the rear doors and the men jumped out.

"Shit," said Koloss, echoing Baumann's thoughts.

"I feel it in my bones that something happened."

"All of that is unimportant right now. We can investigate the causes later, once we have found out the facts." The pastor wasn't easily rattled. "Right now the most important task is to ensure no one gets caught and no connection will be made to our parish."

"Understood." Baumann turned to his comrades. "You know what to do. Get outta here and get yourselves an alibi for the last two hours."

"It's probably prudent if we don't meet for a few days and don't stop for drinks at our regular pub tomorrow either," said Reinhard, who had been silent until now. It was clear to see how deeply the mission's failure affected him.

"On the contrary." Koloss looked at him seriously and said in a voice surprisingly gentle for a man of his size, "We continue just as before: beer at our regular pub tomorrow evening, as if nothing happened."

"I agree with Koloss." Baumann had learned early on that routine was non-suspicious. People usually got caught when they changed their habits. Or due to an unfortunate coincidence, which one could never completely rule out, though one could minimize the risk by not deviating from the daily routine.

"Matze, I'll see you at the workshop in the morning."

"Sure, boss." Matze said goodbye, followed by Reinhard and Manfred. Koloss left the premises a few minutes later, since they didn't want to be seen together near the Swedish parish – because that wasn't a habit.

As the last one Baumann made his way home, deeply worried about the people who had been so close to setting out on their journey to freedom.

CHAPTER 30

Sophie nearly screamed out loud when she spotted Eugen among the arrested. Their eyes met for a second before he lifted his chin and turned his head away. He would never betray her.

A burning sense of guilt shot through her veins. It was solely her fault that he had been arrested. She had been so convinced of Operation Swedish Furniture that she had urged him to seize the opportunity to escape.

If only she had never mentioned a word about it, he would still be safely hidden somewhere in Berlin. Desperate sobs threatened to bubble up in her throat. What had she done? She had driven her beloved Eugen straight into the arms of his henchmen.

A voice inside her spoke up: *It's not your fault. Eugen made the decision himself.*

But I told him about it, if he hadn't known...

Then he might have done something else or been caught during an inspection.

He's always so careful, surely nothing would have happened to him.

You don't know that. So many Jews fall into the trap every day. Eugen was never truly safe in Berlin.

Will I ever see him again?

Sophie's inner voice had no answer to that and fell silent just in time for her to turn her attention back to the events unfolding outside.

With a bleeding heart, she watched as the Jews were pushed into the delivery van. Just before Eugen disappeared inside, he gazed in her direction and their eyes met one last time. He twisted his lips into that charming smile she had fallen in love with.

I love you, she mouthed silently.

Then he was gone. Perhaps forever.

To keep her hands busy, Sophie rummaged in her handbag for a mirror and a lipstick. As she did so, she observed a blonde woman breaking away from the group of Jews and starting a discussion with the guards.

Pretty brave, Sophie thought as she lowered her hand and waited to see what would happen next. To her great surprise, the SS men grabbed the woman by the arm and roughly pushed her onto the back seat of the police car next to Sophie.

"Phew, that was close," the blonde whispered, as she turned around and widened her eyes in horror when she discovered Sophie. "They caught you too?"

Instant alarm bells rang in Sophie's head. This woman was either terribly stupid or... a spy. No matter which was true, Sophie was on her guard. She had no intention of compromising herself.

"I don't recall us being on a first-name basis," she said with all the haughtiness she hated in her mother.

"What kind of person are you?" A flash of uncertainty crossed Blondie's face, as Sophie mentally dubbed the woman, before it immediately disappeared. Her expression smoothed into an innocent gaze. "You're Theresia, aren't you?"

Sophie knew this innocent look; she had used it countless times herself when caught doing something unladylike as a teenager. Blondie would have to try much harder if she wanted to catch Sophie off guard. By now, she was one hundred percent convinced that Blondie was a spy. Perhaps she was even the one who had betrayed the operation.

Sorrow, anger and disgust made bile rise in her throat, yet she strove to maintain a neutral expression. Even if she couldn't save Eugen's life, she at least wanted to expose this woman and render her harmless.

"No, I'm not Theresia. Who are you?"

"Come on now." Blondie looked conspiratorially in all directions. Most of the SS men were just getting into the delivery van, which then drove off. Two of them stayed behind. They stood next to the police car, smoking. "They can't hear us."

"I have nothing to hide."

"Really, Theresia?" Blondie raised her eyebrows, placing a hand on Sophie's arm. "You can tell me the truth. If we compare our cover stories, we can help each other get out of this unscathed. We're in the same boat, after all."

Sophie pulled her arm away, suppressing a sharp retort. She wasn't so easily fooled by a lady who wouldn't even give her name. "And here I was thinking I am in an automobile."

The sheer confusion in Blondie's gaze was delectable. If she hadn't been sitting on the back seat of a police car of all places, Sophie would have savored her victory.

"Very funny." Blondie composed herself soon enough. She peered seemingly disinterested out of the window, toward the SS men who lit themselves a second cigarette and didn't seem to be in any hurry at all.

"Someone betrayed us," Blondie exclaimed. "If you're not Theresia, then who are you? Is the bouquet your recognition sign?"

"You watch too many spy movies. The bouquet is for my injured friend." To prevent Blondie from asking further questions, Sophie went straight on the counterattack. "What are you doing here anyway?"

Blondie smiled smugly. "You can't fool me. Those SS men out there know exactly who you are."

Sophie wondered how Blondie could know this, as no one but she had mentioned the code name.

"I can help you, but you have to tell me the truth." Blondie implored her with big, innocent, trust-seeking blue eyes.

Alarm bells shrilled in Sophie's head. No matter who or what this woman was, she wasn't trustworthy. She looked at the SS men, hoping they would put an end to this charade. However, they seemed more interested in their smoke break than in interrogating their prisoners.

At that precise moment, Sophie caught a head movement from Blondie toward the SS men. She needed no more proof that the other woman was in cahoots with the Nazis.

There was only one thing that might help: play the aristocrat.

"Now listen to me, honey." Sophie let her gaze wander disparagingly over the other woman's cheap dress. She might be pretty and able to charm the opposite sex, but she lacked the money for true elegance. Which was probably the reason why she worked for the Gestapo.

Sophie's fingers glided to the double-strand pearl necklace around her neck, hidden under her blouse. Nonchalantly, she revealed the necklace and played with the pearls. The effect on Blondie was priceless.

She's one of the girls who aspire to greater things. By any means necessary. Sophie knew this type, whose sole purpose in life was to snag a rich or powerful man—preferably both—to enjoy the leisurely life of a high-society lady after the wedding.

"Of course, the men out there know who I am. And you would too if you were familiar with society. I am the Countess of Borsoi."

Blondie's jaw literally dropped. "So you're not Theresia?"

"I'm afraid I must disappoint you. My name is Sophie." She smiled at Blondie. "And you are?"

Visibly confused, Blondie shook her hand. "Thea Dalke, nice

to meet you." Then she seemed to realize that she hadn't wanted to reveal her name and bit her lip.

Sophie intentionally stayed silent, filing away the name to report to Pastor Perwe later.

Meanwhile, Thea had regained her composure. She put on a false smile and said in a forced chipper voice, "It's a pleasure to make your acquaintance, Countess."

Sophie barely managed not to roll her eyes. "The pleasure is all mine."

"Would you happen to have a hair ribbon for me?" Thea asked a few seconds later, tossing her long blonde hair over her shoulder. "I must have lost mine when those brutes dragged me away."

Sophie's hand automatically moved toward her jacket to check if the telltale ribbon was there, even though she vividly remembered throwing it away. A shiver ran down her spine as she stopped herself at the last second, hoping Thea hadn't noticed the twitch of her hand.

Once again, she thanked her mother for the many years of dreadful etiquette lessons in superficial conversation. Who would have thought that these talents would serve her so well one day? While Sophie had never achieved the mastery of her mother, whom nothing and no one could induce to show emotions in public, she had a few tricks up her sleeve.

"I'm so very sorry, Thea. As you can see, my hair is far too short for a ribbon."

"Not even an orange one?" Thea persisted. But Sophie was prepared. Since she was certain Thea worked for the Gestapo, nothing she said could throw her off balance.

"Whatever made you think of that?" Sophie examined the other woman as if considering something. "Do I look like a woman who can wear orange? Such a bold color would suit your complexion, not mine. By the way, that pale green dress doesn't suit you at all, it makes you look washed out. Or is it just the excitement?"

Thea stared at her with her mouth hanging agape, while Sophie deliberately opened her handbag. It was a calculated risk, because she was aware that Thea would peek inside, hoping to spot the ribbon. At least this way, she showed the informant that she had nothing to hide — the ampules with the cough syrup were safely stored in the secret compartment beneath the false bottom.

As if she had no other worries in life, she rummaged for her lipstick and a folding cosmetic mirror before reapplying her lipstick. Let Thea tell her handlers that Sophie was an arrogant, conceited aristocrat who cared about nothing but her appearance.

Indeed, Thea turned her head away. This seemed to be the agreed-upon signal, because the two SS men flicked away their cigarettes and approached the car.

Sophie slipped lipstick and mirror back into her handbag, mulling over her next steps. Just before the two men got in, she decided to put an end to the charade. She was tired of the spectacle. So she opened the passenger door, took her handbag and bouquet, and strolled toward the Oberscharführer.

"Herr Oberscharführer. Either you arrest me or you let me go."

He stared at her in bewilderment and for a second, Sophie feared he would club her down, but then he started laughing. "You've got guts, I'll give you that. I like that."

His gaze fell on the flowers in her hand. "Are those for me?"

"I'd gladly give you the bouquet, Herr Oberscharführer. Regrettably that's not possible. You surely remember I told you the flowers are for my injured friend. Unless you wish for me to return to the forest and pick a new bouquet?"

"Not at all." He raised his hands while looking her up and down as if he could read her thoughts that way.

"Herr Oberscharführer," Sophie smiled. "I'm a nationalist who, despite her noble title, doesn't shy away from contributing her part to the war effort." This was a big fib, because firstly, she had been conscripted for the job at the post office, and secondly, she needed the money to finance her studies, which her parents considered a waste of time. To them, she was just a woman who should focus on finding a suitable marriage candidate rather than enriching her knowledge.

"I didn't know picking bouquets had become crucial to the war effort." The man had a sense of humor, she had to admit, and promptly decided to use this detail to her advantage.

"Maintaining the health of our people is the highest duty of every German," she declared. "For only in a healthy body resides a healthy mind." She smiled at him. "But you're certainly right, Herr Oberscharführer, there are more war-critical activities than caring for injured civilians. I work at the post office, where I sort and forward letters to our brave soldiers in the field. You surely appreciate how valuable these letters from home are for troop morale."

He could hardly dispute the official doctrine without exposing himself to suspicion of undermining the war effort. Therefore he nodded reluctantly.

"So that I can continue to do my part in maintaining our soldiers' fighting spirit at the highest level, I kindly request you let me go."

Again, he burst out laughing and turned to his subordinate. "Well, Schulze, what do you think, should we let the Countess go?"

A shrug was the answer. "It's at your discretion, Oberscharführer. She looks harmless enough to me."

"All right." The Oberscharführer turned back to Sophie. "You may leave, Countess. We've found the Jews hiding in the forest. We'll catch their helpers next time."

He seemed to be waiting for a reaction from her, so she complied. "I thought Berlin has been Jew-free for a long time."

"That's what we all hoped, but like cockroaches, new specimens of this vermin keep crawling out of the woodwork. But don't you worry, we'll exterminate them all." A satisfied grin appeared on his face. "First, though, we'll interrogate the ones we captured until they reveal their helpers. If any of them mentions your name, dear Countess, we'll arrest you immediately."

Sophie stood stock-still, the friendly smile frozen on her face. "I don't associate with such circles."

"Well, then you have nothing to worry about."

"Thank you very much, Herr Oberscharführer." At the last second, she decided to shout "Sieg Heil" for the sake of good form.

The two SS men were visibly pleased. Sophie didn't want to push her luck and hurried away. A few meters before reaching her bicycle, she slowed her steps, unsure if she should leave it behind. However, they had taken her personal information and knew where she lived. Why should she pretend anything?

As she bent over to unlock the bicycle, the police car roared past her. From the corner of her eye, she observed Thea sitting in the middle of the back seat, leaning forward between the front seats.

Definitely a collaborator.

To process her shock, Sophie pedaled home as fast as she could manage. Drenched in sweat, she reached her apartment, threw herself on the sofa and cried her heart out. Afterward, she pulled herself together, washed her face and considered what steps to take next.

She urgently needed to report to Pastor Perwe; he and everyone else involved in Operation Swedish Furniture must be beside themselves with worry. Automatically, she reached for the telephone receiver and dialed the first three digits of the number she knew by heart.

Just as she was about to put her finger in the next digit, she hung up and stared at the telephone. Calling was too dangerous. You never knew if the line was tapped. Even if Sophie said nothing incriminating during the conversation, the mere fact that she was communicating with the Swedish parish after her close encounter with an arrest might trigger uncomfortable investigations.

There was no valid reason why she should call Pastor Perwe right now – except to warn him. The Gestapo would draw the same conclusion.

Sophie bit her lips as she racked her brain trying to figure out how to warn the pastor without implicating herself. At last she remembered Reinhard, who had recommended her to Perwe in the first place.

He was the son of a wealthy industrialist and his father was a good acquaintance of her family. Visiting him would be inconspicuous. After looking up his address in the phone book, she hopped on her bicycle and set off to report the news.

CHAPTER 31

Hertha was finally feeling better and was allowed to play with her brothers in the garden. Holger, in particular, could barely conceal his relief over the fact that she hadn't died.

He was convinced Hertha's smoke poisoning was entirely his fault, even though Pastor Perwe had tried to convince him otherwise. Deep in his heart, Holger knew even the pastor considered him guilty; he was just nice enough not to say it out loud.

Today, though, was different. As usual, the adults hadn't mentioned a word, because they probably thought the children would let something slip. Pah, they didn't know how well he could keep quiet. After all, Holger and his siblings had been hiding for over half a year now. During all that time the SS hadn't found them, which had to count for something.

All day long, an unusual tension hung over the parish, which Holger felt deep in the pit of his stomach. Lars, usually so cheerful, barely greeted him before he disappeared late in the afternoon.

Even Svenja, with whom Holger practiced Swedish for an hour every day without exception – after all, he wanted to be able to communicate in his new home – had brushed him off under the pretext of having too much work to do. That might be true, but she had her hands full every day and that had never been a reason not to quiz him on vocabulary while she was chopping vegetables or peeling potatoes.

"What do you think is making everyone act so strange?" Holger asked.

"Who's acting strange?" Hans didn't look up from the tower he was building out of stones, which swayed precariously. Hans had set out to break a new height record. Similar to a game of Mikado, he had pulled stones from the lower area – windows, he claimed – to place them higher up on the tower.

Meanwhile the tower had reached a size that made Holger's stomach quibble. He nudged Hertha. "We'd better take a few steps back. Otherwise, we'll be buried under the stones when this thing topples over."

Hans didn't seem to hear them. He was biting his lower lip in concentration and didn't even wipe away the beads of sweat on his forehead.

"He never notices anything anyway," Hertha said, lowering her voice to a whisper. "I know what's going on today."

"You do?" Holger gazed at her doubtfully. He hated it when his little sister knew more than he did, except when it came to animals, because no one could match her knowledge in that area.

"When I was helping peel potatoes, I overheard Frau Perwe talking to Svenja." Hertha drew herself up to her full height, revealing a gap-toothed smile. "If you sit very still and don't make a peep, the adults tend to forget about you."

"What did she say?"

At that moment, Hans's tower came crashing down with a rumble. Several stones rolled up to Holger's feet. Sighing, he bent down, collected them and carried them over to Hans.

"I was so close to setting a new record." Hans showed with his thumb and forefinger how little he had missed it by.

"Then you'll just try one more time," Hertha said in her know-it-all manner.

After they had collected all the scrambled stones for Hans, Holger asked his sister, "So, what did Frau Perwe say?"

Aware of her own importance, Hertha beckoned him closer and whispered in his ear, "The escape to Sweden is happening this evening."

A sharp pang stabbed through Holger's gut. If Hertha hadn't been injured, which was his fault, they would be on their way to freedom with the others.

"Oh," was all he managed to say, since the sting of guilt sat too deep.

"You don't have to be sad." Hertha stood on her tiptoes so she could put her hand on his shoulder. "We'll get on the train the next time."

"Yes, we will." Holger forced himself to smile, though it came out more like a grimace. A secret transport to Sweden wasn't comparable to building a stone tower. Who knew when – or if – such an opportunity would present itself again?

Sometime after dinner, the parish's delivery van drove into the yard. Normally, Lars used it for all kinds of errands, especially for buying food. Today though, Lars and Baumann hopped out without opening the doors to the cargo area. Holger was about to run up to them and ask about the success of the operation when he caught sight of Lars's stony expression and jumped back, startled.

He bumped into Hans, who complained, "Watch out, you almost ruined my tower."

Hertha, though, grabbed Holger's hand. She reminded him more of his mother every day, even speaking in the same tone: "Oh dear, that doesn't look good at all."

Great! As if his feelings of guilt and constant worry weren't enough to deal with, now tears were welling up in his eyes because he missed Mutti so much.

Baumann said goodbye to Lars. Both ignored the children

completely and marched away. Since no one told them to go to bed, they continued to play in the yard until late at night. Suddenly the gate bell rang. They quickly hid and waited to see who Svenja would let in.

"Do you know her?" Hertha asked.

"No." Holger had never seen the slender woman with hip-length brown hair before. Svenja led her to the pastor's office, where the other adults had disappeared to hours earlier.

"Should we eavesdrop?" Hertha asked.

"I thought that was forbidden?" Holger hadn't forgotten how she had reprimanded him at the Lembergs' house.

"Frau Goldmann said that sometimes we have to do forbidden things to survive. Now is such an opportunity."

It wasn't the first time Holger wondered where Hertha got all these clever sayings from. Deep down though, he knew: she parroted whatever Mutti, or in this case Frau Goldmann, said. "Alright. Come with me. We'll pick daisies."

Holger had scouted out the perfect spot where they could sit inconspicuously and listen in. Directly under the window to Pastor Perwe's office, which was always open in this heat, grew a narrow strip of green daisies.

"Oh, yes. We'll make a hair wreath." Hertha enthusiastically jumped at the opportunity.

Holger was getting worried she might have forgotten they were supposed to be eavesdropping and would chatter incessantly as usual. But his fear proved unfounded. As soon as they turned the corner of the house, Hertha put her finger to her lips. "Not another word from now on."

Holger all but laughed out loud; after all, he wasn't the one who couldn't keep his mouth shut for more than five seconds. "I'm quiet as a mouse."

"...I'm a friend of Reinhard's," said a high-pitched voice that must belong to the stranger.

"What can I do for you?" The pastor's voice was laced with hesitation.

"Theresia came to visit Reinhard."

The midwife? What does she have to do with this? Holger thought.

"We haven't heard from her in a long time. Do you have a message for us?"

For a few seconds, it was quiet, then footsteps approached in their direction. Instinctively, Holger and Hertha pressed themselves closer to the wall to avoid being seen. Otherwise, they would either be sent away or someone would close the window.

Holger listened with bated breath. The footsteps stopped. Then they moved away again. Thank God, the window was still open.

"Theresia wants you to know that the baby died during childbirth. Only the mother could be saved."

Holger involuntarily gasped. *The poor baby.*

"Why wasn't I called to perform an emergency baptism?"

"There wasn't enough time. However, I was instructed to tell you there's an expectant mother who's causing a lot of trouble. Her name is Thea Dalke. She seems to be having complications and it's not clear who the baby's father is."

Holger shook his head. The eavesdropping was pointless. The adults upstairs were rambling on about pregnant women, so they wouldn't learn anything about the outcome of tonight's operation.

He signaled to Hertha that they should leave, just as the door opened and closed again. Not wanting to risk walking around the corner of the house exactly when someone came out, he held up his hand to stop Hertha.

She must have heard the door too, because she stood frozen in place.

"This is bad. Very bad," Svenja murmured.

"We have to assume the Jews attempting to escape were caught and are being interrogated by the Gestapo." The pastor's voice dripped with concern.

"Fortunately, none of them know who was involved on our side and there are only rumors about the church's involvement in general. There's no evidence."

"What about the Countess?" Svenja asked.

"She's fine. Otherwise, she wouldn't have been able to visit Reinhard."

It was a mystery to Holger how the pastor knew these things. Certainly not from the woman who had just visited.

"We need to wait until the dust settles." That was Frau Perwe's voice. "I'm sure the Countess will pay us a visit and tell us the details as soon as she feels it's safe."

"In the meantime, we need to find out what's going on with this woman, Thea Dalke. If I correctly understood, she's an informant working for the Gestapo. In the worst case, she infiltrated our group of escapees beforehand and betrayed the operation."

Hertha's eyes widened and she waved her hands about wildly. Holger shook his head in warning.

"Lars, when you run errands tomorrow, discreetly ask around if anyone knows anything about her." With these words the adults left the pastor's office.

After the door closed, Holger counted to twenty before taking Hertha's hand and pulling her around the corner of the house into the courtyard.

"I know who Thea is," Hertha whispered excitedly. "She used to be David Goldmann's girlfriend."

"How come you know that?" Holger doubted whether he should believe his sister.

"Amelie told me. He was very sad because she married another man."

Holger shook his head. Animals loved Hertha, but it was news to him that people also revealed secrets to her, which they normally preferred to keep to themselves.

"Honestly, it's true." She put her hand over her heart. "I swear."

"We have to tell the pastor."

"But then he'll find out we were eavesdropping and might send us away." Hertha pulled her head between her shoulders.

"I'll think about how we can best proceed. Now let's go find Hans and get some sleep."

Much to his own chagrin Holger was a tiny bit relieved that the refugees had been arrested. At least now he didn't have to feel guilty that he and his siblings had missed the opportunity to escape.

CHAPTER 32

After the failed Operation Swedish Furniture, Baumann and his comrades temporarily suspended their illegal activities, with the exception of leaving the railway wagons open as a hideout for illegals.

He was itching to learn more about the circumstances. According to the grapevine, Thea Dalke, also known as "Blonde Poison" and herself Jewish, had betrayed the operation.

Baumann balled his hands into fists. If he got his hands on that skunk, he would personally wring her neck. How low could a person sink? Until now, he had considered the Gestapo henchmen to be the lowest scum of humanity, yet a Jewish woman who betrayed her own people to that very scum? The mere thought made him want to retch.

He spat on the ground and lit a cigarette before making one last round through the factory hall right before closing time, locking all the doors. The few workers who stayed until nightfall exclusively used the main exit.

Back in his glass booth, his gaze swept across the workshop hall, checking everything was in order, before he put on his jacket and walked to the exit gate. There he spotted someone he certainly hadn't expected to see.

"Hey, Kessel, what are you doing here?" Baumann waved to his former worker. He had taken a liking to the talented and bright lad, who was about the same age as Baumann's daughter.

Even today, the incorrigible boy wore his reversible jacket with the star on the inside – possibly still believing Baumann knew nothing about his shenanigans. But David couldn't fool an old hand like him.

"Baumann, do you have a few minutes?" Kessel called out.

"Of course. Come on in." Baumann walked over to the new gatekeeper and asked for a visitor's pass for Kessel.

"Isn't it a bit late for a visit? The administration staff left an hour ago," asked the loyal Nazi after glancing at the wall clock in his booth.

"It is. But I've been waiting for him all week. It'll only take half an hour." Baumann suspected that Kessel hadn't come for chit-chat.

Thanks to Kessel's Aryan mother and the many other housewives who had protested in front of the Rosenstrasse transit camp, he'd been liberated. But his freedom was precarious. If he'd dared to show up here, he probably needed help.

The gatekeeper handed Kessel a visitor's pass ordering sternly, "Only half an hour."

"Will do." Baumann motioned for Kessel to follow him.

As soon as they were out of earshot, Kessel said, "They didn't have visitor passes before."

Baumann sighed. "Nowadays the workshop feels like a prison. You can't take a step without having the bloodhounds on your heels. Honestly, what do they think? That we're stealing locomotives or something?"

Kessel's guilty expression told Baumann that his words hit pretty close to the truth. *So he needs something.*

As usual, the workshop hall was deafeningly loud. Men carried engine blocks to the various repair stations, others hammered or welded to bring the worn-out machines back to life. After Baumann closed the door of his glass booth behind him, he took a deep breath before asking, "So, what are you doing here?"

Instead of coming clean, Kessel hemmed and hawed.

Baumann observed him with narrowed eyes. "You're not in trouble, are you? I heard about your liberation."

The lad visibly relaxed. "We were released from the transit camp, but weren't allowed to return to our old jobs. Probably so that former colleagues don't ask questions."

Baumann rubbed his chin. "The regime is afraid of the people. I sensed that when I and a few of the old boys participated in the protests."

The main credit for the successful liberation of their relatives belonged to the housewives who had protested for their families day in and day out in front of the Rosenstrasse camp. Still, Baumann felt a sense of pride in having contributed his bit to ensure that all inmates – Aryan-related Jews or mixed-race individuals like Kessel – had been released after about a week.

"Thank you." Kessel's lips trembled.

"You don't need to thank me. We share the same opinion about our government." Baumann winked at him, whereupon Kessel came out with his request.

"I was wondering if you might have any wire ends to spare."

"What for?"

The boy's ears turned bright red, he cleared his throat and whispered, "To build a radio transmitter."

"Hm." Baumann rubbed his chin. "What exactly do you need?"

"Enameled copper wire, a diode and cables. Anything you can spare."

"We can't spare anything, remember?" He grinned at Kessel. "But I'll give you the stuff anyway. I reckon it's for a good cause."

"A very good cause."

Baumann poured himself a cup of lukewarm coffee from the thermos before adding, "Better I don't know about your plans. The fence still has a hole –"

"You know about that?" By now, not only Kessel's ears burned bright red; his entire face was glowing like a lighthouse in the fog.

"Did you really think I don't notice what goes on in my workshop?"

"I... I was so careful..."

"You can't fool an old coot like me. After you left, Matze took over equipping the wagons with water and food."

"All this time, I was so proud of keeping my activities secret from you." David fumbled around before taking a deep breath and looking Baumann in the eye. "Not because I don't trust you, but because I didn't want to cause you trouble."

"Yep. Which is exactly the reason why I don't want to know what you're up to. You do your thing and I do mine. If you get caught, I haven't got a clue and know nothing about you. I can't snoop around the premises and notice every little detail, I've got enough on my plate." Baumann winked at him.

"Thank you so much. I'll make sure not to get caught and only take small pieces no one will miss."

"Good luck." There was nothing else to say, so he accompanied Kessel to the entrance gate, where the gatekeeper was impatiently looking at the wall clock, although the visit had lasted no more than fifteen minutes.

Baumann returned to the workshop. To ensure Kessel wouldn't have to break in and possibly leave traces, he unlocked the bolt on the back door before calling it a day. In the meantime, he was in a hurry to make it to the regulars' table with his comrades on time. During the entire march to his destination, he mulled over whether he should let Kessel in on his resistance activities.

It wasn't a matter of a lack of trustworthiness. The lad definitely had what it took and would be a great help for the pastor. What worried Baumann too much was Kessel's personal situation. As a half-Jew he suffered enough from Nazi harassment; Baumann didn't need to expose him to additional risks.

A stab to his heart reminded him of his daughter, who was eking out an existence in some concentration camp. He wanted to spare Kessel that fate – or at the very least, he didn't want the lad's deportation to the East to burden his conscience.

As he arrived at the pub, the others were already waiting.

"Finally! We thought you were chickening out," Manfred teased good-naturedly.

"Me? From a bottle of beer? You don't know me very well." Baumann raised his hand, signaling to the waitress that the next round was on him.

"Something to celebrate?" asked Koloss.

"That we're alive and the war will soon be won." They all wanted the war to end. But unlike the Nazis, Baumann and his comrades hoped the Allies would win and end the nightmare of the Third Reich.

When the beer stood in front of them and they had toasted each other, Reinhard spoke up. "I have news from the pastor."

"You don't say." An exciting tingle seized Baumann's gut. From Reinhard's expression, he could tell it was good news.

"There's another Swedish family that needs help moving." Reinhard grinned like a Cheshire cat.

"I'm in." For Baumann, there was no question whether he would participate in a second escape attempt.

"Me too," said Koloss matter-of-factly, before leaning back and eyeing Manfred, who was looking sheepishly at his beer.

Manfred shook his head. "I can't. My boss has become suspicious due to some other stuff and has initiated an investigation. The entire department is under observation."

"It won't work without the seal." Baumann felt the excitement drain from his bones.

"If I could, I really would..." Manfred waved it off. "The SS is snooping around our place. Besides, I suspect the secretary is collecting and passing on information. She's a true party loyalist."

Koloss slammed his giant paw on the table. The bang was loud enough to cause the other patrons to stare at them.

Baumann glared at him.

"Sorry." Koloss turned around and said apologetically to the room, "Trouble with the wife."

He earned some mocking mixed with understanding looks before the other patrons returned to their own conversations.

"Get a grip on yourself," Baumann hissed. He was worried about his friend. The constant tension was getting to the normally gentle giant, and lately he had frequently been losing his temper. For a man of his size, who was able to punch through a door with one blow, this inevitably led to unwanted attention.

Koloss cast a contrite gaze at his calloused hands. "Won't happen again."

Baumann doubted that. For the moment, he let the matter rest, but he made a mental note to have a word with Koloss in private. With his outbursts, he was not only endangering himself but also the entire network.

The quick thinker Reinhard had used the pause in conversation to come up with a solution to their problem. "So, Manfred can't make the seal at his office, right?"

Manfred nodded dejectedly.

"But you know how to do it and you could make one if I organized the equipment needed?"

A hopeful gleam appeared in Manfred's eyes. He might often come across as arrogant, but he certainly wasn't a shirker. "Assuming I have everything I need, then yes."

Reinhard grinned. "My old man won't like it one bit, if we borrow his blacksmith's workshop."

"Then we'll have to make sure he never finds out." New courage filled Baumann's soul.

"Manfred and I will discuss the necessary details in private later. Better you don't know about it."

"You're right." Koloss ordered another round of beer. "Now, this is a reason to celebrate."

CHAPTER 33

BERLIN, AUGUST 1943

One day Lars said to Holger: "Today we're going to try again."

It took several seconds for Holger to understand what the sexton was alluding to. "You mean the escape to Sweden?"

"Exactly." The flaxen-haired man ran his hand over his head. "The last attempt failed, because we were betrayed. This time we're doing it differently. We're only taking people who are hiding in the parish and have had no contact with the outside world for at least a week."

Holger thoughtfully rubbed his chin, just as his father always did when he was thinking. He spoke in a fake deep voice, hoping to sound grown-up. "That's a good plan. What do you need me to do?"

Lars grinned and patted Holger on the shoulder. "Tell your siblings we're leaving tonight. Pack your belongings in laundry bags, which you'll get from Svenja, and wait until I come to get you."

"Will do."

THREE CHILDREN IN DANGER

"You'll ride with me in the delivery van. It's way too far for you to walk with the others." Holger was about to protest, but Lars raised his hand with a grin. "Especially for Hertha, who isn't quite back on her feet yet."

Holger had also noticed that his sister became out of breath much quicker than before the fire and needed to rest more often. The pastor had assured him these after-effects of smoke inhalation would disappear over time.

"Get ready!" Lars ordered before he left.

"Yes, sir." Holger ran to his siblings, who were playing at the other end of the courtyard. Or rather, Hans was building a castle out of stones and Hertha was giving unwelcome advice. "Listen up. I've got great news."

Hans carefully placed the stone in his hand on top of the tower before turning around with shining eyes. "Mutti and Vati have returned?"

"No." A lump formed in Holger's throat. "Tonight we're leaving for Sweden."

"Oh, yes!" Hertha cheered, while Hans made a disappointed face.

"What's wrong? Aren't you happy?"

"I am, but..." Hans looked back and forth between the stone castle and his brother. "How will Mutti and Vati find us there?"

Darn! Holger hadn't thought of this detail. He wrinkled his nose. "We'll figure something out once we're in Sweden."

"I'm not joining you," stated Hans. "I'm staying here and waiting for our parents' return."

"If Hans stays, I'm staying too." Hertha took a step toward Hans and clutched his arm.

Holger's enthusiasm vanished into thin air. Without the two of them, he didn't want to go to Sweden either. They had sworn to stay together forever. However, he also understood it was becoming increasingly dangerous for them in Germany, even within the confines of the Swedish parish.

Rumors abounded that Thea wasn't the only traitor who had

gained access to the parish's underground network. Almost on a daily basis, Gestapo informants knocked on the door, if Lars' stories could be believed. Gestapo officers visited the pastor about once a week under some pretext, always on the lookout for Jews hidden on the premises.

And then there were the bombs. Night after night they rained down on Berlin; a second direct hit on the parish was only a matter of time. Holger racked his brain trying to figure out a way to convince his siblings that escape was their only chance of survival.

"We can't stay here." He gazed at them sternly. "It's become too dangerous. Only in Sweden will we survive the war."

"But... our parents," Hans objected.

"When the war is over, we'll return," Holger said with a firmness in his voice he didn't possess. "Besides, Pastor Perwe can tell our parents where we are. They might even join us in Sweden."

Happy about his brilliant idea, he beamed at his siblings: "We'll all live in Sweden together."

"Do they have rabbits in Sweden?" Ever since Rufus perished in the fire, Hertha often asked about their rabbits Kuschel, Wuschel, and Puschel. Back then, when Jews had to have their pets put down, David's sister Amelie had saved the rabbits' lives by illegally bringing them to her Aryan aunt.

Although Holger didn't know if it was true, he said with absolute conviction, "Sweden is known for its many rabbits. And squirrels."

"How cute!"

Taking advantage of her enthusiasm, he asked: "So, are you in?"

Hertha threw an uncertain glance toward Hans. "Only if Hans is on board."

Hans grimaced. "But we'll write a message for our parents this very instant and hand it over to the pastor."

"We'll do that." Holger breathed a sigh of relief; that had

been a close call. Looking after his siblings was harder than herding a sack of fleas.

Late in the afternoon, Lars sought them out. "Come with me. It's time." He led them to the delivery van, where he gave them juice to drink.

Hans sniffed the glass and returned it untouched. "I don't like it."

"Don't you want to drink just a little? The journey will be long." Lars held out the drink, but Hans shook his head.

"We're taking a bottle of water with us. Besides, I'm not thirsty."

Holger gave his brother an annoyed look. Hans always had to be difficult. In contrast to his brother, he eagerly drank the sweet juice to the last drop. Due to the bitter aftertaste, he paused and asked: "What is this?"

"It'll help you sleep better on the train. Now get into the van, under the bench and not another word."

As soon as the three had crawled under the bench, Lars covered them with a thick woolen blanket. After the first breath, Holger suppressed a gag, because the scratchy thing smelled so disgustingly musty. Shortly after, he heard heavy footsteps and people sat down on the bench.

Holger lifted the blanket a crack to peer out, but he could see nothing except black boots. After a few minutes, it became unbearably hot beneath the woolen blanket. He didn't know what was worse: the sweat running down his back or the rumbling of the delivery van. With every bump in the road, Holger bounced painfully up and down.

Fortunately, the ride didn't last long. As soon as the vehicle stopped, the rear door was unlocked and the children were allowed to crawl out from under the blanket.

"Don't venture out yet," said a man who was at least twice as big as the others next to him. "We wait for Lars to give the signal, then you run behind me to the train."

Holger's jaw dropped as he looked at the paws that were easily as big as Hertha's head.

"Understood?" asked the giant in a gentle voice that didn't fit him at all.

"Yes, sir." It wasn't long before the giant opened the door, jumped out and lifted the children down one by one, while his colleagues were sprinting toward the train.

"Go. Run," the giant ordered, then he was gone.

Holger ran the approximately fifty meters to the tracks, where Baumann stood, grabbed him under the arms, and lifted him into the open wagon. It all happened so fast Holger didn't even realize what had become of Hans and Hertha.

Again his jaw dropped as he noticed the giant standing directly in front of him, swiftly depositing him in an open crate. In a flash, Hans appeared next to him and before they even sat down, Hertha's flailing legs showed up in the opening.

The giant leaned in, handed them their bags with their belongings as well as a small brown bottle. "This is cough syrup. Take it if you need to cough, because when the train stops, you mustn't make a sound."

"And during the journey?" Hans asked.

"Better not then either. If you must talk, only whisper very, very quietly." The face disappeared and a wooden lid was placed over the opening. Seconds later, hammer blows sounded. The wooden crate they were sitting in was nailed shut.

To ward off the rising panic, Holger fumbled for the air holes in the lower third of the wooden walls. He breathed out in relief when his fingers found one. His biggest worry was suffocating in this crate.

He had once seen pictures of people who had been put into coffins alive and buried. He certainly didn't want to experience such a fate firsthand.

"It's so dark in here," Hertha complained.

From outside, muffled sounds reached his ears. Footsteps. Snippets of words. Rattling. Scraping. Next, there was hammering as the remaining crates were nailed shut, finally more footsteps and a thud indicating the wagon door was closed.

Holger held his breath. There was no turning back now. They were stuck inside the crate for better or worse. It became quiet. After a jerk that smashed him against the wall the train set into motion.

"We're moving," he whispered.

"Yes, we're moving," Hertha replied slowly. Her usually bright voice sounded tired.

Holger's eyelids were getting heavy too, even though it was early in the evening. He remembered Lars's words. "So you can sleep better." He was just wondering whether Lars had put sleeping syrup into the juice when he dozed off.

At some point, he woke, as his head banged roughly against the wall of the crate. The train was no longer moving. Confused, he opened his eyes and looked around. In the complete darkness, he couldn't see his own hand in front of his face. Thus, he carefully felt along the wooden walls until he sensed a gentle breath of air. At least they wouldn't suffocate.

Nevertheless, a panic attack threatened to choke him. The walls of the crate seemed to be closing in on him, getting tighter and tighter, until they finally crushed him. Bile gathered in his throat. Feeling sick, he desperately tried to suppress the gag reflex while his fingers continued to wander along the inside of the wooden crate. Suddenly he bumped into something soft and warm.

"Ouch," came Hans's voice.

Relieved, he continued to feel his way through the complete darkness until he found his brother's hand and gripped it tightly.

His fear vanished in an instant. The train jerked on its way again, so he leaned in Hans's direction and whispered in his ear: "Do you know how long we've been on the road?"

"Not exactly. But quite a long time."

"I fell asleep." Holger moved his limbs as best as he could in the confined container.

"There was sleeping syrup in the juice. That's what Svenja told Lars. I didn't want to drink it."

"You should have told me," Holger scolded him reproachfully.

"It was better that you slept, otherwise you would have been afraid."

"I'm never afraid."

"Oh, really?" Hans mocked, as he liked to do to annoy Holger.

Holger was about to slap his cheeky little brother. Regrettably, there wasn't enough room in the crate for a scuffle. Out of necessity he swallowed his wounded pride.

Hans, too, seemed to have come to the conclusion that this was neither the right time nor place for a quarrel, because he added in a conciliatory tone: "I didn't want to sleep because one of us has to keep watch to make sure nothing happens to the others."

Luckily, Hans couldn't see in the darkness that tears were welling up in Holger's eyes. "That's actually my job."

"You do it all the time. You're allowed to rest once in a while."

They both fell silent. The rattling of the train was the only sound, apart from Hertha's steady breathing. She seemed to be sleeping deeply and soundly, which was probably for the best.

The full weight of responsibility for his siblings pressed on Holger's shoulders, while at the same time, an inner satisfaction spread through his limbs, since he had managed well so far.

He must have dozed off again, because a squealing sound startled him. The train jerked violently before coming to a complete halt.

"Hans?" he whispered softly and nudged his brother's arm; Hans didn't move. A wave of panic squeezed the breath out of his lungs. Hans hadn't suffocated, had he?

Holger gasped for oxygen, convinced he was about to die painfully. Much to his surprise, his lungs filled with air – admittedly warm and stale, but air, nonetheless.

Just as he was about to lean back against the wall of the crate, feeling calmer, voices from the outside reached his ear. Shortly after, the wagon door was yanked open. Daylight filtered in through the hair-thin cracks in the wood.

"What's in there?" asked a deep voice.

"The household goods of a Swedish family returning home. Here are the papers."

Holger held his breath, fearing the man might open the crates to check inside. Frozen with fear, he wondered what would happen if Hans or Hertha woke up or screamed in that very moment. He mulled whether he should quickly wake them or wait and hope for the best. Then he decided to let them sleep.

Suddenly, the footsteps sounded close.

"Were the contents checked?"

"Yes, sir. Customs in Berlin did that. I have the report here. After the check, the crates were nailed shut in the presence of the customs officer and the wagon sealed. No one could have smuggled anything in or out."

"Good. Let's move on." The footsteps retreated; presumably the people left the wagon and climbed onto the platform. Then there was a thud, the wagon door closed, and it was pitch black again. Holger continued to hear strange noises for quite a while.

At some point, Hans woke up and nudged him.

To be safe, Holger pressed his mouth to his brother's ear, in case someone had remained in the wagon and whispered, "Two men were just in here checking the cargo. But they left, at least I think they did."

Hans nodded without making a sound.

They sat together, tense and quiet as mice, listening. Eventually, Holger's muscles started to burn and he stretched his limbs.

"We're moving again," Hans whispered, barely audible.

Holger had noticed that too. The train was rolling. Very gently. *As if walking on eggshells.* After a short time, it stopped again. Muffled snippets of conversation drifted in from outside, which he couldn't understand.

Could this be the ship already? Holger didn't dare ask his brother the question as long as voices could be heard nearby.

Hans seemed to be thinking the same thing. He took Holger's hand and made a wave motion with it.

So he also believes we're on the ship. Very gradually, a warmth spread inside him. Lars had explained that the train ferry sailed under a Swedish flag, partly so it wouldn't be attacked by the Allies in the Baltic Sea. The thought drove the comforting warmth from his limbs as he imagined the ship being torpedoed and them slowly sinking to the sea floor in their crate, where they would miserably drown. Even if they managed to open the crate, it wouldn't help, because none of them knew how to swim.

His breathing became ragged until Hans's hand came to rest on his leg. It felt incredibly good, giving him strength. He pulled himself together; his younger siblings must not know that he was afraid.

At some point, it became quiet. A steady humming set in, which reverberated deep in the pit of Holger's stomach.

"Those are the ship's engines," Hans whispered. "We've cast off."

"Hooooonk." A long, muffled ship's horn cut through the air.

"We're leaving the harbor."

"How do you know all this?" Holger asked.

"I read it in a book about diesel engines." While Holger preferred to read adventure novels, Hans stuck his nose into technical books no one else would voluntarily pick up, let alone read or understand.

"How long will it take until we're in Sweden?"

"I don't know exactly, it depends on the ship's maximum speed, wind force and direction as well as the current. Let's assume the freighter makes fifteen knots and the distance to Stockholm..."

Holger only half-listened as Hans calculated the duration of the crossing using a complicated formula. A budding nausea demanded his full attention. With each roll of the ship, the nausea intensified, causing him to retch again and again.

"You need to lie flat, that helps," suggested Hans.

"How is that supposed to work in this crate?"

"Right. I didn't think of that." Hans seemed to be pondering. After a heavy sigh, he continued. "Unfortunately, all other tips against seasickness won't help you either."

Holger convulsively swallowed the rising bile every few seconds because he absolutely did not want to vomit inside the crate. Desperately he wheezed, "Come on, tell me, maybe there's something useful!"

"Eating ginger is supposed to help. Or looking at the sea. Otherwise, it seems to go away on its own after a few days."

"A few days?" Horror squeezed the air from Holger's lungs. He would never be able to endure that long.

"But we're not traveling several days. Besides, they'll surely let us out of the crate as soon as we've passed the three-mile zone and are in international waters. You'll see, then you'll feel better right away."

"Do you genuinely believe so?"

"Absolutely. At least that's what the pastor told Lars when they were planning the operation."

Another wave of nausea prevented Holger from responding. He had always thought Hans was interested solely in architecture and technology, but apparently his brother had been more involved in their escape than Holger had suspected.

Just as he thought he was going to throw up, someone kicked him in the shin.

"Hey. Stop that, Hans," he scolded.

"It wasn't me," Hans defended himself.

"I'm so hot," Hertha complained in a sleepy voice.

"It won't be much longer. We're already on the ship."

"Really?" The relief was audible even in her whisper.

Before he could answer, there was a loud thud. It must have been the wagon door.

"Shh," Holger whispered. The three children remained stock-still for endless minutes. He was so focused on not making a sound he completely forgot about his nausea. What if the Nazis had come aboard and were forcing the ship to turn around? No, that couldn't be. He tried to reassure himself: *It's surely not the Nazis. We've been at sea long enough. Hans said they have no authority in international waters. Just how long does it take to sail through the three-mile zone? Why three miles anyway?*

Suddenly their crate wobbled precariously and the lid was lifted off. Holger stared into the smudged face of a sailor.

"These are children," the seaman muttered in surprise. "Where are your parents?"

Holger was proud that he had diligently practiced Swedish in the Victoria parish and therefore understood the sailor. He shook his head. "We without parents."

The man quickly recovered from the shock. "Well then, come on out."

Holger's legs were stiff from sitting motionless so long; it took several attempts until he managed to laboriously stand up. He was immediately lifted out of the man-high crate. Hans and Hertha followed right behind. Hertha rubbed her eyes sleepily as soon as she stood beside him.

While someone pulled the nails out of the other crates, the sailor gave the children a hand signal to follow him. Holger's stomach churned again as he swayed down the narrow passage between the containers.

He barely made it to the end of the deck, where a woman in a Red Cross uniform stood, holding a list in her hands. Upon reaching her, he couldn't hold it in any longer and vomited directly at her feet.

"Oh, dear, you're seasick," she said in excellent German. "What's your name?"

Holger was too miserable to answer and was infinitely grateful when Hans stepped in. "I'm Hans Gerber, and these are my siblings Holger and Hertha."

"Where are your parents?" the friendly woman asked.

"They're not here, the SS took them. Can you please pass on a message to Pastor Perwe in Berlin once we arrive, so he knows where to send our parents as soon as the war is over?"

A mix of sympathy, horror and amusement flitted across the woman's face before she answered in a serious tone, "Don't you worry. I'll take care of it."

Meanwhile, the other refugees were trickling in. As far as Holger could tell, about half of them were in the same desolate state as he was, while the other half seemed unaffected by the ship's rolling movements.

The Red Cross worker waited until everyone had assembled, before she led the group up the stairs until they emerged into the sunlight on an open deck high above the waterline. In the fresh air, Holger flopped down on the first empty spot on the deck and looked up at the clear blue sky. As Hans had predicted, the terrible nausea dispelled after a while and his freshly emptied stomach grumbled just slightly. When his brain functioned almost normally again, Holger finally dared to hope they had succeeded in escaping the Nazis.

Sometime later, the Red Cross woman leaned over him. "How are you feeling?"

"Much better."

"Can you sit up?"

Bravely ignoring the queasy feeling, he sat up, and she held out a cup of water to him.

"Here, drink this. Take small sips so you won't throw up right away."

Holger drank only a little, always fearful of getting that agonizing seasickness again.

"Thank you." He held out the cup to her before letting his gaze wander. "Where are my siblings?"

"In the mess."

"What, now?" Holger didn't understand why the two would attend a protestant church service after their release on the ship. They weren't usually so pious and avoided mass whenever they could.

The woman smiled. "Unlike you, they didn't get seasick and were very hungry."

In Sweden, they eat during church services? Pastor Perwe had never mentioned that detail. Holger blinked against the sun. He'd think about that later; for now, he had more pressing questions. "Where are we?"

"We've passed the island of Bornholm and are sailing along the Swedish coast to Stockholm. It will take a few more hours."

Since he no longer felt so miserably nauseous, he didn't care how long the journey would take, as long as there was no danger from the Nazis. "You mean we're safe?"

She smiled again. "Yes, you are. Do you see over there?" She pointed to one side of the deck. "That dark strip on the horizon, that's Sweden."

Holger squinted to see better. He might have been imagining it, but there was land visible.

"Even if the Germans have become suspicious, they wouldn't dare to board our ship so close to our territorial waters. After all, Sweden is a neutral country."

The tension dissolved and Holger began to laugh, louder and more carefree than he had in months.

"We're free! We're free!"

CHAPTER 34

The champagne cork popped through the air. Reinhard, who had invited everyone to his father's villa, swung the bottle with a grand gesture and poured a glass for each person.

"I'd rather have beer," grumbled Baumann, while obediently holding up his champagne flute as Reinhard proposed a toast.

"Congratulations, comrades! We've done it! Thanks to your tireless efforts, the first shipment of packages has safely arrived in Sweden."

The small group of conspirators applauded loudly. Baumann looked around; everyone had come: Koloss, Matze and two other helpers. Only Manfred was missing. Just as Baumann was wondering why, the door opened and Manfred strolled in.

"I'm sorry. I had to take a detour, since the street was blocked." The bomb attacks on Berlin were getting worse daily. The long nights in the air raid shelters were a constant source of grief.

Reinhard walked to the long table where a buffet was laid out, took a champagne flute, and poured the rest of the bottle. "Here, take this. I was just about to give a toast."

Manfred stood next to Baumann and everyone waited for Reinhard to continue speaking.

"The pastor sends his greetings and thanks. All the refugees are doing well, especially the three children."

"What a relief!" From the moment they had lifted the children into the crate, Baumann had been constantly worried about their well-being.

"You can say that again." Koloss had also taken the three to heart. "I'm infinitely glad they made it. It wasn't much of a life here, in constant fear and always hiding."

Even Manfred, who usually maintained an emotionless demeanor, nodded. "They deserved it. It's a shame they lost their parents."

"You don't know that for sure," Baumann objected, although he had to admit to himself there was little hope once someone had been deported to the East. If the rumors were true, most Jews went straight from the train to the gas chambers. He shuddered. It was too horrifying to entertain. But thanks to their efforts, at least twelve Jews, including the three siblings, had escaped death.

In the grand scheme of world history, it might not seem like much, but for each of those twelve individuals, it was literally the difference between life and death.

Reinhard joined them with a freshly opened bottle of champagne. "Who wants more?"

Baumann raised his hand in refusal. He couldn't stand this stuff, no matter how much the rich and beautiful raved about it.

"A really good drop." Manfred sipped his glass appreciatively. "Rare these days."

"My old man was prepared and stuffed our wine cellar to the rafters with everything he could get his hands on when the war broke out."

"Where is he, by the way?" asked Manfred.

"On a business trip in Antwerp. Something important. My

mother accompanied him, because she hates being in Berlin. So don't worry, we have the house to ourselves."

Baumann tilted his head. Reinhard was a good one. You couldn't tell he had been born with a silver spoon in his mouth.

"The war has been going on for four years now. Honestly, who among you would have thought it would drag on for so long?" Manfred shook his head.

"Well, I certainly didn't."

"It can't last much longer. The Allied landing in Sicily is the beginning of the end," Matze chimed in.

"That happened over a month ago and where are they? Haven't even arrived in Rome yet." Baumann fluctuated daily between hope and resignation.

"Patience, there's progress. Mussolini was overthrown and arrested, which means Hitler has lost his most important ally." Reinhard put forward this bold thesis.

"You don't really believe that, do you?"

"I'm quite certain Italy will soon sign an armistice. They're fed up with the war and want peace sooner rather than later." Reinhard filled the glasses for the third time.

"Well, I don't know. Sounds too simple to me. There are many fascists in Italy."

"Even fascists value their own lives." Manfred shrugged. "At least those who haven't undergone Nazi brainwashing."

"Yeah, unfortunately, we have far too many blockheads who still believe in the final victory." Instinctively Baumann looked around at Koloss' words, despite everyone in this room being one hundred percent trustworthy.

"Even the most deluded full-blown Nazi should have realized by now that the war is hopelessly lost. They just can't admit it or their entire worldview would collapse. You should see how jittery the bosses at my workplace have become," Manfred interjected. "For weeks now, money and assets have been secretly moved to Switzerland. Plus, escape routes to Argentina are being circulated under the table."

"Of course, they're running away. Cowardly wimps. Not man enough to face the mess they've gotten us all into." Baumann had quite a few ideas about what he would do to an SS man caught fleeing to South America. None of them were appetizing.

"That plays into our hands," said Reinhard. "Because it means the end of the war is near. Until then, we need to pool our efforts and get as many people as possible out of the Nazis' sphere of power. At the same time, we must increase our sabotage efforts and throw sand in the gears of the war machine wherever possible."

"Easy for you to say. You're sitting pretty in an office."

"You can sabotage processes in an office too. Imagine the panic that breaks out, if a list disappears in the mail." Reinhard grinned knowingly.

"The postal service. I could sing a song about it, too." Manfred groaned theatrically. "Letters are constantly disappearing or arriving far too late. We resorted to sending important information exclusively with couriers we trust."

The way Manfred emphasized the word trust made Baumann assume that these couriers' loyalty didn't necessarily lie with the regime. What an excellent opportunity to snoop around unobtrusively in various government offices.

Reinhard asked abruptly, "When are we starting the next operation?"

"Easy there, young buck." Baumann shook his head back and forth.

"We should lay low for a while," Koloss agreed.

"Don't you want to help more Jews to freedom?"

"Of course we do. But we don't want the Gestapo catchin' on to us. Too much of a good thing can be bad."

The corners of Reinhard's mouth sagged in disappointment.

"Why the long face?" asked Matze, who had exchanged a few words with the others present and was rejoining them. "I thought we were celebrating the success of the operation."

"He's just disappointed because we're not immediately planning the next shipment."

"If we want to do that, we need more people." Matze stroked his mustache. "It won't be as noticeable as always having the same people involved."

"Good idea. I already know someone." Baumann had been toying with the idea of asking Kessel for a long time. In recent weeks, he had come to the conclusion that no one in the German Reich was safe anymore: not the Jews, not the communists and not even the upright German citizen who had previously considered himself untouchable.

One wrong word could lead to denunciation and a stay in a concentration camp. Even mothers who mourned the death of their sons at the front a little too fervently risked being interrogated by the Gestapo for undermining the war effort.

"Better not tell us who you have in mind." Manfred took a step back.

Baumann nodded. "I won't. But I'll let you know when it's time to get going again."

That evening, Baumann went home thoroughly satisfied. Their small group might not be able to save the entire world, but a dozen people was a good start.

EPILOGUE

STOCKHOLM, DECEMBER 13, 1943

Holger was incredibly excited. Today was the day of Saint Lucy, the Light Queen. It was a festival meant to bring joy and brightness to the dark winter days.

The three siblings had been living in an orphanage in in the outskirts of Stockholm for over three months. A few days after their arrival, Hertha had befriended the orphanage's rabbits and spent most of her days petting them in their outdoor enclosure.

Holger, too, had quickly settled in. Every free minute, he diligently practiced Swedish and had been very proud when the director of the orphanage allowed him to attend a public Swedish school.

He grimaced, hardly believing that he was looking forward to school and even begging to be allowed to attend. But after a year and a half at home or in hiding, he desperately needed this normalcy.

He didn't understand everything said in class, but he could follow along reasonably well in most subjects. Twice a week, a Red Cross volunteer came and practiced Swedish with him. If he had major difficulties in a subject, he could ask her to explain.

THREE CHILDREN IN DANGER

His Swedish classmates were nice to him. At first, they had been reserved toward the German boy, but soon their curiosity won out and they asked him about his past. His adventurous escape from the Nazis – which he had embellished slightly – soon made him something special in the eyes of his classmates.

For the big Saint Lucy's Day celebration, his school had planned a procession where the Light Queen with her retinue of star boys, Christmas elves, and gingerbread men would walk through the streets of the Stockholm suburb.

Holger was one of the star boys. They had crafted the pointed hat with stars on it in class. They had also been practicing the Saint Lucy song *"Sankta Lucia"* for weeks. Even Hertha and Hans knew it by now.

Holger sighed. His brother still hadn't come to terms with having to leave their homeland. Almost daily, he asked the orphanage director if she had received news from Pastor Perwe about their parents' whereabouts.

Hans wasn't allowed to attend public school because he refused to learn Swedish. He usually claimed that his stay in the country was only temporary, therefore it wasn't necessary to learn the language. Furthermore, he had Holger, and even Hertha, to translate for him.

During the day, Hans spent the hours building various contraptions and pretended to be content with his life. But every night Holger heard how his brother cried himself to sleep when he believed the others to be fast asleep.

At first, Holger had tried to comfort him, but eventually, he gave up—it only dragged him deeper into his own sadness, a weight he could no longer bear. They had defied the odds, surviving when so many hadn't, but what good was survival if it meant carrying this unbearable ache? Hans, too, had to find a way to pick himself up, to move on, to be happy—even if their parents were gone forever.

Of course, he missed Mutti and Vati, too, but the less he thought about them, the less unhappy he became. Life in

Stockholm had so many beautiful aspects. For one, he no longer was forced to wear the hated yellow star and on the street, he was neither spat at nor mocked.

The best thing, though, was that he no longer had to hide. It was a wonderful feeling to simply go for a walk in the neighborhood – without constantly looking over his shoulder to check whether an SS patrol was lurking, ready to arrest him for breaking one of the thousands of rules applying exclusively to Jews.

In the first weeks at the orphanage, he'd woken up several times a night, drenched in sweat, terrified the SS would find him and drag him back to Germany. Thank God those fears were gone. He couldn't remember ever feeling as light and carefree in his life as he did now – despite the hardships that life in the orphanage brought with it.

Another advantage was the lack of air raids – no more nights spent in a musty cellar while plaster crumbled from the ceiling around him.

All in all, Holger was happy and deep in his heart, he hoped that he would see his parents again after the war.

AUTHOR'S NOTES

Thank you for reading **Three Children in Danger**. If you want to know what happens next with Sophie, Baumann, Koloss and the others, sign up for my newsletter and you'll be the first to be informed when a new book is released.

The Gerber children crept into my heart during the first volumes of the German Wives series. You can imagine that I was overjoyed when Frau Perwe told Baumann and David in The Berlin Wife's Vow they had arrived safely in Sweden. So what would be more natural than writing a book about the children's escape?

Perhaps you remember the first book of the War Girl series, Blonde Angel – War Girl Ursula, in which I already wrote about an escape from Germany. Most of the so-called Escape Lines started in France and either went across the Atlantic or over the Pyrenees to neutral Spain and from there via Gibraltar to Great Britain.

There is hardly any literature about escape routes across the North Sea to Sweden or over the Alps to Switzerland. Therefore, I was all the more pleased when I came across an article about the operation organized by Pastor Perwe and his sexton Erik Wesslén.

AUTHOR'S NOTES

The pastor and his sexton created an immense network of helpers. Those in hiding found in the parish a place to go for food, money or clothing. In emergencies, people were allowed to spend several nights in the attic of the parish house or in the basement, until a safe hiding place was found for them.

The two policemen Ahrens and Gruber existed in real life. Their names were Oberwachtmeister Hoffmann and Wachtmeister Mattick from Police Station 155, which was housed in the building opposite the Victoria parish.

They were sympathetic to the pastor's resistance activities and warned him of visits from the Gestapo, who used the station to monitor the Swedish parish. There are different accounts of the agreed upon warning signal: One time a lowered roller blind is mentioned, another time an upside-down flower pot.

The policemen helped with blank forms for various occasions and stamped forged papers for those in hiding to make them look authentic.

The bombing raid during which Hertha was injured actually took place on the night of February 15-16, 1944, when explosive bombs hit the parish and the roof structure caught fire.

Everyone hiding in the parish helped with the firefighting. Pastor Perwe is said to have written the following into his diary about the event: "Everything is covered with glass and soot. There's no gas and no light, the warmth is escaping. Snow is falling into the house. No one was injured – Omnia gratia!"

However he knew another direct hit might happen again at any time and considered how he could bring the people in his care to safety. The opportunity arose when the Swedish embassy planned to return its furniture and files to Stockholm in early summer 1944. This action was the model for the eponymous Operation Swedish Furniture in the book.

To maintain temporal consistency with the other books in the series, I moved both Operation Swedish Furniture and the bomb hit on the congregation forward by several months.

Countess Sophie von Borsoi also has a real-life inspiration:

AUTHOR'S NOTES

Maria Countess von Maltzan. Her autobiography *Schlage die Trommel und fürchte dich nicht* is an exciting contemporary witness account that mentions, among other activities, Operation Swedish Furniture. The countess was an extraordinary woman. For example, she hid at least three Jews in her apartment. One of them was Hans Hirschel, the model for Eugen Habicht. In reality, Hirschel survived the war in his hiding place and the two got married – however, they divorced after a few years.

Both Pastor Perwe and Countess Maria von Maltzan were awarded the title of "Righteous Among the Nations" by the Yad Vashem Holocaust Memorial in Jerusalem.

In the next book, I want to take a closer look at Sophie's resistance activities and Koloss will face serious trouble.

Best regards,
Marion Kummerow

ALSO BY MARION KUMMEROW

Love and Resistance in WW2 Germany

Unrelenting

Unyielding

Unwavering

War Girl Series

Downed over Germany (Prequel)

Blonde Angel: War Girl Ursula (Book 1)

War Girl Lotte (Book 2)

War Girl Anna (Book 3)

Reluctant Informer (Book 4)

Trouble Brewing (Book 5)

Fatal Encounter (Book 6)

Uncommon Sacrifice (Book 7)

Bitter Tears (Book 8)

Secrets Revealed (Book 9)

Together at Last (Book 10)

Endless Ordeal (Book 11)

Not Without My Sister (Spin-off)

Second Chance at First Love (romantic spin-off)

Berlin Fractured

From the Ashes (Book 1)

On the Brink (Book 2)

In the Skies (Book 3)

Into the Unknown (Book 4)

Against the Odds (Book 5)

Margarete's Story

Turning Point (Prequel)

A Light in the Window

From the Dark We Rise

The Girl in the Shadows

Daughter of the Dawn

Standalone

The Orphan's Mother

German Wives

The Berlin Wife

The Berlin Wife's Choice

The Berlin Wife's Resistance

The Berlin Wife's Vow

Escaping the Reich

Three Children in Danger

Find all my books here:
http://www.kummerow.info

CONTACT ME

I truly appreciate you taking the time to read (and enjoy) my books. And I'd be thrilled to hear from you!
If you'd like to get in touch with me you can do so via

Facebook:
http://www.facebook.com/AutorinKummerow

Website
http://www.kummerow.info